D0482396

THE NEW
OLYMPIANS

Also by Kate O'Hearn

The Flame of Olympus
Olympus at War

THE NEW OLYMPIANS

KATE O'HEARN

Aladdin

NEW YORK   LONDON   TORONTO   SYDNEY   NEW DELHI

ALADDIN

An imprint of Simon & Schuster Children's Publishing Division
1230 Avenue of the Americas, New York, NY 10020
First Aladdin hardcover edition February 2014
Text copyright © 2012 by Kate O'Hearn
Jacket illustration copyright © 2014 by Jason Chan
Originally published in Great Britain in 2012
Published by arrangement with Hachette UK
For information about special discounts for bulk purchases, please contact Simon & Schuster
Special Sales at 1-866-506-1949 or business@simonandschuster.com.
The Simon & Schuster Speakers Bureau can bring authors to your live event. For more
information or to book an event contact the Simon & Schuster Speakers Bureau at
1-866-248-3049 or visit our website at www.simonspeakers.com.
Jacket designed by Karin Paprocki
Interior designed by Mike Rosamilia
The text of this book was set in Adobe Garamond.
Manufactured in the United States of America 0114 FFG
2 4 6 8 10 9 7 5 3 1
Library of Congress Cataloging-in-Publication Data
O'Hearn, Kate.
The new Olympians / by Kate O'Hearn. — First Aladdin hardcover edition.
pages cm. — (Pegasus ; [3])
"Originally published in Great Britain in 2012; published by arrangement with Hachette UK."
Summary: "Pegasus and Emily investigate a series of incidents back on Earth, and discover that
the CRU has been cloning Olympians"—Provided by publisher.
ISBN 978-1-4424-4415-7
[1. Pegasus (Greek mythology)—Fiction. 2. Mythology, Greek—Fiction.
3. Cloning—Fiction. 4. Fantasy.] I. Title.
PZ7.O4137New 2014
[Fic]—dc23
2012051367
ISBN 978-1-4424-4417-1 (eBook)

*For Charlie, a white fifteen-year-old carriage horse
that collapsed and died on the streets of New York City,
October 2011. He soars with Pegasus now.*

*It is for Charlie and other abused horses like him
that we will keep fighting and shouting until our voices
are finally heard and the suffering ends. . . .*

THE ROAR OF THE CROWD WAS DEAFENING.
Olympians sprang to their feet cheering on the very
first inter-Olympian soccer match. The Solar Streamers were playing Hercules's Heroes, but this was no
ordinary soccer match. The scene on the field was as
impressive and extraordinary as you would expect on
Olympus.

When Joel first proposed the event, he was amazed
by how many Olympians wanted to get involved. Now,
with a full stadium of spectators cheering him on,
Joel, captain of the Solar Streamers, expertly maneuvered the ball down the pitch and between the legs of
a charging satyr. The half goat, half boy turned and
charged after him as if his very life depended on it.

Joel broke through the defense line and passed the black-and-white ball to his Olympian teammate and friend Paelen, who dashed forward to get into position. The winged boar, Chrysaor, caught up with Joel and drove away the Hercules's Heroes defenders, Mercury and Minerva, while Pegasus flew across the field over a line of centaurs and giants and called to Paelen to pass the ball. With a quick kick, the ball was in the winged stallion's possession.

Emily sat on the sidelines beside Jupiter. She marveled at how adept Pegasus was at a sport he and the other Olympians had only just learned. Pegasus was able to keep moving forward while the ball remained in play between his four hooves.

Suddenly a satyr ducked beneath Pegasus and stole the ball away. Moving swiftly on his goat legs, he kicked it back to his teammates. But no sooner did the opposing team have the ball than a young female centaur on Joel's team made a move that caused the crowd to cheer even louder. Leaping gracefully into the air, she blocked a high kick with her brown equine body. As the ball touched down on the ground, she expertly kicked it forward to Joel.

Running toward the goal line, Joel and Paelen kept the soccer ball moving between them. Finally Joel moved into position to shoot it at the goal.

"Go for it, Joel!" Emily shouted from her seat. "Shoot!"

The opposing side's goalkeeper was a terrifying sight. The Sphinx reared on her lion's haunches, spread her arms and eagle's wings wide, and prepared to block Joel's shot.

With one quick dart away from a young Nirad defender, Joel kicked the ball. It flew in the air and then seemed to arch as if it had a life all its own. It caught the upper bar of the goalposts and flew into the net above the head of the Sphinx.

When the goalkeeper saw the ball enter her goal, she roared in fury and sprang forward, tackling Joel to the ground.

Emily's heart nearly stopped. The Sphinx had Joel pinned down with her large lion paws. She threw back her head, roaring a second time, and raised a fearsome paw in the air, as if to tear into him with her sharpened claws.

"Jupiter, stop her!" Emily cried to the leader of

Olympus standing beside her. "The Sphinx will tear him apart!"

But instead of moving to stop the attack, Jupiter cheered louder and started to applaud. He leaned closer to her. "My dear child, Alexis may be short-tempered, but she knows this is just a game. Joel is perfectly safe." Jupiter paused and looked at all the men in the stands raising their hands and cheering. "I am certain that Joel is the subject of many Olympians' envy."

Out on the field, the players on Joel's team continued to celebrate the goal, unconcerned by the goalkeeper's assault on their star player. Finally the Sphinx brushed back the hair from Joel's eyes, leaned forward, and kissed him full and long on the lips.

"Foul!" shouted Emily as she ran furiously onto the field. Pushing between the players, she shoved the goalkeeper. "Get off him!"

As the Sphinx climbed slowly off Joel, her serpent's tail swished playfully in the air. She narrowed her green eyes and smiled mischievously at Emily. "Is the Flame of Olympus jealous?"

The Sphinx may have looked ferocious and dangerous with her lion's body, eagle's wings, and serpent's tail, but she had the head and upper body of a young woman. In fact, she was breathtakingly beautiful.

Emily paused and looked from Alexis to Joel. Seeing him on the ground with his beaming smile, warm brown eyes, and handsome face, Emily was stunned to realize that she was very jealous.

"Of course not!" she shot back. "But kissing the opposing players isn't part of the game."

The smile never left the Sphinx's face as she padded lithely back to her position in front of the goal. She looked playfully over her shoulder, flicking her long raven hair. "Pity. It should be."

Paelen reached forward and, with Emily's help, lifted the stunned Joel to his feet. As they brushed him off, Paelen stole a look back at Alexis. "Wow!" he breathed. "That was some kiss. You are so lucky!"

The color in Joel's cheeks brightened further as Alexis called, "I will see you later, Joel."

"Don't count on it," Emily fired back. She ignored the soft chuckles coming from the Sphinx and returned her attention to Joel. During his time in

Olympus, he had grown taller and more muscular from all the physical work in Vulcan's workshop. Joel's growth spurt was the cause of much complaint from Vulcan, as he constantly had to enlarge the silver mechanical right arm that replaced the one Joel had lost in the fight against the gorgons.

"Did Alexis hurt you?" Emily asked.

Joel looked back at the Sphinx curiously and then shook his head. "Not at all."

Paelen smiled his crooked grin, then pursed his lips in an exaggerated kiss. "Perhaps bruise your tender lips?"

"What?" Joel cried. He shoved Paelen away as his cheeks reddened deeper. "Stop that. I'm fine! Can we please get back to the match?"

As the players returned to their positions, Pegasus escorted Emily to her seat on the sidelines. The stallion nickered softly, and Emily saw an extra sparkle in his beautiful dark eyes. Pegasus was laughing.

"What are you laughing at?" she challenged.

Emily's teacher, Vesta, approached, overhearing the conversation. "Pegasus believes the Sphinx was correct. You are jealous of her."

"Jealous of Alexis? That's crazy," Emily said. "For one, she's just an overgrown, green-eyed, flying house cat. And for two, Joel and I are friends. That's all."

The smile on Vesta's face grew. "Of course you are, dear. . . ."

"We're friends," Emily insisted as she returned to her seat. "That's all! Now, Pegs, your team is waiting for you; you'd better get back."

Pegasus let out a loud, laughing whinny before trotting back to the field of play to take his position on Joel's team.

As the match progressed, the score remained tied. While the Sphinx was the Hercules's Heroes goalkeeper, Joel's team had a huge orange Nirad called Tirk guarding their end. With his four arms, he proved a capable goalie and rarely allowed the ball into the net.

"That's quite a match going on out there. But I'm not too sure if flying up and down the field is in the rulebook."

Emily jumped at the sound of her father's voice. "Dad!" She threw her arms around his neck. "I've missed you."

He had been away from Olympus with Diana and Apollo for what felt like ages. They were leading a small team back to Earth to determine if Jupiter's ban on visits should be lifted. The Olympians had heard about human advancements and were curious to learn more. Her father went as an adviser and guide.

When Emily released her father, she welcomed Diana with a firm hug. "I've missed you both. When did you get back?"

"Not long ago," her father said. "We went to the palace first and were told about the big match."

He looked at the pitch and whistled in amazement. "When you told me you and Joel were teaching some of the Olympians to play soccer, it never dawned on me who or what would be playing. I've never seen a more fantastic sight."

Emily looked over at the satyrs, harpies, centaurs, giants and some of the Muses out on the field playing alongside winged creatures never mentioned or even imagined in the ancient myths.

"We tried to teach Cerberus to play, but it didn't work," Emily continued. "His three heads kept fighting over the ball and tearing it to shreds. It was the same with the Cyclops. With only one eye, he kept missing the ball and got really frustrated. He even tore down the goal in a rage. Jupiter finally had to ask him to keep score. You can see him over there." She pointed to the end of the field, where the giant Cyclops was updating the scoreboard with each goal. "But most of the other Olympians seem to enjoy the game."

Their eyes were drawn back to the field, where a satyr had broken free of the giant guard and was rushing with the ball toward Joel's team's goal. As she neared the net, Paelen appeared from the left to block the kick. But the satyr was faster and she easily got away from him. With a second quick dart, she kicked the ball between the Nirad's four arms, and it entered the net.

The crowd exploded with excitement and stood cheering. Emily looked around and smiled ruefully at the Olympians. She glanced back to her father. "I don't think they fully understand the concept of supporting one side or the other. Everyone celebrates when there is a goal—it doesn't matter which team made it."

Her father nodded. "Maybe they've got the right idea. We could use more sportsmanship like that back in our world." He focused on Emily again. "You love soccer. Even with your leg brace, you can move just as well as before your leg was hurt. Why aren't you out there playing?"

Emily hesitated before answering. "I didn't feel like playing today. I wanted to watch with Jupiter so I could explain the rules. Not that anyone actually follows them."

Emily watched her father's face, relieved that he accepted her explanation without question. Emily wanted very much to play, but she couldn't. She couldn't because she couldn't trust herself.

Since her return from the Nirad world, where they'd defeated the gorgons, Emily had mastered the power of the Flame that lived deep within her. She could now control it fully. But recently more powers had surfaced. Powers that went beyond the Flame. Where objects moved by themselves, or sometimes, if she became very frustrated or upset, vanished completely. Vesta hadn't mentioned more powers. Emily wondered if her teacher even realized there were others. But too many things were happening around her. Until Emily could better understand and control them, she wasn't going to risk hurting her friends.

The match ended with Joel's team losing by one goal. A celebratory banquet was planned for later that evening. Emily walked with her father and Pegasus back to the apartment they shared with Joel and Paelen in Jupiter's palace.

"I am going to tell Jupiter that I don't think it's a good idea for Olympians to visit Earth. There are just too many dangers. Our world has changed far too much for them now. They had no idea how different or advanced it is."

"But after everything they've heard from us, they're all so anxious to visit," Emily insisted.

"I know," he agreed. "The big problem is that Olympians aren't human. Very few of them look even remotely human. Can you imagine what would happen if a centaur or even the Cyclops were to visit our world? In the past, they were accepted as gods, but today . . ." He paused and looked back to Pegasus. "Look what happened to him in New York."

Pegasus snorted and nickered loudly. Emily

reached over and stroked the stallion's neck. Memories flashed to the surface of her mind. Pegasus had been shot by the secret government agency the Central Research Unit, and taken to their hidden facility on Governors Island. The sight of her beloved stallion lying prone on the floor and struggling for each breath caused a stab of pain in her heart, even now.

Emily looked back at her father and nodded. "It wasn't just Pegasus who was hurt. Look what the CRU did to Cupid. Their helicopters nearly killed him, despite Olympians being immortal. If they stop eating ambrosia, they become vulnerable, and it's too easy for them to get hurt."

"Or captured," her father added. "Personally, I don't think it's a good idea at all. I'm going to tell Jupiter this. Olympians are an amazing people, and I don't want to see anything happen to them."

As they continued to walk down the tranquil, cobbled road, the clopping sound of Pegasus's golden hooves was the only thing to disturb the calm of Olympus. After a long silence, Emily's father spoke again.

"Your aunt Maureen sends her love."

"You saw her?"

He shook his head. "There were CRU agents posted around her building; we couldn't get near her. But I did call and tell her we are fine. She asked a lot of questions, but I'm sure her line is bugged. So I told her we're in hiding but together and safe."

"I wish we could see her again," Emily said wistfully.

"Me too," her father agreed. "Maybe one day soon we can go back for a real visit. Just you and me."

Emily brightened. "That would be wonderful."

When they arrived at their apartment, Emily's eyes flew wide at the assortment of gifts her father and Diana had brought back for her, Joel, and Paelen: clothes, music, and some of Emily's favorite snacks, like salted peanuts and her real weakness, marshmallows. There was even an assortment of chocolate bars just for Paelen.

Emily noticed a stack of newspapers. She had never been interested in the news when she lived in New York, but now that she was living in Olympus permanently, she craved to learn what was happening in her city.

Top of the pile was the *New York Times*. A photograph on the front page caught her attention.

Was that Pegasus?

Emily immediately snatched it up, curious.

Yes, it was definitely Pegasus—but without wings!

She read the caption under the photograph.

Record Breaker! Tornado Warning wins Triple Crown with greatest time and distance ever recorded.

"Tornado Warning?" Emily muttered aloud as she read the article about the winning horse breaking every record in the history of horse racing.

"Look at that face," her father said lightly. "He looks just like Pegasus, doesn't he? His body and legs are darker gray, but if he were all white, it could have been Pegasus. Tornado Warning is everywhere and causing quite a stir. They haven't had a Triple Crown winner like him since Secretariat—and Tornado's even broken his records!"

Emily barely heard the knocking on the door. As her father went to answer it, she continued to scan the article.

"Pegs, you've got to see this." Emily held up the

newspaper for the stallion. "Look at his face. He really does look like you. I mean, you two could be twins!"

When Pegasus looked at the photographs, Emily could sense he was greatly disturbed. Apart from the color, Tornado Warning was identical. His size and shape were the same. All that was missing were the wings and golden hooves. Emily looked at the stallion. "How is this possible?"

"So you have seen the newspapers." Diana had entered the living room and approached Pegasus. "Is there something you wish to tell me? Did you get up to some mischief while you were in Emily's world?"

Pegasus snorted angrily and stamped a golden hoof.

Emily frowned and then shook her head. "That's not possible. Tornado couldn't be his son. Look here, the paper says Tornado Warning is three years old. But Pegasus only came to our world last year."

"But he does look just like you, my friend," Diana said softly as she stroked Pegasus's face. "What else could it be?"

Emily's father, Steve, shrugged. "Maybe he's just a

very handsome horse who happens to look a lot like Pegasus."

Emily studied her father's face and realized he didn't see Pegasus the same way she and the other Olympians did. On the surface, Pegasus could look mostly like a horse, but there was a big difference. It was something that she could plainly see, but her father couldn't. Pegasus was more than a horse, much greater than one. It was in his intelligent eyes and the way he held himself, that created the aura surrounding him that said, *I am not a mere horse.*

Olympus had many horses and some, like Pegasus, had wings. But none of them were remotely like Pegasus. He was unique—until now.

"You're wrong, Dad," Emily insisted. "Tornado Warning doesn't just look like Pegasus, he's identical to him."

Diana put her arm around Emily and gave her a light squeeze. "Well, whatever it is, that horse, Tornado Warning, is in your world while we are all here in Olympus." Diana abruptly changed the subject. "Now, would you like to try on some of the new clothes that your father and I chose for you?"

Emily looked at Diana and saw there was something the tall woman was not saying aloud. A secret message that said they would speak later. She nodded. "You're right. Let's forget Tornado Warning. I want to see what you've brought back."

WHILE EXCITED PREPARATIONS WERE BEING made to celebrate the closing of Olympus's first official soccer match, Emily and Pegasus walked through the fragrant gardens at the back of Jupiter's palace. The air was warm, sweet, and still, and the sun was welcoming but not too hot. Birds chirped in the sky and called a greeting at Emily and Pegasus's approach.

Up ahead lay Jupiter's maze. This was still the best place for Emily and her friends to meet and talk without being seen or disturbed by the other Olympians.

When they reached the center, they didn't have long to wait before Joel, Paelen, and Pegasus's brother Chrysaor appeared. Joel's hair was wet from bathing after the game, slicked back in an effortlessly cool look. Paelen had also bathed to remove the mud and grass stains from the match, but as always his dark hair was unkempt and standing up at odd angles. He was still wearing his winged sandals and had a big grin on his face as he drew near.

"What's up?" Joel asked. "What's the emergency?"

Emily offered the newspapers around. "I couldn't show you these earlier because Dad was in the apartment and doesn't see the problem. Look at the picture and read the headline."

Paelen looked from the front page of one of the newspapers over to Pegasus. His mouth fell open. "He looks just like you! What does this say?"

A frown wrinkled Joel's brow as he read the article. "It's talking about a racehorse, Tornado Warning. He's just won the Triple Crown."

"What is the Triple Crown?" Paelen asked.

Joel continued. "My father was really into horse racing." He looked over to Pegasus wistfully. "I sure wish he could have met you." Joel sighed. "He and I used to bet on the Triple Crown. It's a series of three big horse races that are close together: the Kentucky

Derby, the Preakness Stakes, and then finally the Belmont Stakes. It's really rare for the same horse to win all three. I think the last time was in the 1970s. But Tornado Warning not only won all three races, he's beaten all the records." Joel paused and looked at Emily. "Something doesn't feel right here. Look at these stats." He held up another paper.

Emily peered over and saw a lot of figures she didn't understand. "What's all that mean?"

"It means this is impossible. Look at these racing times. He's got to be the fastest racehorse in history. No horse could run like this."

"But he just did," Paelen insisted.

Beside them, Chrysaor squealed softly, and Paelen lowered his paper so the winged boar could look at the photograph. He grunted and squealed again.

"I do not understand," Paelen asked. "How could this racehorse look so much like Pegasus, run as fast as Pegasus, and yet not be Pegasus?"

Joel shrugged. "If I didn't know better, I'd swear he was a—" A sudden shocked expression appeared on his face, and he shook his head. "No, it's not possible. Are you thinking what I'm thinking?"

Emily was already frightened. The idea had come to her much earlier and left her chilled to the bone. But it was still the only thing that made any sense.

"I'm trying really hard not to," she said. "I asked my dad, and he didn't think so. He said if it were true, Tornado Warning would be white and not gray."

"What?" Paelen asked. "What are you both talking about?"

Emily leaned her head against Pegasus and stroked his neck. "We're thinking that the CRU may have had something to do with this."

Paelen's jaw dropped. "The CRU? How?"

Joel stepped closer to Emily. "It's impossible, isn't it?"

"I just don't know," she said. "But what else could it be?"

"We've got to go back there to find out," Joel finished. "Em, if they can actually do it, we're all in a lot of trouble."

"Enough!" shouted Paelen in frustration. "You are both speaking in riddles, and it is driving me mad! What you are talking about?"

Joel looked at Paelen. "This is going to sound

impossible. But we're thinking that Tornado Warning might be some kind of clone."

Paelen's expression didn't change. Emily realized he didn't understand. "In our world, science is constantly advancing. They are doing amazing things with genetically modifying plants and stuff. What Joel is saying is that while you, Pegasus, and Diana were prisoners of the CRU, they tested you and did experiments. They took samples from you."

Paelen shivered visibly. "It was terrible," he said softly. "They put me in machines, and kept taking my blood, my hair, and who knows what else."

"Exactly," Joel said. "And what I'm afraid of is that they have somehow used those samples to create some kind of clone. A clone is something that is identical to you, created from you, but not you. It's kind of like a twin, but you weren't born together." He crossed over to the stallion and stroked his face. "Tornado Warning looks exactly like Pegasus because he might have been created using cells they took from Pegasus."

Emily's face went pale. "That's crazy, like something out of a fantasy! But if he's a clone, shouldn't he be white like Pegasus?"

"We dyed Pegasus black and brown, remember? What if they are dyeing Tornado Warning gray?" Joel suggested. "I don't know if or how they could have done it, but we've got to find out. Em, we're talking about the CRU. We've seen their facilities. I'm sure they have the capabilities to do it."

Emily shook her head. "But it doesn't make any sense. Even if it is possible, why would they race him and risk exposing their experiments? Besides, the newspapers say Tornado Warning is three years old."

"I can't explain it," Joel said. "But look at those photographs. It's like Pegasus himself was in those races. Those aren't the stats of an ordinary horse."

Pegasus snorted and started to cut deep trenches in the ground. Beside him, Paelen shook his head madly. "No, no, no. This is not possible. You cannot suggest that this racehorse comes from Pegasus. It is unnatural and impossible!"

He stomped up to Emily and pointed at the stallion in one of the photographs "Pegasus has wings. This racehorse does not. If he was created from Pegasus, surely he should have wings!"

Emily nodded. "I thought the same thing until I

saw this." She lowered herself to the soft grass in the maze and started to search through the newspapers. "Here." She pointed at a close-up color photograph of Tornado Warning in the winner's circle. The jockey was still on his back. Beneath the jockey's right knee, there was a trace of a large scar on Tornado's pale-gray shoulder. "Look at that scar. That could be where they removed his wing."

"That is a crease in the paper, nothing more," Paelen insisted. "It does not prove anything."

Joel picked up the paper and studied the image. He shook his head. "This isn't any crease, Paelen—it's a scar. And it proves one thing. We've got to go back there and see that racehorse for ourselves. If the CRU are capable of creating clones, just think of what they could do with your and Diana's DNA."

The enormity of the situation struck Emily like a brick. She looked up at Joel. "Not only Olympian DNA, Joel. Remember, the CRU had captured Nirads as well!"

3

AS THE SUN STARTED TO SET IN OLYMPUS, the soccer pitch had been turned into a huge party ground. Tables were laden with fruit, ambrosia, and nectar as thousands of Olympians gathered to celebrate the game. Torches were lit and shining brightly on the gathering, while the Muses danced and sang for the entertainment of the crowd.

Above the pitch, Cupid led a group of winged Olympians carrying flags and banners. They rose and dipped in the sky, sometimes so low they touched the tops of the heads of those below on the ground.

Cupid spied Emily entering the stadium and swooped down. Folding his large wings neatly on his back, he bowed before her. "Hello, Flame, would you like to come for a short flight with me?"

"Her name is Emily!" challenged Paelen, as he had done hundreds of times before. "When will you finally learn that?"

Cupid smiled radiantly at Emily. "When she tells me so."

Emily held up a calming hand to Paelen and then looked back at the winged Olympian. Nothing remained of the crush she once felt for him. Cupid was just as handsome as ever, but her heart was elsewhere now.

"Thank you anyway, Cupid, but I'd rather stay on the ground for the moment. Perhaps later."

"Of course, Flame," Cupid said, shooting a teasing look at Paelen. "You need only to ask." He kissed Emily's cheek and then leaped confidently into the sky.

"I keep telling you, Emily," Paelen said, "you should have left him as a stone statue in the Nirad world. It would have solved all our problems."

"I thought you two were becoming friends," Joel offered.

"Cupid and me?" Paelen said. "Hardly. I mean yes,

he did help us defeat the gorgons and overcame his fear of the Nirads. But Cupid is still Cupid. He is an arrogant mischief-maker."

Diana joined the group and faced Paelen, her expression stern. "Not too long ago people were saying the same thing about you, little thief."

Paelen shrugged. "Perhaps. But I have changed. Cupid has not."

"Really?" Diana said. "It is said that once a thief, forever a thief. I know there are several Olympians who still count their coins and jewels after you leave."

Paelen's face dropped. Despite everything he had done to help Olympus, there were a great number of Olympians who believed he hadn't changed his thieving ways.

Emily felt for him. What would it take to get them to believe he was different? She also knew that despite his wounded feelings, Paelen was smart enough not to rise to the comment. Diana's temper was legendary. It was better to let the remark rest than say something that would anger her.

Always the policeman, Emily's father came forward to calm the situation. He put his arm around Paelen and then indicated the gathering Olympians on the field. "Look at this place, this is insane! Any excuse for a party. C'mon, everyone, let's have some fun."

Emily wasn't in much of a mood to join in the celebrations around her. Neither were Joel or Paelen. A dark shadow was resting heavily over them. They weren't alone in their worry. Both Pegasus and Chrysaor were showing signs of profound disquiet.

While her father left to gather drinks for everyone, Emily stood with Diana and Pegasus. Joel nudged her gently in the back and whispered, "Ask her now."

Diana's keen hearing hadn't missed the comment. She turned back and looked suspiciously at Joel. "Ask me what?"

Emily inhaled deeply. "Diana, we need to speak with you about something important, but I don't want my dad to know yet."

Diana frowned. "This is about that racehorse, is it not?"

Emily nodded. "It may be nothing. But we need to go back to our world to see if Tornado Warning is something more than a horse. We must get away without anyone knowing."

Her father was walking back to the group, carrying a tray of ambrosia cakes and goblets of nectar.

Diana leaned closer to Emily. "After the party, meet me at the base of the Temple of the Flame. We will speak then."

The party continued well into the night. When it was over, Emily said good night to her father and waited for him to return to his room. When she was sure he'd gone to bed, she left her quarters and headed into the garden to meet her friends.

Pegasus and Chrysaor were already there. After a short time, Paelen and Joel arrived. For speed, they agreed to fly to the temple. As Emily climbed onto Pegasus, Joel settled himself on the back of Chrysaor. Paelen looked down at his winged sandals and ordered them to carry him to the temple. With a quick flap of their tiny wings, they obeyed and lifted him lightly into the air.

Of all the things Emily loved about living in Olympus, the very best was flying on the back of Pegasus. Flying at night was even better. Many times, when her father thought she was in bed, she and Pegasus would sneak out of the palace and spend a long night soaring in the skies over Olympus. Each time they went out, the bright canopy of stars never failed to take Emily's breath away. They always filled her with profound excitement, as though the stars themselves called to her and beckoned her to join them in the sky.

It was these stars that reminded her they were no longer on her world. None of the constellations she knew appeared in an Olympian's night sky. There was no moon, and the stars seemed brighter and much closer.

But this night, there was none of the usual excitement. They launched silently into the air and flew over the dark palace. On the ground below, strange-looking Olympians moved around. These were the citizens who lived their lives only by night.

Emily had learned very quickly not to fear the night dwellers. Though they looked different with their pale skin and huge dark eyes, they spoke very softly and posed no danger to her or Pegasus. She discovered that Olympus was like two worlds in one. A day world filled with sunshine and bright colors and ruled by Jupiter; and then a night world that existed only by starlight, filled with strange, silent beings overseen by Jupiter's brother, Pluto. Olympus at night was the underworld the myths so often spoke of.

Emily looked over to Joel and realized this was the first time he'd ever seen this Olympus. At any other time, he would have asked her lots of questions and insisted on flying down to meet the night creatures. Not tonight. He looked at the night dwellers with curiosity, but remained silent.

Up ahead they saw a bright glow shining in the dark night sky. It was coming from the top of the Temple of the Flame. This was the Flame that gave the Olympians their powers and strength. Without it, Olympus would fall. It was the same Flame that Emily's power fed. She had been born with the living heart of the Flame deep within her. When she sacrificed herself in the temple, her powers were released and renewed the Flame in the temple. It was her connection to the Flame that made Jupiter and all the Olympians so protective of her. Though she still didn't understand how it worked, she did know the survival of the Olympians depended on that Flame continuing to burn. And the survival of the Flame depended on her.

As Pegasus glided lower, Emily was surprised to see three dark figures standing at the base of the temple. Drawing nearer, she saw her father standing beside Diana. His hands were on his hips, and he didn't look happy.

Emily stole a look over to Joel on Chrysaor's back. He glanced back at her. "I think we might be in trouble," Joel said.

Emily was tempted to tell Pegasus to turn around and go back to the palace. But it was too late. With Pegasus glowing in the dark sky, everyone had seen them coming.

When the stallion touched down on the ground before the three figures, Emily frowned. Standing beside her father and Diana was a third figure that she didn't recognize.

Emily's father came forward to help her down from the stallion. "Isn't there something you want to tell me before you sneak away from Olympus?"

Emily's heart nearly stopped. Diana had told him everything. She dropped her head. "I'm sorry, Dad.

I wanted to tell you, but I know you'll want to stop me."

"Darn right I'm going to stop you. Emily, you can't go back there; it's too dangerous. What were you thinking?"

"It's my fault, Steve, not Emily's." Joel stepped in to defend her. "I was the one who suggested we go. We told Diana so at least someone would know what happened to us."

"This is about that stupid racehorse, isn't it?"

"Dad, listen to me, please," Emily begged. "Tornado Warning looks too much like Pegasus and runs too quickly to be an ordinary horse. You know that. If you didn't think so, you wouldn't have brought the newspapers to show us. We need to find out. If there's even a small chance he's a clone, we've got to know. Don't you see? If the CRU can clone him, they can do the same with the other Olympians."

"Or Nirads," Paelen added.

The third shadowy figure came forward. "Do you seriously believe this is possible? The CRU could create New Olympians from our blood?"

When he moved closer, Emily saw how much he

looked like Jupiter and Neptune. But his eyes were more intense and as black as the night sky. His skin was pale as parchment. This must be the third brother, Pluto. He was the owner of Cerberus and leader of the underworld. She had heard all about him, but had yet to meet him.

Emily bowed her head respectfully. "We're not sure, sir." She turned to her father. "Dad, you've seen him on TV. Can you say for sure that Tornado Warning isn't some kind of clone from Pegasus?"

Emily's father combed his fingers through his hair. He looked from Diana to Pluto. He shook his head. "No, I can't. Human science is moving so quickly, I have no idea what they can achieve."

"Don't you see?" Emily pleaded. "That's why we must go back there and see for ourselves. If Tornado Warning is just a horse, we can forget all about him. But if he is actually a clone from Pegasus, then we've got to know. What could the CRU do with an army of cloned Olympians or Nirads? They could take over the world!"

"Or maybe even challenge Olympus," Joel added.

Pluto's voice dropped. "If that horse you speak of

really has been created from Pegasus, all of Olympus will be outraged! Jupiter will go to your world to stop them." He paused before staring Emily directly in the eye. "I will join him. The development of such creatures from our blood must not be tolerated. If this is true and they have created New Olympians, we will have no recourse but to destroy Earth."

4

EMILY LOOKED AT PLUTO IN COMPLETE shock. Could it be true? Would the Olympians really destroy her world? Jupiter had always been so generous and treated her like a granddaughter. Would he actually do it?

"It is true." Diana looked around and started to whisper. "Should my father hear of this, he would not hesitate to destroy your world even before there was proof. I have seen him do it before. Jupiter is capable of anything if it means protecting Olympus and the order of nature."

Emily's father shook his head. "But Earth has billions of innocent people and animals. Jupiter wouldn't destroy all of that just to punish the CRU for doing something stupid."

Diana sighed heavily. "I am sorry, Steve, but he would."

"Apollo has also seen the photos," Pluto added. "He came to me quietly, voicing his concerns. I discouraged him from telling his father. But we are all loyal to Jupiter. If the CRU has done this thing, we have no recourse but to tell Jupiter and let the punishment fit the crime."

"Destroying Earth is too great a punishment!" Steve argued. "Especially if it's just a few people who have done this—and we aren't even certain that they have done anything at all!"

"Which is why we've got to go to see for ourselves," Emily added.

"Emily is correct," Pluto said. "We must let them go see if this racehorse is real or an unnatural creation of your people."

Her father started to pace the area. "All right, but I'm coming with you."

Pegasus nickered softly. He approached Diana and made a long series of sounds.

"Pegasus does not agree," she translated. "He says you must remain here. You and I are scheduled to make our full report to my father following our trip. They will only be gone a very short time. I can make excuses to my father about why Emily and the others are not here, perhaps tell them that they have gone to the Nirad world to visit the queen. But if you leave as well, it will draw my father's suspicions, especially so soon after our return. With all that is at stake, we must not risk that."

"But it's too dangerous," Steve insisted.

"Dad, please," Emily said. "We've got to go. We'll be really quick. You must keep Jupiter occupied and stop Apollo from telling him about Tornado until we figure this out."

"But how can I protect you?" her father said as he pulled her into a tight embrace and kissed the top of her head. "The CRU separated us once. I couldn't bear that to happen again."

"It won't," Joel promised. "This isn't like before. We're not breaking into a CRU facility. We're just going to go see Tornado Warning at a racetrack."

Steve sighed heavily. "I really wish I were coming with you."

"So do I," Emily agreed as she held her father. "But

we'll be careful. I promise. You just keep Jupiter busy so he doesn't notice we're gone."

As the sun started to rise the meeting was called to a halt by Pluto. They agreed to meet at the temple the following evening to prepare for departure.

The next day Emily, Joel, and Paelen packed up their new clothing and a good supply of ambrosia and nectar for the trip. Emily barely got to see her father, as he spent most of the day with Jupiter, Diana, and Apollo, presenting their report. She ached to speak with him, to talk about her fears for their world if Jupiter ever found out.

Until now, everything Emily had done was to protect and defend Olympus; first from the Nirads and then from the gorgons. But now, as she checked and rechecked her backpack, she realized that she, the Flame of Olympus, might be forced to protect Earth from the Olympians.

As night arrived and Emily's father returned from a long day with Jupiter, they waited for Olympus to go to sleep before heading out to the Temple of the Flame.

For the short journey, Emily's father rode with her on the back of Pegasus. She felt his reassuring arms around her and silently wished he were coming with them. But Pegasus was right. He had to stay to keep Jupiter from getting suspicious.

Diana and Pluto were waiting at the temple. As she and her father climbed down from Pegasus, Emily noticed that Pluto was holding a package in his hands.

Diana came forward. "I have told my father that you are all going to the Nirad world to visit the queen. He has no cause to question it. But you must be swift. My father understands your need for independence and freedom, but he does not like it when the Flame of Olympus is away from here."

"I understand," Emily said grimly. "We'll be as quick as we can."

While they spoke, Pluto opened the sack he was carrying, pulled out an ornate leather helmet, and held it up.

Paelen sucked in his breath. "That is your helmet of invisibility! Are you coming with us?"

Pluto shook his head. "No, I must remain here to ensure my brother does not become suspicious. However, my helmet will be joining you on your quest."

"May I wear it?" Paelen asked.

"It is not for you," Pluto said.

"For me?" Joel asked hopefully. "I've read all about that helmet. It's amazing."

Again, Pluto shook his head and said no.

Finally Emily said, "It's for Pegasus, isn't it? So he can travel with us and not be seen."

"I am sorry, no. I wish I could give you something to keep Pegasus hidden, but I have only the one helmet to offer."

"If not us, who is going to wear it?" Paelen asked.

"I am." A voice came from behind them.

Emily turned, and her eyes flew wide at the sight of the Sphinx landing silently on the ground. She folded her eagle's wings neatly and padded forward. As she walked past Joel, she brushed against him like a cat brushing against the legs of its owner at feeding time.

"No way!" Emily cried, feeling her temper rising. "You aren't coming with us!"

"Yes, she is," Diana said sternly. "This is the price you will pay for our cooperation in this. If you insist on returning to your world to see Tornado Warning, then Alexis is coming with you. She has great skills that will keep you safe."

"But she's a—a—" Emily struggled for the right word.

"Careful, child," Alexis warned. She approached Emily and rose up on her lion's hind legs. Her serpent's tail swished in the air in annoyance as she rested her paws on Emily's shoulders. Her claws were drawn. "We are not playing now, Emily. This is very serious. I have been told what is happening. Diana has asked me to accompany you to keep you safe. This is what I intend to do."

"You're just going to spy on us," Emily challenged, forcing herself not to look at the Sphinx's claws so close to her face.

Diana moved forward. "Alexis, get down." She concentrated on Emily. "Alexis is not a spy. It is her job to keep you safe. You are the Flame of Olympus. You must be protected at all times."

"I can take care of myself," Emily replied. "I beat the gorgons. You know I can control the Flame now."

Emily's father stood with her. "Em, we all know

you can control the Flame. But our world is a dangerous place—not just from the CRU." He looked over
to Pegasus. "And I know you'll do everything you
can to keep her safe. But Alexis has special skills that
you don't. Diana tells me she can sense danger before
it comes. She can move silently and swiftly and can
read a person's intentions. She will be an asset you
can't turn down."

Alexis held up a paw. "Thank you, Steve, but
perhaps there is another way to settle this." She
approached Emily. "I will ask you a riddle. If you
answer correctly, I will not go. However, if your
answer is wrong, I will go and you will say no more
about it."

"You want to play a game?" Emily demanded.
"Now? Right before we leave?"

"This is no game," Alexis answered seriously.
"Either you will answer my riddle, or I will join you
without your permission."

"Be careful, Em," Joel warned. "Alexis is the
Sphinx."

"What's that supposed to mean?" Emily said.

Alexis looked at Joel. "Say no more, Joel. This is

between Emily and me." She concentrated on Emily. "Riddle me this . . .

My shallow hills are the faces of kings
My horizon is always near
My music sends men to the grave
My absence sends men to work.
What am I?"

Emily frowned as she tried to work out the simple riddle. Since Alexis was from Olympus, she figured the answer would have to be something Olympian. What shallow hills were in Olympus with a close horizon? None, so it was not a place. The next line was about music. But what kind of music sent men to the grave but absence sent them to work? The Muses sang beautifully, but they never killed with their songs. Who did?

Emily smiled. "I know."

"Tell me," the Sphinx demanded.

"The answer is: the Sirens."

Alexis laughed. "You are wrong."

Emily's temper flared. "No I'm not. The Sirens

send men to their graves in the water, but when they leave, the sailors can get back to work. So it's got to be the Sirens."

"You are wrong," Alexis repeated.

"So what is the answer?"

"That is for me to know and you to figure out."

"What?" Emily cried. "You're cheating. I got the answer right and you don't want to admit it!"

The hackles on Alexis's lion's back rose as the Sphinx narrowed her green eyes. "Cheat? You accuse me of cheating!" She advanced on Emily.

Emily took a step back and raised her hands. She felt the tingling of power flowing down her arms to her hands. The Flame was just a breath away.

"Alexis, enough," Pluto said. "Control yourself. Emily, you too!"

The Sphinx's furious green eyes lingered on Emily a moment longer before she turned back to Pluto. "As you command."

Emily lowered her hands but refused to take her wary eyes off the Sphinx.

Pegasus nickered softly and nodded. He stepped closer to Emily and nudged her in the back gently.

 45

"He says Alexis never lies," Paelen translated. "If you had said the correct answer, she is bound by honor and the laws of Olympus to tell you. Your answer was wrong."

Emily started to protest further until Pluto raised his voice. "This is not open for discussion. The riddle was asked, the answer given. Alexis will go with you."

"But—" Emily cried.

Pluto shook his head. "You are the Flame of Olympus and too precious to risk. Either you will take Alexis with you, or you will not go at all."

Joel leaned over to her. "It'll be all right, Em. With Pluto's helmet, you'll never even see her. We'll just go, see Tornado Warning, and come right back."

Emily looked at Joel, then Paelen, who was nodding his head enthusiastically. It was obvious how much they both liked the Sphinx. Finally her eyes trailed over to Alexis, who was still eyeing her up dangerously. She shook her head. "I have a very bad feeling about this."

5

THE GROUP ENTERED THE BRIGHT, POWER-
ful light of the Solar Stream. This was the passage
the Olympians used to travel between worlds. It was
loud and filled with white energy that caused the hair
on Emily's arms to stand on end. Riding on Pegasus, she recalled her father's fearful face as he watched
her go. She prayed she would be returning to him in
Olympus soon with good news.

Behind Emily and Pegasus was Joel on Chrysaor,
while Paelen flew beside them using his winged sandals. Emily looked back and saw Alexis at the very
rear. The Sphinx's face was grim as her large wings
beat in rhythm with Pegasus's.

When they burst free of the Solar Stream, Emily

was alarmed to feel the sunny warmth of a summer day. What her father said was true. The time between the worlds was completely different. While it was night on Olympus, it was full daylight in the skies over New York City. They had also discovered that when a day passed in Olympus, weeks had sometimes passed on her world.

They had decided to return to the New York area, where the Belmont Stakes, the last race in the Triple Crown, was run. It was the final place Tornado Warning had been seen. When they emerged from the Solar Stream, Emily looked down to see the tall antennae of the Empire State Building pass directly beneath them. She could see tourists on the observation deck. They all seemed to be looking down on the world and failed to notice them. "Pegs, we're too low! Take us higher in the sky!"

Pegasus maneuvered his wings and led the group higher in the sky as he flew uptown over the city. Emily looked back at Joel. He was shaking his head. "That was too close!" he called. "Do you think anyone saw us?"

"I hope not!" Emily called back.

Joel shouted over to Paelen. "Take the lead! Ask your sandals to find Tornado Warning. Let's just take a look at him and get the heck out of here!"

Paelen directed his sandals forward. When he was a length ahead of Pegasus, he called down to his sandals, "Take us to Tornado Warning."

Emily gripped Pegasus's mane tighter and prepared to change direction in the sky. But when she looked at Paelen and then down to his winged sandals, nothing happened. Normally when he gave a command to the sandals, the wings fluttered to let him know they had heard and were obeying.

"Tornado Warning," Paelen repeated. "Find Tornado Warning."

Paelen repeated the command several more times, but the sandals remained unchanged. He looked back at Emily and shrugged. "They do not know where he is."

By now they were moving uptown. On their left, Emily saw the George Washington Bridge. She reached forward and pointed. "Pegasus, do you see that tall bridge over there? Please follow it. It will take us to where we can land." She called forward to Paelen, "Follow us!"

Pegasus veered in the sky. Beneath them, the tall suspension bridge crossed over the Hudson River and led them deeper into New Jersey. As they passed over Fort Lee, Emily saw a large area of dense trees rising to the far right. "Take us down, Pegs. We need to talk!"

After a few minutes of searching, Pegasus found a clearing in the trees. When the stallion neatly touched down, Emily slid off his back. She approached her friends.

"What happened?" she asked Paelen. "Why can't your sandals find Tornado?"

Paelen shrugged. "I do not know. They have never failed me before."

"Are they still working?" Joel asked. "Test them. Ask them to take you to Governors Island."

Paelen nodded and looked down at his winged sandals. "Take me to Governors Island." Immediately the tiny wings flapped in acknowledgment and lifted Paelen off the ground and moved in the direction of the small island off southern Manhattan. "Stop!" Paelen ordered. "Take me back to Emily."

"So they are still working," Joel muttered.

"Perhaps they do not recognize the command,"

Alexis added as she folded her wings and padded up to them. "If Tornado Warning comes from both Pegasus and this world, it may be confusing them."

"That's dumb," Emily said.

Alexis narrowed her green eyes. "Do you have a better suggestion?"

Emily didn't. But she didn't want the Sphinx to know that. She still resented Alexis being forced on them. "If the sandals can't find Tornado, what are we supposed to do? That was the plan."

Joel rubbed his chin. "Well, we can't go back until we've seen that horse. We just have to find him another way. Let's search the Internet to find out where he's racing next."

"How?" Emily asked. "It's not like we can just walk into an Internet cafe—we don't exactly blend in!"

"I wasn't suggesting that," Joel shot back. "We need someone with a home computer. Who do we know?"

"My aunt," Emily suggested. "But she's being watched by the CRU."

"I didn't have any school friends," Joel muttered. "And my foster family didn't own a computer, so no point going back there."

"I know," Paelen offered excitedly. "What about Earl? Perhaps he can help us."

Emily thought back to Earl, the owner of their old hideout, the Red Apple. He had helped them the last time they were in this world. Even after he'd been badly hurt—when the Nirads attacked—he'd done all he could to help.

She looked at Paelen and nodded. "That's not a bad idea. Do you think your sandals could find him?"

Paelen looked down at his sandals. "Take me to Earl."

The tiny wings flapped and lifted Paelen off the ground. There was no hesitation as they carried him over the trees and higher in the sky.

"Paelen, stop!" Joel cried. "Get back here!"

Paelen returned, and Joel looked at the group. "We can't go now, in daylight; we'll be seen. Lord only knows who's seen us already. We arrived too low in the sky over the city. I think we should wait here till dark. It will be safer to fly then."

Chrysaor nudged Joel's hand. He grunted several times. Pegasus also whinnied softly.

"They both agree, Joel," Paelen translated. "It is too big a risk to go now."

"Then it's settled," Emily said. "We wait till tonight, then we find Earl."

The day passed slowly as they sat among the trees waiting for sunset. Emily jumped at every crack and sound from the woods around them. She felt exposed and vulnerable, as though a CRU agent was hiding behind every tree and waiting to burst out at them at any moment.

Every time Emily jumped, Alexis shook her head and tutted. "Did Diana not tell you I can sense danger? Is that not the reason I am here? There is no danger; we are alone in these trees. So just sit there and let me do my job."

Emily sat on the ground beside Pegasus. Joel moved to sit beside her, leaning against the resting stallion's side.

"Alexis is right, Em, just relax. Don't you know who the Sphinx is?"

"A giant cat from the Egyptian desert," Emily said flatly.

Alexis bristled and hissed at the insult. "What did you say? Egyptian? That is not I!"

Joel held up his hand to the Sphinx. "Alexis, calm down. Not everyone in this world knows the stories."

"Then educate her. I will not suffer such insults again!" Without a second glance, the Sphinx wandered into the trees.

"Watch yourself around her," Joel warned. "The Sphinx is very dangerous. The myths say she used to guard the entrance to Thebes. Anyone who approached had to answer one of her riddles. If they got it wrong, she killed them. Some legends say she even ate them."

"Oh, gross!" Emily cried. She looked to where the Sphinx had entered the trees. "Wait, how could she eat them? Okay, she does have a lion's body and claws, but she has a woman's head. How could she?"

Paelen answered. "You have not seen her teeth."

"Yes, I have," Emily said.

Paelen shook his head. "No, you have not. If you had, you would not be asking the question. Alexis has two sets of teeth: her talking teeth and her eating teeth. She has long, sharp fangs that extend down. When she is finished eating, she can retract them like claws."

"Just like a vampire," Emily muttered.

"But a lot more dangerous than a vampire," Joel said. "If the myths are true, she was sent to Thebes by Juno, Jupiter's wife. The Sphinx was only ever defeated once—when Oedipus guessed the right answer to her riddle. It's said that she killed herself when he did."

Pegasus nickered softly. Paelen translated. "No, she did not kill herself. She simply returned to Olympus. But she is one of our best guards. Pegasus knows you do not like her and that she is not particularly fond of you. But he says we are very honored to have her with us. We are in safe hands."

"That's if Emily doesn't do something stupid and drive Alexis to kill her!" Joel added.

Emily looked at Joel and felt a sting. "If she tries anything, I'll burn her up!"

Paelen's eyes flew wide. "You must not say such a thing. The Sphinx is Juno's favorite. There would be no stopping her rage if you destroyed Alexis, even if you are the Flame of Olympus. Please—"

"Calm down," Emily said. "I wasn't serious. I could never hurt Alexis, even if she does drive me crazy!" She directed her attention to Pegasus. "You know that too, right, Pegs? I won't use my powers to hurt anyone *ever*!"

"Except maybe the gorgons," Joel added as he nudged her playfully.

Emily shoved him back. "That was different. They started it and turned you all to stone. I had no choice. Apart from them, I don't want to use my powers against anyone, ever again."

Paelen relaxed visibly. "That is a relief. I would hate to see a war start between you and Juno over Alexis."

Emily said nothing. There was already a huge weight on her shoulders, knowing she might have to fight Jupiter to protect Earth. She wasn't about to pick another fight. Sitting beside Pegasus, absently stroking the feathers on his wings, she worried about the future.

As the summer sun moved steadily overhead and started to descend in the west, they changed into their "Earth" clothes. Paelen beamed as he looked down at his jeans and T-shirt. "I do look human, do I not?" he asked proudly.

Emily smiled at her friend's eagerness to blend in, despite the fact that he was wearing jeweled sandals with wings instead of sneakers. "You look great."

Emily struggled to get her jeans up over her silver leg brace. She hated that she still needed to wear it. But the damage the Nirads had done to her left her unable to walk without it.

Across the small clearing, Alexis was refusing to put on the T-shirt Emily had given her to cover up her naked front.

"I will not do it," Alexis said. "I have never had to wear anything before—even when I was last in your world. I will look ridiculous."

Emily bit her tongue. A lion-woman with eagle's wings and a serpent's tail was worrying about looking ridiculous if she wore a T-shirt?

"Things have changed," Emily grunted, struggling to fasten her jeans. She crossed to the Sphinx and then looked over at her friends. "Not to mention you are distracting Joel and Paelen, and we need them to focus."

"No," Alexis said. "I will not wear this. Not unless you answer another riddle."

Emily groaned. "Not again."

"If you insist on me wearing clothing, I will only do it when you answer correctly."

The Sphinx moved closer to Emily and narrowed her green eyes.

"Riddle me, riddle me ranty ro
My father gave me seeds to sow
The seed was black and the ground was white
If you riddle me that
You'll escape my bite."

Emily asked Alexis to repeat the riddle. Black seeds with white ground. After the last riddle, she knew the answer wouldn't be clear or easy. One thing was sure, it would have nothing to do with planting at all. White ground and black seeds . . . What made the ground white? Snow! Finally she had a thought and snapped her fingers.

"I know! It's coal in a snowman's eyes!"

Alexis smiled and threw away the T-shirt. "Incorrect. I do not need to wear this."

"What is it, then?" Emily demanded.

Alexis shook her head. "It is not my place to tell you the answer."

Emily threw up her arms in frustration and walked back to Pegasus. When she passed Joel, she shook her head. "Will you please talk to her?"

Color rose in Joel's cheeks. "Um . . . well, I . . ." He looked awkwardly over to the Sphinx. "I know you've got Pluto's helmet and all, but it might be best if you put something on."

Alexis dropped her head and pouted. "You do not like me. You think I am ugly."

Joel jumped to his feet and picked up the T-shirt. Then he approached the Sphinx. "Alexis, I think you're amazing! But in our world, we tend to cover up. Please, for me?"

Alexis looked at the shirt dubiously. "Fine, but only for you."

Emily watched Joel fawning all over the Sphinx. With her raven-black hair and large green eyes, she was strikingly beautiful. But despite what everyone said, to Emily, Alexis was still just an overgrown, fly-ing house cat!

Emily felt the Flame within her stir. She knew she

could control it and wouldn't let it free. But at that moment she was tempted.

Pegasus gently nudged her. Emily looked back into the stallion's big brown eyes. "Thanks, Pegs," she said softly as she hugged his neck. "But why can't he see it? She's just toying with him."

When the sun had finally set, they packed up their things and prepared to leave. Emily climbed up onto Pegasus. "Okay, Paelen, lead on. Take us to Earl."

With the lights of New York City behind them and all the towns of New Jersey ahead, Emily expected to head due north, back toward Tuxedo, New York, where they'd first met Earl. But once they were higher in the sky, the sandals took them in a southern direction.

"Did Earl tell you where he lived?" Joel called to Emily.

"In Tuxedo," Emily called back. She turned on Pegasus's back and pointed in the direction they'd come from. "But that's way back there. Where do you think we're going?"

"Guess we'll find out soon enough."

As the moon rose high and full above them in a sky

filled with stars, Emily settled down on Pegasus for a long flight. The air was warm and getting warmer the farther south they traveled. Beneath them, they watched towns and city lights passing. Yet Paelen's sandals continued without a break.

After a time, the lights of civilization stopped and they passed silently over a tall, heavily wooded mountain range with only the occasional car headlights to break the solid darkness below.

"Em," Joel finally called, "do those look like the Blue Ridge Mountains to you?"

"Don't know," she admitted. "I've never traveled any farther south than New Jersey."

"Well, I've gone down to Florida, and this looks familiar."

Emily was unsure how long they had flown. But with the passing of the moon overhead, she knew it had to be most of the night. Just before dawn, with the air becoming warmer and sweeter with the fragrance of flowers and salty sea air, Paelen's sandals finally started to descend.

They were heading down toward a densely populated neighborhood filled with houses running along a canal. With the pink rays of dawn rising in the east, Emily noticed several homes with their lights already on. There was some light traffic on the roads as commuters started their journeys to work.

"I don't like this," Emily called to Joel and Paelen. "We could be seen."

Paelen looked over his shoulder. "But this is where Earl is."

Within minutes, they were gliding over a row of homes.

"Don't land in front!" Joel called. "Paelen, if it's one of these homes, land in the backyard."

Paelen repeated the order to his sandals. Soon they were touching down in the grass of a small backyard along the canal. Palm trees were blowing in the soft, warm breeze, and the sound of morning songbirds filled the soupy, humid air.

Emily looked around nervously. "I really don't like this. We're too exposed here." Pegasus was still glowing in the predawn light. She pointed to the house directly across the canal from them. "Look, their lights are on. If they look outside, they can't miss us."

"Then let's not stay out here," Joel said. He looked

at Paelen. "Are you sure this is the right place?"

"I am not, but the sandals are certain."

Alexis fluttered her wings into position and scanned the area. "I have never been here before. The air is delicious. Where are we?"

Joel looked around. "Looks and smells like Florida to me."

"Florida?" Emily repeated. "Are you saying we flew over a thousand miles in one night?"

Pegasus nickered softly, and Chrysaor squealed as they moved closer to the back of the house. "They say we should seek cover before the sun is fully up," Paelen translated.

Joel approached the sliding glass door at the rear of the house. "I hope your sandals are right," he muttered softly, "or we're about to ruin someone's day."

"Someone's whole life, you mean," Emily added.

The door was locked. But one of the benefits of having an artificial arm made in Vulcan's workshop was that Joel now possessed amazing strength in his silver right arm.

With a quick, sharp tug, the lock on the door snapped and the glass door slid open.

"Everyone inside," Joel whispered.

As the biggest, Pegasus went first. But even with the glass door fully open, the winged stallion was too large to fit through the doorway. Joel, Paelen, and Emily had to push Pegasus from behind to force his whole body and wings through the opening.

"C'mon!" Joel grunted. "One more good push should do it."

Pegasus whinnied in complaint as he was shoved painfully through the glass door. With a final effort, the stallion made it through the tight opening, but not before losing several feathers.

As Chrysaor and Alexis trailed in behind the stallion, Emily and Paelen ran around the yard gathering Pegasus's lost feathers, now blowing in the breeze. A large feather blew into the canal just as Emily reached for it.

"Go and get it," Paelen said as the feather floated on the surface.

"I'm not going in there," Emily protested. "You go get it."

Paelen shook his head. "Not me. I do not like water. You should go."

"And I don't like alligators," Emily said. "I've heard Florida canals are full of them."

Paelen looked at her in shock. "So you wish for me to be eaten by creatures in this water?"

"No, of course not, but being Olympian, I'm sure the alligators would leave you alone."

While they argued, the feather drifted farther away. Finally Emily raised her right hand. She concentrated on the feather while summoning the Flame. A tight beam of fire shot from her hand and burned up the feather. When it stopped, all that remained was steaming water.

Emily looked at Paelen and rubbed her hands together. "That's fixed. Let's catch up with the others."

When they were all gathered in the small living room, Emily stood beside Pegasus, stroking his neck to let her powers restore his lost and damaged feathers. "Sorry about that, Pegs," she said softly. "But we had to get you in here. I don't think any of us realize just how big you are until something like that happens."

Pegasus nickered softly and nodded.

 65

Moments later Alexis raised her head and hushed Emily. "There are two humans stirring in this dwelling."

"Two?" Emily repeated.

Alexis let out a ferocious roar. In the blink of an eye, the Sphinx launched into the air, and soared over Emily's head. A strange, choked voice behind her screamed as Alexis knocked to the floor a long-haired man wearing a brown bathrobe.

Emily received her first look at Alexis's eating teeth as the Sphinx stood on the man's chest and prepared to kill him. They were a terrifying sight. Huge, sharp canines filled her mouth as her jaw unhinged to allow her to open her mouth wider than Emily had thought possible.

"Alexis, no!" Joel cried. He ran up to the Sphinx and knelt down beside her. "Please don't kill him! We know him. He can help us."

When the Sphinx looked over to Joel, Emily saw her eyes were almost as scary as her teeth. The color was gone, and all she could see were enlarged black pupils. A low, deep rumble continued from the Sphinx's throat. Emily understood what Diana meant about Alexis being a good security guard. She was terrifying.

Finally the Sphinx's pupils returned to normal and her teeth retracted. She climbed off, but remained close and poised to strike.

Joel helped the man climb shakily to his feet.

It took a moment to recognize him because he'd changed so much. His hair was long and shaggy and he had a mustache, but it was him. "Agent T!" Emily cried. "What are you doing here?"

"Me?" the CRU agent challenged. "What the hell are you doing back here? And what is that thing you've brought with you?" He pointed a shaking finger at Alexis.

"Thing?" Alexis repeated as her soft growls grew considerably louder. "Did you just call me a thing?"

It was Agent T all right. He still possessed the same arrogance and defiance that all CRU agents had. If he wasn't careful with the Sphinx, that attitude would get him killed. Emily stepped forward to stop the disaster before it started. "This is Alexis," she introduced quickly. "She is the Sphinx of Olympus."

Agent T groaned. "More damn Olympians? Not again."

A second man charged into the room. "What's going on in here?"

Emily turned and saw Earl standing in the doorway. Like Agent T, he had changed since the last time she saw him. His light hair was dyed black and his beard was gone. They were obviously trying to disguise themselves to hide from the CRU. But there was no mistaking the sparkle in his eyes. There were no traces of the severe burns he'd received at the destruction of the Red Apple rest stop.

"Earl! I'm so glad to see you!"

Earl's eyes flew open at the sight of Pegasus and the others crammed into the small room. "Emily!" He ran over and scooped her up in his arms. "I've been so darn worried about you!" His eyes went to everyone in the room. "About all of you."

"We're doing good," Joel answered. "But we really need your help."

"Help?" Earl said as he crossed to Pegasus and patted the stallion's neck. "Hiya, big fella." He turned back to Joel. "What's wrong?"

Emily looked from Earl to Agent T. "Actually, I'm glad you are here too, because we think the CRU are involved with something horrific."

Agent T stepped away from the Sphinx and approached Emily. "Whatever it is, I don't want to know about it. I haven't been with the agency since you started that mess up in Tuxedo, New York. The CRU have been searching for us ever since. Earl and I are in hiding. We've changed our names countless times and had to take awful jobs just to survive. Look at this dump. I've got multiple degrees and was a high-ranking CRU agent. What am I doing now? Because of you, I'm a janitor."

Emily bristled. "Don't go blaming us. We didn't start that mess in Tuxedo—you did, when you took my father!"

Agent T stood defiantly erect. Despite his messy long hair, tattered robe, and bare feet, he was still an imposing sight. "We wouldn't have taken your father if you hadn't caused all that trouble in New York. Do you have any idea how much chaos those Nirads caused us? We had to buy off most of the city officials and threaten the newspapers."

"That wasn't our fault either!" Emily cried.

Pegasus nickered softly. Paelen came forward and put his hand on her shoulder. "Emily calm down. That is in the past. Pegasus says we must focus on our mission."

Emily looked back at the stallion and nodded. She took a deep, steadying breath. "You're right."

"So why are you here?" Earl asked. "What have the CRU done now?"

Joel answered. "We think they may have created a clone from Pegasus. It's that racehorse who won the Triple Crown."

"Tornado Warning?" Earl asked. "You think that there horse was created by the CRU?"

Emily nodded. "He's too much like Pegasus."

"But cloning ain't possible," Earl insisted. "I know he's broken records and all, but it can't be. Besides, Tornado is gray."

Agent T stood beside Earl. "A horse can be dyed," he said. "Look at what these kids did to Pegasus last year. And I'm afraid to say, cloning is very possible. The CRU scientists have been doing it on a small scale for years. If they had enough genetic material from Pegasus, it would be the obvious thing to do."

Earl's eyes flashed open and he snapped his fingers. "Hey, do you think them others could be—"

Agent T shook his head and flashed Earl a quick warning. "Later . . ."

Emily studied Agent T's face and Earl's reaction. Something was going on between them. Just as she was about to ask, Chrysaor came forward and knocked Agent T backward as he made several loud and angry squeals.

"Don't you squeal at me, pig!" Agent T fumed as he recovered. "I'm not the one doing it. I told you, I left the CRU."

"Chrysaor, please," Joel said. "Losing your temper isn't helping." He concentrated on Agent T. "Why would they do it?"

Agent T gave the winged boar a final threatening look before saying, "Olympians are much stronger than humans." He paused and looked at Pegasus, Chrysaor, and Alexis. "And it seems most of you can fly. Think about it. What could the CRU achieve if they had an army of laboratory-created Olympians?"

Shock tore through the room like wildfire. Pegasus

pounded the tile floor with a golden hoof while Chrysaor squealed in rage. Paelen's face went ashen, and Alexis roared and drew her claws.

"Quiet!" Agent T ordered. "Do you want the neighbors to hear? They'll call the police and we'll all be captured."

Emily stood in silence, fearing the worst. If Jupiter had heard that one comment, there would be no stopping him. "They wouldn't, would they?"

"They could and they would," Agent T insisted. "That is what the CRU do. Use new technology to create weapons to better equip our military."

Emily shook her head. "You don't understand what this means! If it's true and the CRU is building an army of cloned Olympians, it will mean the end of everything."

Earl put his arm around Emily. "Calm down, I can't hardly understand you. What do you mean the end of everythin'?"

"Your world," Paelen finally said. "If the CRU has created Olympians, Jupiter will destroy the Earth."

6

BEFORE LONG, EVERYONE WAS GATHERED together to eat. Though they had ambrosia, Pegasus and Paelen also ate a whole box of sugary breakfast cereal and introduced Alexis and Chrysaor to the joys of glazed doughnuts.

While they ate, they told Earl and Agent T everything that had happened since they left the cabin in the woods and had gone to the Nirad world to fight the gorgons. Earl whistled in disbelief.

"Gorgons? Them snaky-haired women from the stories? They are real? They was the cause of all that trouble?"

Emily nodded. "They wanted to take over Olympus and tried to get me to use my powers to kill Jupiter.

When I wouldn't, they turned all of us to stone."

"For real?" Earl cried. "Just like in the stories?"

Again Emily nodded.

"What happened?"

"Emily melted the stone around her," Paelen added. "Then she melted the gorgons."

"You melted the gorgons?" Earl repeated.

Emily shrugged. "I lost my temper and kinda unleashed my powers. The Flame did the rest."

"Then she used her powers to turn us back from stone," Paelen finished.

Earl whistled. "Boy, I sure woulda liked to have seen that!"

Agent T was rubbing his chin. He looked around at the odd assortment of Olympians in the room. "Tell me something. The myths, are they all true? Everything?"

Joel leaned forward. "Seem to be. They're not exactly the same, but close. From what I've learned, the Olympians used to come here all the time."

"Why?" Earl asked.

"Because you were interesting," Alexis answered. "We were studying you."

"You were studying us?" Agent T asked incredulously.

"Of course," Alexis replied. "You were a savage people, always going to war. We found you fascinating. But you were contaminating us with your violent ways, so Jupiter stopped all visits to your world. He had hoped you would learn from your mistakes and embrace peace. From what I have seen and heard, you have not."

"Who is he to judge us?" Agent T shot back. "Or to decide if we can exist or not?"

Alexis narrowed her eyes. "He is Jupiter."

Earl looked over to Joel. "What about you? What happened to your arm?"

Emily sighed. "That's my fault."

Joel shook his head. "No, it's not. The gorgons did this to me, not you." He turned to Earl. "When I was stone, I fell over and my arm smashed. Emily tried to heal me, but it wouldn't work." He held up his silver right arm and wiggled his silver fingers. "Vulcan made this for me in his forge. I don't know how it works. There are no electronic parts and if you look, you can't see any joints for the fingers. But it's better and much stronger than my real arm. The only thing is I can't feel with it. But at least it can't be hurt."

Agent T leaned closer and studied Joel's arm and hand with the kind of intensity that disturbed Emily. She'd seen that same expression when he was in the laboratory with the wounded Pegasus on Governors Island. "The CRU would love to get hold of that thing," he mused softly. "Can you take it off?"

Joel shook his head. "Nope. It's attached to me now."

"So if they wanted it, they'd have to surgically remove it from you," Agent T muttered.

"The CRU is not going to see it!" Emily shot back. "They've caused enough trouble already. If they've created clones, Jupiter is going to destroy this world."

"Don't be ridiculous," Agent T spat. "If Jupiter is so pro-peace, he wouldn't destroy this planet just because the CRU may have created a few clones. He couldn't."

"You don't know Jupiter," Joel said. "He is very protective of the Olympians."

"And the order of nature," Emily added. "It's true that in the past some of the Olympians had children with humans. But that was natural. Clones being created in a lab are different. Diana and Pluto know about this and why we're here. If it's true, they won't stop Jupiter."

"Ah, yes—Diana," Agent T said. "Interesting woman. How is she?"

"Still angry," Joel said. "Even more so now that this has happened."

Agent T shook his head. "This is insane. A few Olympians can't possibly come to Earth to destroy the whole planet. You may be powerful, but we have weapons and we will defend ourselves."

Pegasus was standing beside Emily, munching on his large bowl of cereal. He raised his head and nickered.

"You cannot defend yourselves against Jupiter," Paelen translated. "He would not even need to come to your world to destroy it."

Emily looked at Pegasus and frowned. "He wouldn't?"

Both Pegasus and Chrysaor started to make sounds.

Paelen raised his eyebrows. "I did not know this."

"What?" Emily asked. "Paelen, what did they say? How would Jupiter do it?"

"He would open the Solar Stream and turn it on Earth."

"What?" Joel cried. "The Solar Stream?"

Earl frowned. "Ain't that the special superhighway you guys use to come to here?"

Paelen nodded. "Jupiter has control of it. All he needs is to combine his powers with his brothers', and they can redirect the Solar Stream. When they are gathered together, they are called the Big Three. And collectively they have the power to shift its direction. Instead of it opening up beside your world as it does now, they would point it at your world. The energy of a billion suns would obliterate your planet in an instant."

Emily sat in stunned silence. How many times had she traveled within the Solar Stream without really thinking about what it was or how it worked? It was just a means of transport. She never imagined it could be turned into a weapon of mass destruction.

"We've traveled through the Solar Stream lots of times," she said to Earl and Agent T. "You can feel its power when you're in it."

"We've got to stop him," Earl said.

Agent T shook his head. "Wait! You are all jumping the gun. Right now, this is only speculation. There is no proof that the CRU have done anything at all. But even if they have, I am certain we could reason with Jupiter."

Alexis sat up on her haunches and rested her front paws on the table right beside Agent T. She narrowed her eyes at the ex–CRU agent. "Jupiter cannot be reasoned with when the sin is too great. If your people have created New Olympians, nothing will stop him. He can and will destroy this world."

"They are not my people anymore," Agent T said as he leaned closer to her and stared defiantly into the Sphinx's green eyes. "I am not responsible for what they are doing now."

"Once a CRU agent, always a CRU agent," Alexis growled.

Earl looked at everyone around the table. "We've got to find Tornado Warning and pray to God he's just a horse and not an Olympian clone."

"And if he is a clone?" Agent T posed.

Emily looked Agent T squarely in the eye. "Then we must stop the CRU before Jupiter finds out."

• • •

After breakfast, Agent T took Joel, Paelen, and Chrysaor into his small office to use his computer to search for Tornado Warning. Emily helped Earl clear the table.

"I was shocked to see Agent T still with you," Emily said to Earl as she washed a breakfast bowl.

"I ain't got much choice. I can't get him to leave me alone," Earl said, picking up a cloth to start drying. "Lord knows I've tried! I don't know what the heck you kids did to him. Last I saw, he was crazy for Cupid. But I wake up in the cabin and he's there and you guys are gone. He said Cupid told him he was my brother and that he's going to protect me forever. I can't hardly go to the toilet without him checkin' to see if it's safe first."

"Cupid shouldn't have done that," Emily said.

Earl sighed. "I may complain a lot. But the truth is he ain't that bad once you get to know him. I ain't never had a brother, and it's kinda nice. And he's saved my life more than once. He knows how them CRU folk work. He's kept us one step ahead of them. I'd have been a goner long before now if it weren't for him."

Emily dropped her head. "I'm really sorry about that. It would have been better if you'd never found us at the Red Apple. You'd have your old life back."

"Hey, hey, hey," Earl said softly. "Don't you go frettin' about that. I bless the day y'all came into my life. If I hadn't met that big fella out there"—Earl stepped through the door and stroked the stallion's face—"and the rest of you, my life would have been a lot emptier. Even though you left, I still felt part of you. It's kinda like you're my family that's gone on vacation but would come back one day. And look—here you are.

"And now I get to meet even more interesting people, like this pretty lady here." Earl approached Alexis. The Sphinx was sitting on her haunches and came up to just past his waist. "That Olympus must be one amazing place if folks like you are there."

Alexis's green eyes sparkled, and she smiled demurely. "Thank you, Earl. It is a pleasure to finally meet a human who appreciates true beauty." She shot a look at Emily. "Some people only regard me as a . . ." She paused. "What were the words you used, Emily? Oh yes, now I remember: an overgrown, green-eyed, flying house cat."

Emily's face reddened. She hadn't thought the Sphinx knew what she'd called her.

Earl turned to Emily in shock. "You didn't!"

Emily shrugged. "Well, I . . ."

"It is all right," Alexis said as she patted Earl's hand with her large paw. "I understand fully. She is jealous of me. She knows I am the better woman."

Emily inhaled sharply. "I am not jealous!"

Alexis looked up at Earl and nodded. "She is."

Beside them, Pegasus nickered.

"It's not funny, Pegs," Emily said.

Suddenly Joel appeared in the room. His face was ashen. "Em, you've got to see this. We have a big problem!"

Emily followed Joel into the small office.

Chrysaor was deeply troubled. The large boar was shaking his head back and forth and fluttering his coarse brown wings. Agent T was at his laptop computer, furiously tapping away on the keyboard, while Paelen was tearing through a scrapbook. Joel approached a large bulletin board on the wall. Newspaper articles were pinned all over it.

"What's that?" Emily asked.

"We've been keeping a record of Olympian sightings," Earl explained.

"What sightings?"

"Look." Joel pointed at a newspaper clipping. There was a blurry photo at the top of the article that looked like it had been taken with a security camera. The headline read: WOMAN WANTED FOR MURDER.

Emily peered closer and her jaw dropped. "That's Diana!" She looked back at Earl. "Why didn't you tell us about this earlier?"

"I started to," Earl defended himself.

"But I stopped him from mentioning it," Agent T finished.

"Why?"

"I wanted to know why you were here first." Agent T stood up and walked toward Emily. "But if this isn't the real Diana, these sightings and the clone theory must be linked."

"It can't be Diana," Emily insisted. "What's this woman done?"

"She is wanted for robbery and murder," Agent T said.

Pegasus whinnied loudly while Emily cried, "What?"

Agent T nodded. "I saw this article a few months

back and thought Diana had returned to Earth. Earl and I have been searching for any unusual stories that suggest it could be Olympians."

"Until y'all came back today, we really thought this was her," Earl added. "I ain't never met the lady myself, but Tom has. He says she's strong and mean enough to do this."

"Tom?" Emily asked.

Agent T nodded. "My real name is Thomas. I know what Diana is capable of. I was the one who supervised the tests on her when we had you at the Governors Island facility. When I saw this article, I was convinced she was back."

"We swear it wasn't her!" Joel said. "Yeah, she was here for a quick trip with Apollo and Emily's father, but there's no way that's her. They were being inconspicuous, and anyway, she just wouldn't!"

Agent T rubbed his chin. A troubled expression crossed his face. "Then this may be further evidence that the CRU have created clones. But if it's true, how are the clones on the loose? First there was Tornado Warning and now these sightings. I know for certain the CRU wouldn't be releasing them into the community. That would be too dangerous and raise far too many uncomfortable questions. The clones must be escaping somehow. But how are they getting around CRU security systems?"

Emily turned back to Pegasus, who was standing at the threshold. "It says the mysterious woman and her large accomplice broke into a jewelry store. They killed the owner and several employees and then stole a lot of jewels. The article says there was a walk-in safe at the back of the store. They don't understand how, but the heavy door was ripped off and the contents taken. It also says that there was one survivor of the massacre. He claimed that the woman's accomplice was a monster. It had four arms. Its face was covered, but it was huge and super-strong. It ripped the door right off the safe. He said he got a look at one of the creature's hands, and it was dark gray."

"That's a Nirad!" Paelen said.

Earl looked at Agent T. "I told you so! You wouldn't believe me when I said it could be a Nirad."

"When you told me, Olympus was still at war with the Nirads. It wasn't logical for Diana to be working with one. That they could be clones was never a consideration."

"But it is now," Joel said.

Emily nodded. "The article says the police think the man was in shock and didn't understand what he was seeing. They say the accomplice had been wearing a costume. There is a nationwide hunt for them going on right now."

In the doorway, Pegasus whinnied loudly. He pounded the floor with his hoof and tore a large hole in the carpet. Chrysaor squealed loudly. After their heated exchange, Paelen translated. "They believe this is confirmation of our worst fears. We know for certain that this wasn't Diana or a Nirad—they would never kill so senselessly. The only explanation is that they are creations of the CRU. This world is in even more danger. If Jupiter were to find out . . ."

"We know," Agent T shot. "He'll destroy us."

Alexis was scanning the photos in the newspaper clippings. "There have been multiple sightings of this Diana woman all over the country. The riddle is this: Is that the same woman appearing in all these different locations, or is there more than one?"

"It is not just Diana," Paelen said as he pulled a paper from the scrapbook. "It appears I have been up to mischief as well." He held up an article with a mug shot of a teenager who looked just like him. The boy was holding up a sign with a series of numbers beneath it. Though the face was Paelen's, the expression in the eyes was very different. The boy's eyes were wild and terrified.

Paelen handed the article to Emily. "What does this say?"

Emily read the story. "It seems this boy was caught after breaking into a chocolate shop. They found him on the floor, ravenously eating an entire tray of chocolates. The police caught him and took him to the station. It says the boy never spoke a single word and appeared petrified. After he was booked and photographed, he attacked the guards and managed to escape. One witness said he was superstrong and tossed everyone around like they weighed nothing. He then seemed to squeeze himself through an impossibly small window. They are still looking for him but think he's left the area."

"I thought that was you in that article," Earl said

to Paelen. "But if it ain't, then we're all in a heap of trouble."

"I swear it is not I," Paelen insisted. "Though I must admit, I do like chocolate. But had it been me, I would not have been caught."

"Emily, where did that story happen?" Joel asked.

Emily scanned the article. "Las Vegas." She looked back up to the wall and the article with the woman who looked like Diana. "Where was the jewelry store?"

"Salt Lake City, Utah," Joel read. "And this one has Diana in Denver, Colorado. And here is a sighting in Virginia."

"We've found articles about them from all over," Earl said. "If they ain't the real Diana and a Nirad, where are they coming from?" He looked at Agent T. "What CRU facility could be creating clones?"

Agent T shrugged. "I don't know. There are multiple facilities all over this country. We also have several others scattered around the world. Any one of them could be doing it."

"Just how big is the CRU?" Joel asked.

"It's massive," Agent T answered. "It's larger than the CIA, FBI, and FSA combined."

Emily sucked in her breath. "How is that possible? I don't understand how they could be so big and no one really knows about them!"

"That's the way it was set up. I was recruited into the CRU straight from college. They have been around since the 1930s. They don't answer to the president or Congress. They're completely self-governing and independent."

Silence filled the room as everyone tried to digest the new information. Until now, no one had any idea just how large and dangerous the CRU really were. Finally Alexis approached Agent T. She raised herself up on her haunches and placed her paws on his shoulders. Her claws were out as she held her furious face centimeters from his. "Tell me now. How do we find out which facility is creating these Olympians?"

"There is only one way I can think of," Agent T answered, again meeting the Sphinx's challenge without fear. "We've got to find that racehorse. If he is a clone, we'll find his owner and demand to know where he got him."

"Did you find Tornado Warning?" Emily asked.

"Yes and no," the ex–CRU agent answered. When

the Sphinx released him, he reached for the pages he'd printed. "There are countless articles about him. After the Triple Crown win, his owner reported that he's retiring him. Tornado Warning is at his home stables at the Double R Ranch in California. His owner is a man called Rip Russell. He says he's putting the stallion out to stud."

"Stud?" Emily cried. "If he is a clone of Pegasus and they start to breed him . . ."

"There could be a lot of winged horses being born," Paelen finished.

Pegasus went mad. The stallion pounded the floor and reared up in fury until his head struck and cracked the ceiling. He kicked a hole in the wall behind him and screamed before trotting down the short hall into the room, where he took his rage out on the furniture in the room.

As a coffee table shattered to splinters, Emily ran up to him. "Pegs, calm down!" she soothed. "Please, you can't let anyone hear you!"

Pegasus snorted and continued to pound the floor, shattering the white tiles beneath him. Chrysaor ran up to the stallion, trying to calm him down.

"I promise you we won't let that happen," Emily said. "We'll go out there and stop them."

"We will," Joel agreed as he and the others followed. "We won't let them do this."

Emily looked desperately to the others. "Should we go now? We could use the Solar Stream to get there."

Alexis shook her head. "That would not be wise. We have been here longer than expected already. If we enter the Solar Stream, it may arouse Jupiter's suspicions. If you wish to protect this world and remain hidden until we solve this riddle, we must travel by other means."

"But we can't fly over three thousand miles in one night," Emily said.

"No, we cannot," the Sphinx agreed. "We must avoid being seen."

"That's easy for you to say," Emily challenged. "Pluto gave you his helmet of invisibility. But that won't help Pegasus or Chrysaor."

Pegasus nickered. Paelen said, "He says we have no choice. We must find Tornado Warning before he reproduces. We can fly by night and hide during the day."

"So it's settled," Agent T said. He turned to Earl. "Pack up, we leave tonight."

Everyone turned to the ex–CRU agent.

"What are you all looking at?" Agent T challenged. "You don't expect me to sit idly by while you kids determine our planet's future, do you? I may be ex–CRU, but I still care for this world. I have skills and specialist knowledge you'll need. If the CRU really are behind this, who better to help than me?"

7

AFTER MUCH ARGUING, IT WAS FINALLY agreed that taking Agent T and Earl with them would be the best option. With the CRU still pursuing them, it was time for the two men to move on anyway. Agent T also voiced deep concerns that the Olympians may have been spotted in the Florida skies before they arrived. He drew out all his weapons and prepared to fight. While Agent T guarded the inside of the house, Alexis put on Pluto's helmet and prepared to watch the exterior.

When she first donned the helmet, Emily feared it didn't work. She could still see the Sphinx. But when the others couldn't see Alexis, they concluded that this was another one of Emily's hidden powers.

Emily watched the Sphinx go into the backyard. Alexis spread her wings wide and launched into the air and flew up to the roof of the small house. There she settled to watch for any approaching danger.

Exhausted from the long night, the others settled down for some much-needed rest. Pegasus was too upset to settle, but stood watch over Emily and the others as they slept.

At sunset, Pegasus woke Emily and Joel. Paelen was already up and eating ambrosia cakes smothered in honey, cherry jam, half a bag of sugar, and chocolate syrup. Emily was surprised to find the Sphinx working closely with Agent T. The two had laid out maps on the dining room table, and using Agent T's compass, they were plotting their course to Ramona, California, where the Double R Ranch was located.

As she rose from the sofa and stretched, Emily studied Pegasus. The stallion had calmed some, but his eyes were still too bright and alert. The news of Tornado Warning going out to stud had badly affected him.

"Are you all right, Pegs?" she asked softly as she stroked the stallion's neck.

Pegasus looked at her. Deep in his eyes she saw the vision of the two of them soaring in the night skies over Olympus. This was Pegasus's dream: to be back safely home with her.

"I wish we were back there too," Emily agreed. "I hate what the CRU might have done. But we'll stop them, Pegs. I know we will."

Pegasus nudged Emily, and she hugged his neck tightly.

"Is he all right?" Joel asked as he came up.

"He will be," Emily said, "once this is over."

Joel reached out and patted the winged stallion. "Pegasus, we could be wrong, you know. Tornado Warning could just be a very fast racehorse. And that woman the police are looking for? She may just look like Diana. Who knows, we could be back in Olympus in a day or two and laughing about this."

Emily knew Joel too well. He was saying this for Pegasus. Deep in his heart, he didn't believe it. But she was grateful to him for trying.

"Joel's right, Pegs," she agreed. "It could all be a strange coincidence."

In the dining area, Agent T was marking a course

95

on the map. He looked up at Emily and Joel. "Good, you're up. Earl's in the kitchen. Grab yourselves something to eat; we'll be leaving shortly. We've got a long flight ahead of us." He reached over and picked up a large sweatshirt and then a pair of gloves. "Joel, I've got these for you. Put it on and wear the gloves."

"You want me to wear a sweatshirt in this heat?"

Agent T nodded. "Unless you want the world to see that magical silver arm and hand of yours, you'll do as I say."

Emily and Joel continued into the kitchen. She looked back at Agent T. "Who put him in charge?"

Joel followed her eyes. Agent T was back in deep discussion with Alexis. As they listened, they heard the Sphinx and ex–CRU agent discussing security measures and what they would do if they were opposed. Emily was shocked to hear them not only getting along—they were in complete agreement. If anyone tried to stop them, they were prepared to kill.

She looked at Joel. "I guess that's what puts them in charge."

When they were ready to go, they filed silently into the dark backyard. Instead of forcing Pegasus through the glass door again, Earl and Agent T took it off its tracks and opened it up completely. Pegasus fitted through without a problem.

Emily invited Earl to ride with her on Pegasus, while Alexis offered to carry Agent T. As the group took to the air, they flew as high as the humans could withstand. With the light of the moon and Agent T's compass to guide them, they started the long journey west.

Earl whooped and cheered like a kid at riding Pegasus. His excitement was infectious, and he kept Emily in fits of laughter as he waved and called to Paelen and then over to Joel on Chrysaor. Even after several long hours, Earl was still enjoying the ride.

As the long night slowly passed and the sky behind them started to lighten, Agent T finally directed Alexis down lower in the sky. Passing through the clouds beneath them, they saw the streetlights of a large city below.

"If our calculations are correct, that should be Baton Rouge, Louisiana," Agent T turned back and called to them. "We're going to pass over the main city and find somewhere to stop on the other side of it. Understood?"

Everyone called their agreement. Before the dawn arrived fully, they flew down closer to the ground. Emily saw early-morning traffic on the interstate highway directly beneath them. Following its path, they came across the last motel in the area.

Alexis glided lower and finally chose a spot to land in an open field behind the two-story motel. Earl climbed off Pegasus first and helped Emily down. Joel climbed stiffly off Chrysaor and looked around. "Are we sure we want to stop at a motel? Wouldn't it be safer to find some woods or something?"

Agent T shook his head. "No. That would be a mistake. Out in the open you feel exposed and never truly rest. For what we are facing, we need to stay fresh and sharp. Alexis, Pegasus, and Chrysaor especially need to recover after two long nights of heavy flight. We need somewhere private for them to rest their wings."

Emily hated to admit it, but Agent T was right. She could see Pegasus was tired. His wings were drooping a bit and his head was down.

She looked at the others. "He's right. You need your rest."

Agent T stepped up to Earl. "Come with me—it's the usual cover story. We're two brothers who've driven all night. Our car broke down and it's in the garage. We'll get a double room at the very back and say we need to sleep all day and don't want to be disturbed."

Earl nodded and looked to the others. "Y'all stay here. We've done this before. As soon as we get the room, we'll come for you."

Emily stood beside Pegasus as they waited for Earl and Agent T to return. Joel and Paelen came up to her.

"Do you think we should trust Agent T?" Joel asked. "He was with the CRU. What if he turns us in to get his job back?"

Alexis was lounging on the ground. Her eyes were closed, and she was enjoying the fragrance of the predawn air. "He would not do that," she answered softly. Rising, the Sphinx padded closer to the group. "He may not like you," she said truthfully. "But he will not betray you. There is too much at stake."

"How can you be so certain?" Emily asked.

Alexis cocked her head to the side and narrowed

her green eyes. Emily was certain that if she could, the Sphinx would have put her hands on her hips. "Are you suggesting I do not know my job? That after all this time, I cannot read a human's intentions?"

Emily sighed. She shook her head tiredly. "I'm sorry, Alexis. I didn't mean to insult you. But you don't understand what the CRU did to us."

"Especially Agent T," Paelen added.

The Sphinx calmed and sat down. "No, I was not there and do not know what he did," she admitted. "But I do know the man who has been riding on my back all night. He is changed. Whether it was Cupid's charm or the realization of what the CRU have done, I do not know. But he is on our side. Tom will be a great ally."

Emily looked at Joel and raised an eyebrow. "Tom?"

Paelen caught Emily's arm. He shook his head. "Do not say more. She is tired and worried like the rest of us."

The arrival of Agent T cut off further conversation. "All right—we've got a double room on the ground floor, just in from the end." He concentrated on Alexis. "We'll use Pluto's helmet to get you into the room one at a time. People are starting to move around and check out. No one but Earl and I must be seen."

One by one, the helmet was used to sneak the Olympians into the cramped motel room. Once again, Pegasus had difficulty squeezing through the narrow doorway. But with help, the invisible stallion was finally shoved through.

The DO NOT DISTURB sign was hung on the door, and the two mattresses were pulled off the beds and put on the floor to create a more comfortable sleeping space for everyone. Before long, everyone had fallen into a deep, exhausted sleep.

When Emily woke up, there was still light coming from behind the curtains. She looked over and saw Pegasus was also awake. "You okay, Pegs?" she whispered softly.

The stallion pressed his muzzle to her hand. His eyes were still bright and alert. There was no mistaking it. Pegasus was scared. Despite what Joel had said before, Pegasus didn't believe it either. Deep inside,

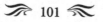

the stallion knew that somehow, Tornado Warning was part of him.

Emily rose to use the bathroom. In the tight, crowded room, she had to climb over Pegasus. Then she stepped over Joel on the other mattress. But as she put her foot down, she trod on Chrysaor. The winged boar squealed and complained loudly.

"Sorry! Go back to sleep," Emily hushed, as she gave him a light pat. She looked around to see if his squeals had awoken the others. Satisfied that they remained asleep, Emily continued her obstacle course to the bathroom. But as she entered, she found Alexis lounging on her back in an overflowing bathtub.

"Did your father not teach you to knock?" Alexis demanded.

Too stunned at the sight of the Sphinx in the bath, Emily backed out of the room and shut the door quietly behind her. Paelen was awake and smiled at her.

"She's been in there half the day," he whispered.

Irritated by the need to use the toilet, Emily muttered, "I thought cats hated water."

"I heard that, Emily!" Alexis called from the bathroom.

. . .

Hours later, everyone was up and moving around. Joel was introducing Paelen and Chrysaor to the joys of cable television. Paelen held the remote and was learning to channel surf. "Pegasus, move out of the way—you are blocking my view!" he complained as he tried to see around the large stallion. There was just so much to watch, he couldn't settle on one station for more than a minute or two. "This is amazing," he cried as he started to follow a science-fiction movie. "We must get this in Olympus!"

Chrysaor squealed loudly in protest when Paelen changed the channel again. He tried to snatch the remote from Paelen.

Joel looked at Emily. "Do you think Jupiter would go for satellite or cable TV?"

"Neither," she laughed as she watched her friends enjoying their first television experience.

On the bed behind them, Agent T was counting out his remaining money. "Earl, how much cash do you have left?" he asked.

Earl opened his wallet and pulled out two ten-dollar bills. "Twenty bucks, that's it."

Agent T looked at Emily. "Did you bring anything from Olympus we can sell?"

"No, we didn't expect to be here this long. The plan was to get a close look at Tornado Warning and then go right back."

Agent T sighed. "We have ninety-seven dollars left. That won't get us another room, let alone a lot of food."

"Well, we can't go back to Olympus for more," Emily said.

Alexis finally emerged from the bathroom. Her dark hair was up in a towel, and she was struggling to pull on a T-shirt with her paws. As Emily helped her finish getting dressed, the Sphinx's eyes settled on Paelen. "It is lucky that we have a very good thief among us."

Paelen looked up. "I am not a thief anymore," he complained. "Why will no one believe me?"

Agent T rose from the bed. "Because we need a good thief right now, and you're elected."

Paelen handed the remote to Chrysaor and came closer. "What do you need?"

"Money," Agent T said.

"And food," Earl said. "We can't all eat the ambrosia; you Olympians need that."

Paelen nodded. "I will go. How do I find money? The last time we needed it, Cupid won a costume competition. I do not know if there is another such competition around here."

"I'll come with you," Joel volunteered. "Your sandals can carry us both. And if Alexis will let me, I'll use Pluto's helmet to stay invisible while you use your talent to stretch yourself out and fit into wherever we need to go."

The Sphinx carried the helmet over to Joel. She smiled warmly. "Anything for you. You just ask and it will be my command."

Emily balled her hands into tight fists. As she did, the ceramic lamp on the table beside her exploded.

"What the hell?" Earl cried as he jumped away from the flying pieces.

"Sorry," Emily quickly said. "My hand accidentally hit it."

"That wasn't your hand," Joel challenged. "That lamp blew up!"

Emily was shaking in fear as her new powers

surfaced again. She couldn't let the others know about them. Not now, when the world was at stake. "No, Joel, it was me. I hit it. Now, are you going or not?"

He nodded but continued to inspect the remains of the lamp. "Yeah, we're going." Finally he looked at Agent T. "Do you know how much money they keep in bank machines?"

"More than enough," the ex–CRU agent said. "But they are built tough. I doubt you'll get into one before the police catch you."

"I've got this," Joel said as he held up his silver arm. "All I need to do is get it open. Paelen can do the rest by slipping in and getting the cash."

Agent T nodded. "Try it if you want, but be careful. Those things are heavily alarmed. If that doesn't work, you're going to have to go somewhere else. Try to find a pawnshop. They always have a lot of cash in them. But be warned. The owners are usually armed, and there are going to be cameras everywhere."

"That's why we're taking this." Joel held up Pluto's helmet. He looked over to Paelen. "The sun is down; let's go."

8

WHEN JOEL AND PAELEN LEFT, WITH LITTLE
do to but wait, Emily took a bath. As she lay back
in the tub, she was glad to finally take off her leg
brace. Though it helped her to walk, it was heavy and
rubbed her skin painfully.

She dozed in the warm water until Alexis entered
the bathroom. "Did your father not teach you to
knock?" Emily challenged, repeating the Sphinx's
words back to her.

Alexis ignored the comment. She shut the door
and approached the side of the tub. "Do you wish to
tell me what happened out there?"

Emily looked away and shook her head. "I don't
know what you're talking about."

"You may fool the others, but you cannot fool a Sphinx. You were angry at me and you caused the lamp to explode."

Emily gasped. Alexis knew everything. "I don't want to talk about it."

Alexis sat beside the tub and put her paws up on the side. "You may not wish to, but you are going to. I know you do not like me, and that is your choice. But I took an oath to protect you and this mission. If I see something wrong, I am going to act upon it. So you might just as well tell me, because I am going to find out anyway."

"Aren't you going to give me a choice?" Emily asked. "Bargain with a riddle or something? If I get the riddle wrong, I tell you, but if I get it right, you leave me alone?"

"Not this time," Alexis said. "You must tell me what happened."

Emily dropped her head and sighed. She looked into the penetrating green eyes of the Sphinx. "I have more powers, and I can't control them," she admitted. "When Vesta first told me about the Flame, she said I'd learn to control it, and I have."

Emily lifted her hand out of the water. She summoned up the Flame, and it burned brightly and painlessly in the palm of her wet hand. "I can do anything I want with the Flame now."

"But . . . ," the Sphinx prodded.

"But these new powers are unpredictable, and they really scare me. Sometimes I can move things. Sometimes items disappear and I can never find them again. And sometimes . . ."

"Sometimes they explode," the Sphinx finished. "Why haven't you told anyone? I am sure Vesta and Jupiter would be very interested to know."

"I was going to," Emily said.

The Sphinx tilted her head to the side.

"Eventually," Emily finished. "But then Dad came back with the papers, talking about Tornado Warning, and that became more important."

"More important than making things disappear or destroying them?"

"I know," Emily said. "But if I told anyone, I couldn't have come back here. And look what we've learned so far."

Alexis sat back and dropped her paws to the wet floor.

"I do understand, Emily. Your dedication to Pegasus and this world is a credit to you. But you have endangered everyone you care for by not telling Vesta and letting her try to help you control these new powers."

Tears came to Emily's eyes. Now used to the explosive danger they posed, she kept the sea-green handkerchief with the embroidered Pegasus that Neptune had given to her close. It alone had the power to contain her tears so they couldn't do any harm. She reached for it and gently dabbed her eyes and watched the tears slipping into the secret pocket. "I'm just so scared. What am I supposed to do?"

The Sphinx reached out with her large paw and stroked Emily's head. "This must be very difficult for you: to be a child and yet so powerful. I can imagine your life and Jupiter's must have been very similar. But he learned to control his powers; I am confident you will do the same. All I can suggest is that until you learn to master them, you do your best to control your temper."

Emily looked down into the water until Alexis put her paw under her chin and drew her head up. She leaned closer. "Emily, people are going to come and go in your life who you may not like and who may annoy or upset you. You must learn to tolerate them. It appears that extreme emotions trigger your powers."

Emily sniffed and nodded. "You're right. I'll try."

Alexis shook her head. "You must do better than try, Emily. You must succeed—if only to protect your friends."

The Sphinx rose and moved for the door. "I have heard it said among humans that when they are upset, they count to ten. May I suggest you try doing the same?"

As she was about to leave, Emily called to her. "Alexis, wait!" When the Sphinx paused, she continued, "Please don't tell anyone about this. I don't want my best friends to be frightened of me."

"I won't tell them," Alexis agreed. "Not unless your powers become too unpredictable. Emily, I am here to protect them, too—even if it means protecting them from you."

When Emily emerged from the bath, she found Earl and Agent T chatting softly while Pegasus, Chrysaor, and Alexis were glued to an old Elvis Presley movie on TV. Alexis was roaring with laughter.

When Elvis started to sing, Alexis sighed dreamily. "I am in love. I must find that man."

While stroking Pegasus, Emily wondered if she should tell the Sphinx that Elvis had been dead a long time. But before she could say a word, there was a soft knock on the door.

Agent T sprang from the bed. He opened the door a crack, peered out, and then let Joel and Paelen into the room.

Joel was carrying two large pizza boxes, while Paelen had other bags of groceries. Emily immediately noticed that Paelen was covered in hundreds of tiny cuts.

"What happened to you?"

Joel started to laugh. "He was eaten by a bank machine!"

Paelen shot him a dirty look. "We had some difficulty getting the money out of the machine. Joel was able to punch a hole in it, but when I stretched out and entered it, the metal cut me to pieces."

"Were you able to get any money?" Agent T asked.

Paelen handed over a thick stack of twenty-dollar bills.

While the money was counted, Emily reached out and touched Paelen. As she traced lines along his deep cuts and gashes, her powers started to heal him. Within moments, his skin was back to normal.

"Excellent," Agent T said. "This should get us safely to California." He looked around the room. "Everyone eat; we've got a long night ahead of us."

The night passed slowly as the group made their way west. Before long they had flown over Louisiana and were crossing Texas. As they finally reached New Mexico, Emily and Earl marveled at the sudden appearance of clusters of golden light from towns and cities in the seemingly endless darkness beneath them.

Eventually they landed outside an old motel. Joel was excited to discover they were on the outskirts of Roswell, New Mexico. "This place is famous! It's where they claim aliens crashed in the 1940s," he explained to Paelen.

"Aliens did crash here," Agent T confirmed. "Where do you think we get some of our modern technology and weapons from?"

"When I was first captured by the CRU, Agent J

and Agent O kept calling me an alien," Paelen said.

"That was our first thought," Agent T explained. "It was easier to believe you were an alien than Olympian because we knew already that aliens existed."

"And now?" Emily asked.

"Now we know that Olympians exist as well. Though if you ask me, since Olympus is another world away from Earth, technically, you could still be called aliens."

Exhaustion from the long flight caught up with them as they piled into the small motel room. The sun rose, crossed the sky, and finally set in the west while the group slept. As the last of the daylight faded, they awoke and prepared for the final leg of the journey to California.

"I hope we are not here much longer," Paelen said as he ate his last ambrosia cake. "You know what happens when we go too long without this. Even with sugar, we become weak and vulnerable."

"With luck, we'll be going back tomorrow night," Joel said, munching on his burger and fries. "Once we see Tornado for ourselves and prove he's just a horse, we're free to go back."

"And if he really is a clone?" Emily asked.

"Then we are all in trouble," Agent T said darkly, "not just the Olympians lacking their food."

The final comment settled heavily in the air as the group used Pluto's helmet to exit the room without being seen. They gathered together behind the old motel.

"All right," Agent T said, "by my calculations, if we put on more speed, we should arrive at Ramona before dawn. That will give us time to find the Double R Ranch to see Tornado Warning for ourselves. What happens next is anyone's guess. I don't like not knowing, but we don't have much choice."

As Emily climbed on Pegasus, it felt like lead was settling heavily in her stomach. This was it. Within a few hours they would discover the truth. But even before they saw Tornado for themselves, somehow Emily already knew the answer. He wasn't a horse. Tornado Warning was a clone of her beloved Pegasus, created by the CRU.

9

WITH EACH POWERFUL WING BEAT, EMILY felt her tension grow. She looked at the others flying around her and, in the dim light of the stars, was able to see their expressions were the same. Paelen was leaning forward as his winged sandals carried him onward. His arms were crossed over his chest and his expression grim. Even Earl stopped chatting and sat quietly behind her on the back of the stallion. They were all sharing her fears.

As they flew over mostly desert with very little popu-lation, without the fear of being seen, Alexis directed the group lower in the sky. Up high, the temperatures were much colder and it was hard on Joel, Earl, and Agent T. Emily was no longer bothered by the cold, but for most of the trip when they traveled over populated areas, she had felt Earl shivering behind her.

Continuing through the night, the landscape beneath them changed. From the sharp cliffs and mesas of Texas, New Mexico, and then Arizona, they were entering a region of rolling mountain ranges that was the entrance to California. It was still all desert terrain, and yet it looked so different.

Ahead of them, Alexis and Agent T continued to lead the way. The ex–CRU agent was holding his compass in one hand and struggling with a map in the other. He gripped a small flashlight in his teeth. Despite how she felt about him, she was grateful he was here. It was true. He did possess skills they needed. Without him, the trip to California would have been much more difficult.

After they had been flying for several hours, Agent T directed everyone lower. They were surrounded by mountains on either side that climbed high in the sky. Though it was still dark, they could now make out shapes and structures.

Soon they came upon a small town. Most of the lights were off, and there was no traffic on the road.

But almost immediately Emily felt a change in Pegasus. The stallion was snorting and his ears flicked back.

"Are you all right?" Emily called forward.

Pegasus didn't react. Peering closer, she could see his nostrils were flared and his eyes were wide and bright. She also noticed his glow had increased. "What is it, Pegasus?"

"We are near Tornado Warning," Paelen explained as he flew closer. "Pegasus can sense him and he does not like it."

Beneath her, Pegasus started to tremble. Chrysaor flew on the other side of the stallion and started to squeal at his brother.

"What's happening?" Joel called.

"Pegasus can feel Tornado Warning. We're getting close." She leaned forward and patted his neck again. "Just take it easy, Pegs."

"I don't like this," Earl said. "He may be an Olympian, but Pegasus is still a full-blooded stallion. We may be in for a lot of trouble."

Earl voiced what Emily was trying hard not to. For the first time ever, Pegasus was starting to frighten her. Something was driving him on. If that something was Tornado, what would he do when they met?

Emily got her answer much more quickly than she expected. Pegasus sped up. He left the others far behind as he tore through the town and started to follow along a dark road. In the predawn light, Emily saw a chain-link fence surrounding a large property. They flew over a tall gate that was the entrance. Emily barely had time to read the sign, DOUBLE R RANCH.

Directly ahead were multiple paddocks. Farther in the distance, they saw several dark shapes that were buildings. But Pegasus kept going. He flew right over the top of the first set of stable blocks and outbuildings without slowing down. Finally Emily saw their destination. It was a large, squat, circular stable at the very center of the property.

Even before Pegasus landed, they heard sounds coming from inside the stables. The horses were awake and screaming. It was almost like the first time they'd visited the carriage stables in New York. But this was different, because one voice rose higher and more furious than the others.

"That's got to be Tornado," Emily said. "He knows Pegasus is here."

Pegasus hit the ground in a full gallop. Emily had to cling to his mane to keep from being thrown off. Earl wrapped his arms tightly around her waist and did his best to stay on the stallion's back.

"Stop, Pegs," Emily cried as the stallion charged forward. "Let us down!"

Pausing only long enough for Emily and Earl to dismount, Pegasus charged forward. Glowing brilliant white, the stallion ran up to the locked stable doors. He reared high in the air as his golden hooves tore through the doors like they were made of paper.

"Pegasus, stop!" Emily screamed as she watched him losing control. The stallion threw back his head and screeched in fury as the doors came free of their hinges. Without a pause, he stormed into the stable.

Emily and Earl charged in behind Pegasus just as the others landed on the ground behind them.

"Emily, wait!" Joel called. "It's too dangerous!"

But Emily had to stop Pegasus before he did something to endanger them all.

Pegasus's glow lit the darkened stable enough to see that it was a huge circle with an open center ring for training. Countless stalls lined the circular walls.

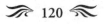

Their doors were solid on the lower half, with bars on the upper. There were horses at the front of each. Eyes bright, they were shrieking and kicking at the tall doors to get out. But despite their strength, the doors were holding. All but one.

Light blazed through the bars as its occupant glowed almost as much as Pegasus. He was kicking at the sealed door, and large cracks formed on the outside.

"It's Tornado Warning!" Emily cried. "Look, he's glowing just like Pegasus!"

Pegasus was on the outside of the stall door, kicking at the wood in fury. His eyes were wild and enraged. This was not the stallion Emily knew and loved. Pegasus had gone insane.

"Pegasus, no!" Emily cried. "Stop!"

If he heard her, he gave no sign. Within moments, the wood of the door shattered and Tornado Warning charged out of his stable. Rearing up, the two glowing stallions attacked each other with all the fury they possessed.

Pegasus's wings opened and smashed at Tornado's head, knocking him into the large open training ring.

"Pegasus, stop!" Emily howled as she ran closer.

"Emily, no!" Alexis cried. Racing forward, the Sphinx slammed Emily to the ground and pinned her down with her large paws. "They will hurt you if you go near."

"Let me up!" Emily howled. "I've got to stop them!"

"You cannot stop them!" Alexis shouted. "Not even Jupiter could!"

"I've got to try before they kill each other!"

"How?" Paelen ran up to her. "Look at them! I have never seen Pegasus fight with such fury before. Even his brother cannot stop him!"

Chrysaor was in the middle of the fight, squealing and trying to separate the two deranged stallions. But all his presence achieved was to infuriate Tornado Warning further. The gray stallion rose high in the air and came crashing down on Chrysaor with his powerful front hooves.

Driven to the ground, the winged boar squealed in pain. His cries fed Pegasus's fury as he launched a new attack on Tornado Warning and drove him away from Chrysaor.

"Joel, help me get Chrysaor," Paelen called. They dashed into the ring and dragged the boar away from the fight. Chrysaor squealed and left a trail of blood behind him.

"Please, help him," Alexis said as she let Emily up.

Emily nodded and knelt beside Chrysaor. She saw two deep gashes on his back where Tornado's hooves had cut deeply into his skin. One wing was badly damaged. The boar moaned in pain.

"It's all right," Emily soothed as she gently touched the boar's wounds. "You'll be fine in a minute."

As she healed the damage caused by Tornado, Emily realized that when Chrysaor and Pegasus had fought at the Red Apple, Pegasus had held back. Tornado hadn't. Looking at the wound, Emily understood Alexis's warning. One good kick from Tornado Warning could kill.

When she finished healing Chrysaor, Emily looked up and watched the deadly fight continue. She felt helpless to stop it as Pegasus reared up and kicked at Tornado Warning. But the gray stallion would not back down. He was also rearing and biting at Pegasus as murder flashed in his bright eyes. Each time one stallion's hooves made contact with the other, they cut deep gouges in their opponent's skin.

The furious sounds coming from the fighting

stallions were deafening in the large stable. No one heard the workers from the ranch arriving. A blast from a shotgun fired at Pegasus alerted the group.

"No!" Emily howled as a man raised his gun to fire a second time. Even before Alexis could move, Emily reacted. She raised her hands in the air. No Flame emerged, but the man was lifted over the heads of the fighting stallions and thrown to the opposite side of the stable.

A second armed man followed the first. Emily suddenly realized her powers were reacting without her command or control. She looked desperately back to her friends, who were staring at her in shock. "Stop the men," she cried, "before my powers kill them!"

With the deadly stallion fight continuing in the center ring, Joel and the others took on the men entering the stable. The ranch workers were quickly overpowered and their weapons taken away.

Tears filled Emily's eyes as she watched her beloved stallion attacking Tornado Warning.

As the minutes passed, Pegasus was steadily gaining over Tornado. Despite the racing stallion's strength, he was no match for the enraged Olympian. As Pegasus drove the rearing Tornado back, the gray stallion lost his footing. Falling backward, he hit the ground hard.

Before he could get up, Pegasus used the opportunity to finish the fight. He reared up and came crashing down on Tornado with his lethal golden hooves. Screaming in fury, Pegasus did it again.

"Pegasus, no!" Emily howled. Unable to stop herself, she ran forward. Pegasus was rearing to come down on Tornado a third time when Emily placed herself between him and the fallen racehorse. She summoned the power of the Flame in both her hands and raised them against Pegasus.

"Stop it, Pegasus!" she commanded. "Don't make me burn you!" She raised her hands higher. "Just stop!"

Pegasus's eyes were white and wild with rage. He reared above her with his deadly golden hooves hovering mere centimeters from her face.

"It's over!" Emily cried. "You won!"

Finally something changed in Pegasus's eyes. He suddenly realized what he was doing and to whom. Lowering himself to the ground, he neighed softly.

"Get back!" Emily yelled, still unsure of what he would do next. "Go on, get back!"

Pegasus pawed the sawdust floor. Finally he turned and walked to the other side of the stable.

With her heart still pounding painfully in her chest, Emily looked at the other horses in the stable as they continued to scream and kick their stall doors.

"All of you be quiet!" she shouted.

Alexis and Chrysaor approached the stalls. Their presence seemed to calm the frightened horses. Finally they all fell silent.

Earl flicked the switch that turned on the stable lights. Agent T was holding a gun on the ranch workers and ordered them deeper into the stable. In the bright light, their frightened eyes followed Alexis and Chrysaor as they made their way around the stalls. Finally they went back to Pegasus as he stood away from the others. His head was down and his wings drooped.

"Em," Joel called softly. He and Paelen knelt on the floor beside Tornado Warning.

Emily looked down on the fallen racehorse. Tornado Warning was covered in blood from the deep cuts caused by Pegasus's hooves. His eyes were closed, and he wasn't breathing.

"He's dead," Joel said. "Pegasus killed him."

10

FOR THE FIRST TIME EVER, EMILY WAS FURI-
ous with Pegasus. She didn't think it was possible.
But Pegasus knew how important this was, and yet it
didn't stop him from killing Tornado Warning. She
remembered his blazing eyes when he was rearing
above her. If she hadn't used the Flame, would he
have attacked her, too?

Pegasus hung back, away from Emily. He neighed
softly to her.

Emily looked at him but raised a warning hand.
"Stay back, Pegasus. You've done enough damage
already."

The stallion stopped and quietly left the stable.

"That was unfair," Alexis said.

"Unfair?" Emily shot back. "You saw what he did. Pegasus knew how important it was for us to learn the truth about Tornado Warning. But does he let us see the horse? No, he kills him."

"But we did learn the truth," Alexis said. "The fact that each was driven to kill the other says so. Is it not obvious? Tornado Warning does come from Pegasus. They have the same fiery blood. Neither could tolerate the other's existence."

"Em, look," Joel said softly. "It's true. Here's where they cut off Tornado's wings."

Emily looked to where Joel pointed. She knelt down and traced her fingers along the long, deep scars at the horse's shoulders.

"I'm so sorry, Tornado," she said softly. "You shouldn't have had to die."

"He should never have existed," Paelen said angrily.

As Emily's hand rested on Tornado's side, she felt a flicker of movement. Looking down on the fallen stallion, she placed her second hand on his wounded side.

"Joel, check his eyes," Emily said. "I just felt something."

Just when Emily thought she was mistaken, she felt another movement from Tornado.

"He is Olympian," Joel breathed. "Em, you're healing him!"

As the moments ticked by, more and more life returned to Tornado Warning. It happened more slowly than with other Olympians, but it was happening just the same. Suddenly Tornado took in a deep, unsteady breath.

Pegasus appeared at the entrance to the stables and called over to Emily.

"Remain where you are, Pegasus," Alexis ordered. "Emily is healing Tornado Warning. There will be no more fighting today."

Emily sucked in her breath as Tornado Warning's old wing scars faded and stubs appeared. Then those stubs grew. Wings began to take shape. They filled in and grew feathers. The gray dye that had covered his body faded, and all his wounds were healed.

Everyone was shocked into silence. Tornado Warning was truly identical to Pegasus—including the large wings and golden hooves.

"He's a perfect clone," Joel whispered.

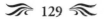

Tornado Warning opened his eyes. He screeched when he saw Joel and Paelen right beside him. In a move too quick to follow, he bit Paelen viciously in the leg.

Paelen howled in pain and jumped away from the stallion.

"Everyone get back!" Alexis warned as she opened her wings, drew her fangs and claws, and faced Tornado Warning. "He may come from Pegasus, but he is nothing like him."

With his eyes wide and wild, Tornado Warning climbed to his feet. He looked back at his wings and for a moment paused with confusion. When they fluttered, he whinnied in fear.

"It's all right," Emily cried. "Tornado, calm down!"

Tornado looked at Emily and stopped. He tilted his head to the side and nickered softly.

At the entrance of the stable, Pegasus neighed back.

Tornado faced Pegasus. He reared, opened his wings, and prepared to charge again.

"Tornado, stop!" Emily shouted. "No more fighting!"

Once again, the stallion's eyes came to rest on her. He dropped to the ground and took a step forward.

"Em, get back," Joel warned.

Emily matched Tornado's stare. She knew immediately he was nothing like Pegasus. But something told her he wouldn't attack her.

"It's all right, Joel," she said softly as she approached the stallion.

Pegasus whinnied loudly from across the stable.

"He says don't touch him," Paelen warned as he rubbed his leg where Tornado had bitten him. "He says Tornado Warning is dangerously insane. He is unnatural and must be destroyed."

Emily turned back to Pegasus. His eyes were bright and his nostrils flared. He was preparing to fight again. "Trust me, Pegasus. He won't hurt me."

She didn't know how she knew, but she did. Emily concentrated on Tornado Warning and stepped up to the stallion. "Easy, boy," she said softly. "You don't want to hurt anyone, do you?"

"Yes, he does!" Paelen shot. "Look what he did to me!"

Tornado took another step forward and reached out to Emily. His eyes were calmer, and he showed no signs of aggression toward her.

"That's a good boy," Emily said as she gently stroked his soft muzzle. She could see, standing before the stallion, that physically his face was identical to Pegasus's. But there was something profoundly different in his eyes and what she felt from him.

Whenever she was with Pegasus, Emily always felt a sense of peace, calm, and intense intelligence. But with Tornado Warning, it was a mix of confusion, fear, and anger. There was no intelligence or sense of peace. She could feel that although he wouldn't hurt her, it wasn't the same for others. It was true: Tornado Warning was dangerously unstable.

With the tension easing, Emily looked back at Pegasus. He was still bleeding from his wounds caused by the fight and shotgun blast. But his head was high and proud, and his eyes were bright.

"Go to him," Alexis said softly. "He needs you."

Emily didn't need to be told. Her anger with Pegasus was gone, and she could feel her connection to him calling her. Pegasus was in pain, and she couldn't bear it. He was her first priority. She looked back at Tornado Warning and held up her hand. "Stay."

But as she walked toward Pegasus, Tornado Warning started to follow. "No, Tornado." Emily stopped and held up her hand again. "I said stay."

"He cannot understand you," Paelen said as his wary eyes watched the racehorse. "He is nothing like Pegasus. He is just a flying horse that cannot communicate and lives only by confused emotion." Paelen took a cautious step toward the stallion. "You cannot understand me, can you?"

Tornado's eyes went wild again as he looked at Paelen. His ears went back, his nostrils flared, and his breathing changed. He started to quiver and paw the ground. He looked ready to attack.

"Em, you're the only one who can get near him," Joel observed, as he and Paelen took a cautious step back.

Emily looked at Tornado and frowned. "Why will he let me touch him?"

"Silly child, do you really not know?" Alexis approached. "You are the Flame of Olympus. Your powers call to him as much as they do to all of us. He is drawn to you as we all are. He does not understand his need for you, but it is there nonetheless. He will not harm you."

"Are all Olympians drawn to my power?"

Alexis nodded. "But do not think it is only your power that draws us. We are drawn to you. Though some of us may not show it, we all care for you."

Pegasus approached Emily, but his eyes remained locked on Tornado Warning. Tornado opened his wings threateningly.

"Stop it," Emily said sharply to the racehorse. "Pegasus needs help and I'm going to give it to him. Stay there and behave yourself."

The tone of her voice stopped further protests from Tornado Warning as Emily crossed the distance to Pegasus. "Oh, Pegs, what am I going to do with you?" She stroked his neck. "You know I'll always love you best. But you can't blame Tornado for being what he is. You should pity him, not try to kill him. Promise me you won't attack him again."

Pegasus reached back to Emily. He nickered softly and tugged at her shirt, drawing her to his head. Emily hugged his face and let her powers heal his many wounds. When they were finished, she kissed him softly on the muzzle. "There, all better."

Across the stable, Agent T called, "Not that this lovefest isn't touching, but we're wasting precious time." He held up his weapon at one of the stable workers they had captured. "You there, tell me, where is Rip Russell?"

The man said nothing as he kept his eyes locked on the Olympians. Alexis walked over to him. She rose on her hind legs and rested her paws on his shoulders. "I do not have patience for your silence. Answer the man."

"Diablo," he muttered as he tried to cross himself.

"Not *diablo*," Alexis corrected. "Sphinx. And I would suggest you not call me that again."

The worker's eyes went large with terror as he looked into the face of the Sphinx. "He is there," he said fearfully, and pointed at one of the men Emily's powers had tossed across the stable. "The one with the gun."

Agent T nodded. "Fine. Alexis, would you please escort him and the others to one of the empty stalls? We don't want any heroes here."

The Sphinx nodded and directed her attention to all the workers. "You heard him," she said loudly. "All of you, into that stall. Now!"

An elderly Mexican man stepped away from the others. "Where do you come from? What magic do you do to Tornado Warning? I have trained him all his life." The little old man touched his head. "He is *loco*—crazy. How can that girl touch him? He has killed two riders already." Emily turned to the worker. "What did you say?" The elderly man nodded. "Tornado Warning is *loco*. He has killed two riders. No one can touch him unless he is drugged."

"You keep him drugged?" Joel was shocked.

The worker nodded. "*Sí*. It is the only way to keep him calm."

"What do you give him?" Agent T demanded.

"Sedatives and sugar," the little man said. "Lots and lots of sugar. It make him more better."

Emily suddenly understood. "No wonder he's so vicious. He's starving. He needs ambrosia."

"What is ambrosia?" the little man asked.

"Never mind," Alexis said as she directed him to join the others in the stall. "Just count yourselves fortunate that I do not kill you for what you have done here. Tornado Warning should not exist." She closed and locked the stall door.

Paelen walked across the ring to where the two men lay unconscious. He rolled over the one they knew to be the owner of Tornado Warning. He started to shake him.

"Time to wake up," he said. "We need to speak with you."

The man started to stir and come around. He gasped in shock as his eyes found Emily standing between Pegasus and Tornado Warning.

"What the hell?" he said.

"Hell has nothing to do with this," Agent T said sharply. "Are you Rip Russell, the owner of Tornado Warning?"

The man climbed shakily to his feet and looked around the stable in complete disbelief. "What are you?" he asked fearfully. "Where do you come from?"

"We ask the questions," Agent T said. "Where did you get Tornado Warning?"

The man's frightened eyes lingered on Pegasus and then went over to Tornado. "Those horses got wings!"

"Yes," Agent T said. "Now answer my question."

Rip looked wildly around the ring. "Where is that devil horse? He was fighting with the winged one."

"This is Tornado Warning," Emily answered as she stroked the winged stallion.

"No, it isn't!" Rip insisted. "Tornado doesn't have wings. But they do."

"Yes, we have established that," Agent T said calmly. "This is Pegasus and that is Tornado. Now, I won't ask you again. Where did you get Tornado Warning?"

"I won't tell you a thing," Rip said, "until you tell me how those horses can have wings."

"Wrong answer." Agent T slapped Rip across the face. "That is me playing nice. One more wrong answer and I will gladly introduce you to Alexis. She's not so patient."

"Who's Alexis?" Rip demanded.

"I am." The Sphinx opened her wings and flew the short distance to where the group was standing. She narrowed her green eyes and stalked up to the man. "I am Alexis. You will answer our questions or you will not live to see the sunrise."

Fear rose on Rip's face. "You're a lion-woman! And you got wings too!"

"You do not miss much," Alexis said sarcastically. "But did you also notice these?" She held up her paw to show her sharp claws.

Rip held up his hands and looked over to Agent T. "All right, all right, I'll tell you anything. Just keep that thing away from me!"

"Thing? " Alexis roared.

Emily saw only the quickest flash of movement from the Sphinx. Moments later Rip Russell was on the ground, crying in pain and grasping his lower legs. His jeans were torn from Alexis's claws, and blood was rising to the surface.

"You were lucky it was only your legs," Agent T warned. "One more remark like that and I won't stop her." The ex–CRU agent knelt down beside him. "Now tell us. Where did you get Tornado Warning?"

"My cousin," Rip gasped between gritted teeth. He was clutching his bleeding legs. "My cousin gave him to me."

"Where did he get him?" Emily asked.

Rip cursed and sat up. "I just knew it! I knew this would come back to haunt me!"

"Explain," Agent T ordered.

Still grasping his legs, Rip Russell started to speak. "Ten months ago I was living on a broken-down farm in northern California. I had a couple of racehorses

but could never catch a break and win anything. One day outta nowhere, my cousin calls me. He says he's got a sure thing. All I had to do was raise a foal and then race him. He said we would split the winnings."

"And you agreed?" Agent T asked.

"Wouldn't you?" Rip answered. "So a month later, he brings this tiny white foal to me. It had bandages all over it. But even with the bandages, I could see it was quality horseflesh. So I took it. I was given instructions to keep it fed on sugars and other sweet foods. I was also told to dye the foal gray for racing, since no one races white horses."

Agent T frowned. "How could you race him? He had no papers to prove his pedigree."

"That part was easy," Rip said. "All I had to do was find a registered gray horse that we could substitute for him. It took some time, but we found one that looked a lot like him, with the same cowlicks and everything—he was called Tornado Warning. Then all I had to do was wait for the foal to grow up. Which he did superfast. So we switched him for the real Tornado Warning and by six months of age, he was winning every race we entered him in."

"What happened to the real Tornado Warning?" Emily asked.

"There couldn't be two in case we were found out. So I had him destroyed."

Emily's hand went up to her mouth. "You killed him?"

Rip shrugged. "Hey, this is horse racing. I did what I had to do."

Agent T sat back on his haunches. "That was a grave mistake. What did your cousin tell you about the foal?"

Rip shook his head. "Nothing. I was just told to race him and to keep him colored gray. That I did. And he is one amazing racehorse. Tornado Warning is the fastest horse in the world."

"He's the fastest because he isn't really a horse. He's a clone of Pegasus!" Emily shot back. "Didn't you ever wonder about the bandages? Didn't you care that they cut off his wings?"

Rip held up his hand. "Hey, I didn't know nothing about that. I just thought he'd had shoulder surgery."

"Yes!" Emily cried. "To cut off his wings!"

Her raised voice caused Tornado Warning to

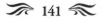

whinny and pound the ground furiously. His eyes went wild.

"Keep that monster back!" Rip cried.

Emily left Pegasus and stepped up to Tornado. "Easy, boy. I'm sorry I raised my voice." At her touch, Tornado Warning calmed. He even let Pegasus move closer.

She looked back at Pegasus. "See, Pegs, you don't have to fight him. He's fine."

Emily stood between the two stallions, with one hand resting on each of their wings. Beneath her fingers, Tornado was calm. But she could feel Pegasus trembling. He wasn't happy with the attention she was giving the clone.

"Where did your cousin get the foal?" Joel asked.

"I swear I don't know," Rip said. "He's an agent with the Central Research Unit. I had no idea he was working with horses."

"The CRU." Agent T nodded and looked back at Emily and the others. "That explains everything. If his cousin was working on the clone project, he'd know just how powerful Pegasus was and how powerful the clone could be. If he has a high rank, it wouldn't be impossible to smuggle a very young foal out of a facility. A clone like that could make a fortune."

"He has," Rip said. "We've made millions from Tornado. Especially after the Triple Crown win. When he goes out to stud, there is no telling what we could make."

Pegasus's ears went back, and he whinnied angrily. He pawed the ground furiously, causing Tornado to shy back and open his wings menacingly.

"Easy, Tornado," Emily calmed. "Pegs, please. We get that you're angry. But you can't upset Tornado. There's no telling what he'll do."

"Can he understand us?" Rip asked as his wide eyes watched Pegasus.

"Yes," Joel said. "And he's furious that you were putting his clone out to stud."

"I didn't know he was a clone!" Rip insisted. "I just thought he was a horse!"

Agent T reached out and squeezed the man's wounded legs. "Where can we find your cousin?"

"I—I—I don't know how to reach him. He works at Area 51!"

"Oh God, this gets worse by the moment." Agent T started to pace and combed his fingers through his long hair.

"Isn't Area 51 where they develop all the new military aircraft?" Joel asked.

Agent T nodded. "Yes, it's an air force base. But it also holds the country's largest CRU facility. That's where we have been keeping all the debris from the Roswell alien crash. That facility has the highest security of all the US locations because it's got the most developed laboratories. Governors Island was an open theme park and the facility at Tuxedo was a children's playground compared to it."

"Where is it?" Emily asked.

"The Nevada desert," Agent T said. "At a dried-up lake bed, Groom Lake. It's a good hundred miles from Vegas. I've only been there once, and that was more than enough. I couldn't wait to leave it. For as bad as we were at Governors, they are much worse there."

"So could they be the ones creating the clones?" Emily asked.

Agent T nodded. "Most likely. I should have

thought of that first. The laboratories at Area 51 would be the best equipped to create and manage the clones."

"They aren't managing them that well if the clones keep escaping," Joel said.

"I've got to get in there and see just how many clones they've created," Agent T mused. "Maybe I can stop this before it goes too far."

"You mean *we've* got to get in there," Emily corrected.

Agent T shook his head. "Not the Olympians here and especially not you. You have powers far too dangerous for them to get hold of. This all started when the CRU captured Olympians. What might they achieve if they caught hold of you?"

Alexis shook her head. "No one is going there, especially the Flame of Olympus. We did not come here to enter a CRU facility. Our mission was to see Tornado Warning and then return. We have done that. Here is Tornado Warning. We now know he has been created from Pegasus by the CRU. Our mission is complete. We must now return to Olympus and report our findings to Jupiter."

"No!" Emily cried. "If we do that, Jupiter will destroy the Earth."

"This world's fate is already sealed," Alexis said darkly. "The CRU decided it the moment they created Tornado Warning."

"There must be another way!" Agent T insisted. "It can't end like this. Please, Alexis, let me try to get in there and save my world."

Emily was stunned to see Agent T begging the Sphinx. He was always so tough and hard, even around her. Now there was genuine fear and desperation in his eyes. "I was with the CRU for almost twenty years. Look how I have changed. We all can. Please, you must let me try."

"I am truly sorry for you, Tom," Alexis said. "But nothing can save this world. The CRU have committed an unforgivable crime. It is my duty to return to Olympus and tell Jupiter the truth."

A HUSH FELL OVER THE STABLES. EMILY looked at the shocked faces around her. She continued to stroke both winged stallions as she collected her thoughts.

Tornado remained oblivious to the danger he was facing, but Pegasus knew. He nickered softly and pressed his face to Emily. Chrysaor's head was bowed, and he was pawing the ground.

Finally she spoke. "I won't go back."

Everyone turned to her.

This was it, the moment of choice. For days Emily had wrestled with the dilemma. What would she do if it came down to a choice between Olympus and Earth? Faced with the terrible decision, Emily made her choice. She would choose her world over Olympus.

"You can't change my mind," she continued. "If Jupiter decides to destroy this world, he's going to have to destroy me with it."

Pegasus nickered and looked at her in shock.

"I'm sorry, Pegs. You know how much I love Olympus, and you know I would do anything to protect it. But I love this world too. I came from here. I can't let Jupiter destroy it just because a few people have done something really stupid."

Joel and Paelen stood beside Emily. Chrysaor took up a position next to Pegasus. They crossed their arms and stood defiantly before the Sphinx.

Alexis glared at the group. "You are all being unreasonable. We told Diana, Pluto, and Steve that we would be right back. We have been here too long already, and our presence in Olympus will be missed. We must return and report our findings."

"Go back if you must, Alexis," Emily said. "But I won't let Jupiter destroy this world without a fight."

Alexis huffed and her tail swished the air. "Would you please speak with her?" she told Pegasus. "Tell her this must happen. These humans must be punished for what they have done."

Emily looked at Pegasus. The time had come for him to make his choice as well. Would he stay with her? Or would he side with Olympus? She knew how tough this must be for him. But as she watched his eyes closely, she saw no hesitation. Pegasus moved closer to Emily and stood beside her. He nickered at Alexis.

"You also, Pegasus?" the Sphinx said in disbelief. "You would betray your own people for this world? They have sinned against you most! Tornado Warning was created from your stolen blood. Do you not want vengeance for that crime?"

Emily's heart flushed with emotion for the stallion. Pegasus was going to stand with her, no matter what. She pressed herself to his side and faced the Sphinx.

"Please, Alexis, help us," she continued. "This doesn't have to turn into a battle. I have the power to destroy Area 51 if I must." Emily looked at her friends. "We all do. But maybe it won't come to that. Maybe we can stop everything and save this world."

Alexis looked at the group standing with Emily, ready to fight for the world. Her eyes found Pegasus. "Is it really true, Pegasus and Chrysaor, sons of Neptune? You will turn your back on your people for this place?"

Several long nickers and squeals confirmed their decision. "They both agree they are not turning their backs on Olympus," Paelen whispered to Emily and Joel. "Pegasus believes we can stop this before it goes too far."

"Is that your final decision?" Alexis asked.

Pegasus nodded and pounded the ground.

The Sphinx started to pace before the group. Her wings were fluttering, and her tail swished back and forth. "This is bad," she said softly to herself. She kept looking at Emily. "Very, very bad indeed."

She sighed heavily and sat down.

"So be it."

Emily's heart was in her throat. "Are you going back to Olympus to tell Jupiter?"

The Sphinx sighed again. "I should. But I promised Diana I would be your guardian. I would fail in that duty if I were to abandon you here to face

Jupiter's wrath alone. Like it or not, I must remain to keep you safe."

"Thank you!" Emily cried as she ran forward and hugged the Sphinx tightly.

"Do not thank me, Emily," Alexis said gruffly. "I have sided with you against my better judgment. I have a feeling I will live to regret it."

The sun was up fully before they were ready to leave. As more and more workers arrived on the ranch, they were marched into the stallion barn. All the workers, including Rip Russell, were now locked in two large horse stalls. Alexis kept watch and warned the workers what would happen if they made a move against her or her friends.

Outside the barn, Earl and Agent T hooked up a large four-horse trailer to a brand-new white pickup truck. Agent T was still insisting that the safest thing for everyone would be for Emily to use her powers to destroy the racehorse.

Emily refused. They would take Tornado Warning with them to keep him from being turned out to stud. After they fed him a breakfast of sugary foods and heavy tranquilizers, the winged racehorse was bridled, and Emily led him into the first box in the trailer.

"Now, what are we going to do with all the men? They're going to tell the police as soon as we leave," Joel said as he closed and secured the back door to the horse trailer.

"Maybe I can convince them not to," Emily suggested. "Especially if we explain what's at stake." She walked toward the barn.

"It would be more effective to kill them," Alexis purred. "But we can try your way first if you insist." She followed Emily back into the stallion barn to see to the workers who had been locked in the stalls.

With Pegasus and Alexis standing outside the stall, Emily entered the one holding Russell and several of his men. She tried to reason with him, explaining that if the police were called and they were captured, the leader of Olympus would destroy the world. But she could see in his face that after all he had seen and heard, he didn't care. All Rip could see was them taking away his only means of making money. That and his brand-new truck and trailer.

Shaking her head in defeat Emily turned to leave the stall. But as she did, Alexis cried a warning.

"You're not taking my horse!" Rip shouted.

Emily turned back in time to see him order his men, "Grab her!"

Rip lunged forward and knocked Emily to the ground as his men surrounded her, just as Alexis flashed into the stall. Those who followed Rip's orders were soon to learn just how strong, fast, and lethal the Sphinx of Olympus truly was.

Russell was the first to feel her wrath as Alexis tore him off Emily. The Sphinx unhinged her jaw, and her eyes went black as she drew her teeth. She barked at Emily, "Close your eyes!"

Doing as instructed, Emily put her hands over her face. She heard screams filling the air around her, mixed with the sound of Alexis roaring as the Sphinx defended her against the attacking men.

Emily curled into a tight ball and tried to block out the terrible sounds. Moments later she sensed movement. Reaching out her hand, Emily felt Pegasus's front legs before her. His back legs were behind her, while his wings were hanging down the sides.

She realized he was standing over her and protecting her with his whole body.

Just then she heard Earl and Agent T running into the stall.

"Emily, are you all right?" Earl said.

She nodded. She started to move, but Earl stopped her. "Keep your eyes shut; you don't want to see this." He helped her climb out from under the stallion.

"Pegasus, take her out of here," Agent T ordered. "And keep the others out as well. We'll take care of this."

Earl guided Emily out of the stall and hoisted her up onto Pegasus's back. "Go on ahead. We'll be out in a moment."

As the stallion carried her out of the stable, she could hear the horses screaming and kicking their stall doors. When they reached the outside, Pegasus nickered softly.

"I'm okay, Pegs," Emily said shakily as she slid off his back.

"Em, what happened in there?" Joel said. He ran up to her and looked at the blood on her clothes. "Are you hurt?"

Emily shook her head and looked at herself in

shock. "It's not my blood. It's theirs. After everything they heard and saw, Russell still didn't want us to take Tornado Warning away. He and his men attacked me."

"What did you do?" Paelen asked.

"Nothing," Emily said. "I didn't have time. Alexis did it all. She told me to close my eyes and she dealt with it. It all happened so fast."

Paelen shivered. "That is the Sphinx. When she is on your side, you cannot have a better ally. Oppose her and it is at your peril."

Earl emerged from the stallion stable. He leaned heavily against the side, struggling to stand up.

"Earl," Emily cried as she and the others approached him. "Are you all right?"

He shook his head. "I ain't never seen nothin' like it. The darn fools. Didn't they realize what would happen if they tried anythin'? We warned 'em. We warned 'em all."

"Did Alexis get everyone?" Paelen asked.

He shook his head again. "Don't think so. I saw a couple huddled in the corner of the stall. It looked like they hadn't moved."

Pegasus nickered and Paelen said, "Alexis would only go after those men attacking you. If some stayed back, she would leave them unharmed."

Earl nodded. "She left the others in the second stall alone too. It was just the ones going after Emily that she got." Earl's face turned a darker shade of green. "I'll be fine in a minute," he said. "You kids get ready to go, and I'll meet you at the truck."

"C'mon," Joel said softly as he led Emily toward the vehicles. "Get changed and then we can leave."

12

HOURS LATER EMILY WAS STANDING IN THE trailer beside Pegasus as it was towed across the desert toward Nevada. Chrysaor and Alexis were in an open stall behind them. Tornado Warning was locked in the rear stall, now calm and still from the tranquilizers. Joel and Paelen were up front in the four-seater pickup truck with Earl and Agent T.

Emily hadn't said a word all journey. Alexis had emerged from the stallion barn soaking wet after being hosed down by Agent T. No one but Pegasus, Earl, and the ex–CRU agent had seen what the Sphinx had done, and not one word was spoken about it.

As Alexis dozed peacefully in the clean, dry straw

of the trailer, there was no sign of the monster she had become.

Beside her, Pegasus nickered. Emily gazed into his warm brown eyes and saw the vision of the two of them soaring together in the open skies over Olympus. There was no violence, no blood. Just the sense of peace and joy they shared whenever they were alone together.

"I hope we can do that again someday, Pegs," Emily said softly as she stroked his soft muzzle. She turned and looked out the barred trailer window. The air that blew across her face was dry and blisteringly hot. Though Olympus was warm, it never became uncomfortable. The oppressive heat only made Emily feel worse.

She sat down in the straw and leaned against the wall. She was achingly tired. Pegasus bent down and licked her face. He neighed softly.

"He suggests you get some rest," Alexis translated without opening her eyes. "We have a difficult time ahead of us, and you will need it."

Emily wanted to comment on the difficult time they'd just been through, but thought better of it. The Sphinx was on their side, but barely. It wouldn't take much to drive her back to Olympus and Jupiter.

She lay down in the soft straw at Pegasus's feet. She worried about the time ahead and she worried about what the men from the stables would tell the police. Alexis had warned them that if they told the truth she would return. But would that be enough to stop them?

Despite her worries, the gentle rocking of the trailer and the sweet smell from the fresh straw lulled Emily into a deeply troubled sleep.

"Look at that! I must see this place for myself!"

Emily awoke to see a golden lion's underbelly standing over her. The Sphinx's front paws were up on the barred window frame as she and Pegasus peered out.

"What is this place?" Alexis asked breathlessly.

Emily crawled out from under the Sphinx and climbed shakily to her feet. They were driving along a highway that ran through Las Vegas. The sun was starting to set and casting a golden light on all the windows of the buildings. They were currently passing a tall black building covered in dark glass. There

was a crane on the roof, and it looked like it was still under construction. Just past it was another series of brightly colored buildings. "It's Las Vegas," she answered. "Those are casinos where people gamble and see shows."

As they continued on the road, Emily watched Alexis's excited eyes trying to take in all the sights of the city. She squinted to understand a large billboard hanging down the side of a tall casino. "Elvis . . . is . . . in . . . the . . . building," she slowly read aloud. "Elvis? My Elvis! He is here. I have found him! We must stop!"

Emily hated to shatter Alexis's illusion. "Maybe when this is over, we can come back and see him."

"Wonderful idea," Alexis agreed excitedly. "It will be our reward for saving the world."

Down at the far end of the stall, Tornado Warning was coming out of the sedative daze. He kicked the stall door and whinnied. Emily went over and stroked the racehorse's white face. "How're you doing, boy? It won't be much longer."

Pegasus crept closer, his jealousy obvious. "It's all right, Pegs," Emily said softly. "He's frightened and confused. He doesn't understand what's happened to him."

Despite her comments, Pegasus continued to hover. Tornado's ears twitched back and his nostrils flared. He started to paw the trailer floor and whinny.

"Easy, boy," Emily calmed. "Please, Pegs, get back. You're upsetting him, and I don't know what he'll do here in the trailer."

Pegasus backed down. He snorted angrily and turned away from Tornado. He walked to the far end of the trailer and kept his back to Emily.

"I believe we will need to sedate Tornado Warning again." Alexis carefully approached the stall. "He is upsetting Pegasus. In these tight confines, that would not be good. Pegasus is doing his best to contain himself. But even he has his limits."

Emily agreed. She climbed the small ladder that ascended into the "granny's attic" of the trailer and crawled along the overhang that went over the truck bed. Emily started to pound on the trailer's front wall, hoping that Paelen, with his sensitive hearing, would hear her and let Agent T know they needed to stop.

The message was received. Soon the truck and trailer were pulling over to the hard shoulder of the highway. When they stopped, Emily went up to the barred window and waited for someone to appear.

"What's up?" Earl asked as he came to the window.

"Tornado Warning is coming out of the drugs and he's really upsetting Pegasus. We need to give him some more before they start fighting again."

Earl nodded. "Well, we're pretty cooked up in the truck. This place is like an oven! How people can live here is beyond me. We were all talkin' about stoppin' to pick up some supplies and something to drink. I think now would be a good time."

"Definitely," Emily agreed.

With the promise of a pit stop, Earl went back to the cab of the truck. "Did you hear that, Pegs? We're going to stop for some food. We'll also sedate Tornado again, so he won't bother you," Emily said.

The stallion's eyes were large and bright, and he was quivering. Emily put her arms around his neck. "I know this is hard for you, Pegs. But I'm asking you to stay calm for a bit longer."

Chrysaor had been lying in the straw but now approached his brother and squealed softly. Pegasus nickered back. But when Emily looked to Alexis to translate, the Sphinx simply shook her head and remained silent.

After a time, the trailer turned off the highway and they entered the suburbs of Las Vegas. Alexis remained at the barred window, curiously taking in everything and bombarding Emily with questions.

They finally turned into a shopping center with a huge supermarket. Agent T parked the trailer, and everyone climbed out. The moment Emily left the trailer, Tornado Warning started to whinny loudly and kick at his stall door. This caused Pegasus to whinny in response and paw the floor.

"You'd better stay in there with them," Joel warned. "I don't think it's safe to leave those two alone together."

"I will stay with you," Paelen volunteered quickly. "I'd rather not go in after my last supermarket visit." It had been a CRU trap. Emily could fully understand his reluctance.

"Joel and I will go." Agent T handed the truck keys to Earl. "If anything happens, get everyone away from here."

Alexis came out of the trailer wearing Pluto's helmet so only Emily could see her.

"Where are you going?" Emily asked.

"I sense no danger here and wish to see what is inside this strange place." Alexis touched the ex–CRU agent's leg. "Tom, do you mind if I join you?"

"Not at all," Agent T said, and actually smiled. "Just stay close to me."

Emily noticed a definite change whenever he was speaking with Alexis. His tone was much softer and friendlier. Had the Sphinx's charms actually warmed his cold heart?

More loud whinnies from Tornado Warning forced Emily back into the trailer. Paelen and Earl followed her in while the others went shopping.

Little was said as they waited, and they all felt the tension pressing down on them.

Agent T and Joel returned with a shopping cart full of food. An excited Alexis reported all the things she had seen, smelled, and heard at the supermarket. She was more like a child than the fearsome creature she had become at the Double R Ranch. She and Agent T laughed as they retold the story of Alexis's tail accidentally knocking over a display and the perplexed expressions on the faces of the people who couldn't see her or understand how it happened.

Tornado Warning was fed first as they put more heavy tranquilizers in his chocolate ice cream. Once he had eaten his fill, everyone else climbed into the trailer and settled down to eat.

"Well, this is it." Agent T stood. "In a couple of hours we'll be in Rachel, Nevada. That's only a few miles from Area 51 and the entrance to the CRU facility."

"Then what?" Joel asked. "Does anyone here have any suggestions about what we do next? "'Cause I sure don't, and it's driving me crazy."

Emily shook her head. "Not this time. It seemed so clear last time because we were getting my dad back. But now . . ."

"But now we've got to see how many clones the CRU have created and if we can stop them," Agent T finished.

"Exactly," Emily agreed.

"Well, we won't know until we get there," Earl said as he too stood. "And we ain't gonna get there unless we get movin'."

"Before we do . . ." Agent T said. He concentrated on Emily. "Did you see that tall, black tower-like building when we first arrived in Vegas?" When Emily nodded, he continued, "We've all agreed that we're going to use that as a meeting place if anything goes wrong. If we ever get separated, head to the top of that black tower. Understood?"

Emily nodded.

"Good, let's go."

Under a blanket of stars, they left Las Vegas and made their way along the Extraterrestrial Highway that ran deep into the desert. When they arrived in Rachel, it was a surprise to see that the place was actually considered a town. It was more like a mobile home park. There were no houses, and the only business in the area was one motel with a small restaurant. Like everything else in Rachel, it was nothing more than a series of mobile homes parked closely together.

While Earl and Agent T went inside to arrange accommodation for the night, the others gathered outside the trailer.

"Hey, Em, did you catch that name?" Joel pointed at the restaurant.

"Little A'Le'Inn." Emily read the sign. "What else would you call it this close to Area 51?"

Paelen walked over to a flying saucer mounted on a tall pole. It was surrounded by brightly colored lights. "What is this?"

"It's supposed to be a UFO." Joel explained to a confused Paelen about alien spacecraft.

"So that is what the CRU thought I came to your world in when they had me at Governors Island?" Paelen frowned and looked even more puzzled. "It is not very big. How did they think I would have fitted in there?"

Joel and Emily laughed.

"That's only a model." Emily put her arm around him. "A real spaceship would be much bigger."

Paelen didn't look convinced. "If there were aliens, surely they would use the Solar Stream and not have to come here in these things."

Agent T returned with a key to one of the mobile homes. He leaned closer and kept his voice low. "Only you Olympians use the Solar Stream. The other aliens we have captured use vehicles like these."

Emily looked at the ex–CRU agent in shock. "How many have there been?"

"Quite a few," he said cryptically, but then changed the subject. "We got a mobile home for the night and can drive the trailer right up to it. Then I want us all to go into the restaurant and behave like one big, happy family."

"But I am not hungry," Paelen said.

"It doesn't matter," Agent T said. "This is the only place to eat within fifty miles. You can bet there will be workers from Area 51 coming here. Some of those will be with the CRU. And if I am completely honest, I would suspect that some of the people who work here are with the military. What family would come to stay and not eat at the only restaurant in the area?"

Emily frowned and looked around nervously. "But why would someone from the military work here at a restaurant?"

Agent T sighed and shook his head. "After everything you have seen and learned about the CRU, you still don't understand? Emily, think. This is the only place to eat that's anywhere near Area 51. Rachel,

Nevada, attracts every kind of person, from alien fanatics to reporters and conspiracy theorists. It's only logical that the military and especially the CRU would have a plant working here to check out the people who might be coming to the base. So let's just go in there and behave like travelers passing through."

They headed into the small restaurant. Alexis, wearing Pluto's helmet, stayed close to Emily, Joel, and Paelen as they looked around at all the pictures and UFO memorabilia on the walls. There were display racks selling Area 51 T-shirts. Coffee mugs had aliens and AREA 51 written on them. Computer mouse pads had the Area 51 warning sign on them, and there were several books written about the secret base. Even the menus had little aliens on them and were offered for sale.

There were a number of people sitting at the bar and at the tables, eating and talking softly. A group of men were playing pool. Music filled the air and the mood was light.

As they settled at a large table and their orders were taken, the middle-aged waitress smiled and casually asked why they were there. "Come to see the aliens?"

she asked Joel playfully. "Maybe see the entrance gate to Area 51?"

Agent T smiled and laughed lightly. "My kids and brother want to, but we've got a schedule to keep. We're moving a couple of horses farther up north. But we thought it'd be fun to come this route. We've heard of this place and wanted to see it for ourselves."

Earl put down his menu and asked, "So have you ever seen anythin' in the sky here?"

The waitress shrugged. "I don't look."

Emily thought that was an odd answer but remained silent. She watched the waitress closely. Although she smiled and chatted in a friendly manner to all her customers, there was something troubling about her. The woman's answers were too rehearsed, and there was a hardness around her eyes. She stood like she had a pole up her back and wasn't allowed to lean or slouch.

Alexis was also suspicious. When the waitress returned to the kitchen to place the orders, the invisible Sphinx followed her in. Alexis returned several minutes later and quietly told Agent T that the waitress had gone into a room and spoken softly with someone. Though she couldn't hear everything that was said, the waitress did mention the family traveling north with a horse trailer.

"So far so good," Agent T said. He looked at the others at the table. "Just act natural."

As their food was delivered, Emily was impressed with the act Agent T put on. He was nothing like his normal self. He smiled readily, told silly jokes, and even had a sparkle in his pale-blue eyes. He acted exactly as a father should. Emily wondered what he would have been like if he had never joined the CRU and instead had had a family. She imagined her own father might have even liked him.

When they left the restaurant, everyone paused to look up at the star-studded sky. It was breathtaking and almost as beautiful as when they were flying up in it. Over to the south, they could see the glow of Las Vegas.

The temperature was noticeably cooler than in the day, and the air was filled with the sounds of the desert. Coyotes howled in the distance, while insects chirped and small animals scurried through the scrub.

As they made their way to their mobile home, they

heard other motel guests moving around and heading toward the restaurant. Dogs were barking loudly in their pen, not too far from where the trailer with Pegasus and Tornado was parked.

"I hope the dogs don't bark all night," Emily said. "I was planning to let Pegasus out of the trailer to stretch his wings. But I don't want him drawing attention to us."

"Pegasus will have to remain where he is," Agent T said darkly. "I don't want him taken out here."

Emily noticed that the ex–CRU agent seemed agitated. "Is something wrong?"

"I have a bad feeling."

"As do I," Alexis agreed. "Coming here may have been a mistake."

Emily looked around fearfully. "Should we leave and find somewhere else to stop?"

Agent T shook his head. "That would definitely draw too much attention to us. We've just got to be extra careful. Let's get to the trailer and we can talk."

Before climbing into the trailer, Earl and Joel went into the small rented mobile home and turned on the lights. They closed the curtains and made it look as

if there were people settling down for the night.

Soon everyone was gathered together in the horse trailer. Tornado Warning remained locked in his stall. The lights were off, and everyone spoke softly.

"This place is crazy," Joel said. "There's no TV or telephone in the mobile home. What are you supposed to do for the night?"

"Sleep and then get out," Agent T said. "They don't want people spending any time here. Especially this close to an active military base." He looked over to the Sphinx. "Alexis, we need all your skills right now. Let me know if you hear or feel anyone approaching the trailer."

The Sphinx nodded and sat up higher. She split her attention between the meeting and listening for sounds outside.

Agent T shook his head. "This is going to be more difficult than I thought. There were a lot of military people in that restaurant tonight. The tension is high. Something big is going on at the facility."

Earl looked at his friend. "I didn't see no military folk."

"They were there," Agent T said. "You've got to

know what you're looking for. Like I told you, I visited Area 51 some years ago. Security was tight back then. But not like this. We're going to have to watch ourselves."

As the group talked, Alexis turned her head sharply. She held up a paw. "Someone is approaching."

Emily felt a flutter of fear. The power within her stirred and started to rumble, with the prickling of the Flame reaching her fingertips.

In an instant, Agent T changed his manner. He leaned closer to the group and laughed loudly. "And you know what?" he called. "Your granddaddy never found out it was us who'd put the outhouse on the barn roof!"

He laughed louder and signaled the others to join in. He nodded at Earl.

"That's right," Earl added, joining in the laughter. "Momma knew, but she never told Daddy. To this day he still believes it was the boys down the road. . . ."

As everyone laughed, Alexis waved her paw in the air, indicating they should continue. She crept closer to the side of the trailer and pointed at the wall. "He is right here," she mouthed.

Tiny flames burst from Emily's fingertips as her

fear increased. She tried to call the Flame back, but it wouldn't obey. Pegasus nudged her, trying to get her to calm down.

Joel looked at the flames as they flickered several centimeters above Emily's fingers. He laughed louder. "So, Uncle Earl, is it true what Dad told us? That you and him went fishing with dynamite?"

"Sure did," Earl agreed brightly. "That's the best darn way to get the big ones."

Suddenly there was a loud knocking on the trailer door. Agent T motioned for Pegasus and Chrysaor to hide in one of the stalls. He nodded at Emily's hands. She put them behind her back.

"Who's there?" Agent T called lightly, returning to the role of the friendly father.

A man's voice came from outside the door. "Is everything all right in there?"

Agent T went to the door. "Of course. Everything is fine," he said, opening it. "Why do you ask?"

The man was holding up a flashlight. Emily could see his face. It was hard and cold as he tried to peer in past Agent T. "Someone reported strange sounds coming from here. We keep a secure motel. I

just wanted to make sure everything was fine."

Agent T swept his hand back to invite the man to enter, and Emily's heart nearly stopped. She balled her hands into tight fists to keep back the Flame.

"Of course," Agent T said. "We understand. But my horses get a little spooked if they spend too long in the trailer. So my kids and I are spending some quiet time with them before bed. Would you like to come in and see for yourself?"

Alexis was pressed back behind the door. Her eyes were bright and her claws drawn. She was poised to strike.

The man took the first step up into the trailer when a voice called him. He paused for what seemed like an eternity as they waited to see if he was going to enter. Finally he stepped back down onto the ground. "Sorry to have bothered you folks tonight. We're just being careful."

"We understand completely," Agent T said. "Have a good night." The ex–CRU agent stood at the door for a few minutes, watching the man go.

Joel looked at Emily. "You can turn that off now," he said, indicating her burning fists.

Emily calmed down and drew the Flame back into herself. "I don't like it here. Maybe we should fly to the facility right now and see what's happening and get out."

Agent T closed the door and returned to the group. He shook his head. "They're suspicious enough already. We make one move and we'll expose ourselves. We have to plan this very carefully. This base has got ground and air sensors that pick up visual, audio, and heat traces. I know for a fact that by the time anyone gets within three miles of the gate or any of Area 51's property, the authorities have seen them and know just about everything there is to know about them. This isn't Governors or Tuxedo. This place has the highest security of all the facilities in the world. Even the president of the United States can't get in here."

"What do we do?" Paelen asked.

"We use our heads and not our emotions," Agent T said coldly. His eyes rested on Emily. "And you, young lady, must control those powers of yours. We can't have you setting things alight until we're ready."

"I know," Emily said, dropping her head. "Normally I can control them. But knowing that guy was just outside, it kind of got away from me."

Agent T's penetrating blue eyes bored into her. "Just like at the hotel in Baton Rouge with the exploding lamp? And what about at the Double R Ranch? It appears your powers get away from you a great deal."

"Yeah, what happened at the stable?" Joel added. "Those two guys went flying! And you told us to stop them before your powers killed them."

Emily realized she'd been exposed. "I'm so sorry," she started. "But I think I've got more powers than just the Flame, and I can't control them. Sometimes they get away from me completely."

"Why didn't you tell us?" Joel demanded, looking hurt. "Don't you trust us?"

Emily shook her head. "That's not it and you know it! I didn't say anything because we have bigger things to worry about. I thought I could keep them hidden until we got back."

"What are these new powers?" Paelen asked. "What can you do?"

Emily hated to tell her friends about her powers. She didn't want them to discover she was even more of a freak.

"I can move things," she started. "And sometimes they kinda explode."

"Like the lamp," Joel said.

Emily nodded. "And sometimes—but not very often—objects will disappear completely and I never see them again."

"Do they turn to ash like the gorgons did?" Paelen asked.

Emily shrugged. "Not really; they just sort of disappear."

Alexis sat down beside her. "Emily will soon learn to control these new powers as she can control the Flame. In the meantime, we must all help her remain calm and focused so her powers do not escape her again."

"Which is why we *must* plan our next move very carefully," Agent T said. "We can't let Emily lose control. Agreed?"

Everyone nodded and agreed to help her. Looking at their determined faces, Emily wondered why she had been so worried about telling them.

"Back to the problem at hand," Agent T continued. "I know for certain they have taken our vehicle details down and checked us out. The fact that we are still free means that someone at the Double R Ranch followed our orders and told the authorities we're moving horses. We are safe for the moment."

"That or they're raising an army against us," Joel said.

The ex–CRU agent shook his head. "No, with the base this close, they could be here in minutes. We're safe for the time being. I think our best course of action is to take a drive out to the base's gates in the morning and see what it's like in daylight."

Emily asked. "Shouldn't we go tonight while it's dark?"

"We mustn't make rash decisions," Agent T said. "If we overreact, this could backfire on us. We have to plan very carefully. Besides, we're all tired from traveling. We need to be fresh and prepared before we move. Rest tonight, because tomorrow we move against Area 51 and the CRU."

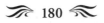

13

EMILY AND EARL REMAINED IN THE TRAILER
with Pegasus, Chrysaor, and Tornado Warning. With
Pegasus close at her side, Emily lay in the straw and
curled into him. Exhausted from the long, hot day
behind her, she quickly drifted off to sleep.

A pounding on the trailer door woke Emily with
a start. Pegasus was instantly on his feet, pawing the
floor and whinnying. In his stall, Tornado Warning
joined in and whinnied loudly. Emily looked out the
trailer windows. It was still dark out, and she couldn't
see anything.

"Stay back," Earl warned. "Let me get it."

Earl reached for the door and peered out. "Oh,
dear Lord!" He jumped down to the ground.

Emily ran to the door and watched Earl struggling to lift Alexis. The Sphinx was collapsed on the ground and covered in blood. He carried her up the three steps into the trailer.

"Close the door and turn on the lights," he ordered as he put Alexis down in the dry straw.

The Sphinx was moaning. "It's all right, Alexis," Emily said softly as she brushed her raven hair away from her face. "You're going to be fine."

Earl ran back to the trailer door. "Stay with her. I'll get the others."

Emily concentrated on the Sphinx. With a lack of ambrosia, Alexis was weakened and vulnerable to be hurt. She looked like she'd been in a terrible fight.

"Are these gunshot wounds?" Emily gasped as she checked Alexis's body and began to heal her. "Who did this?" But the Sphinx was too weak to respond.

As Emily's powers got to work, Pegasus and Chrysaor stood near Alexis's bruised and bloodied head. Pegasus licked her face soothingly.

Joel, Paelen, and Earl crowded around the Sphinx as she stirred and slowly opened her eyes.

"Tom is gone," Earl cried. "He ain't in the room."

"We didn't hear him go," Joel added. "I thought he was still with us. What's happening here?"

With the last of the healing finished, Alexis sat up shakily. Tears were rimming her eyes. "Tom is dead," she announced. "He was killed by his own people at the CRU."

"What?" Emily cried. "How?"

Alexis ignored Emily's question and looked at Earl. "They dislocated my wings. I could not fly and had to run back here. We do not have long before they come for us. Tom told me if anything happened we should get to Las Vegas to hide at the black tower. Go now, get us moving. I can tell you what happened later."

Earl nodded. "You kids stay with Alexis and hold on tight. I'm goin' to move this trailer as fast as it can go."

Moments after Earl left the trailer, they heard the sounds of men shouting and gunfire. The trailer rocked violently as the tires were shot out beneath them, disabling the vehicle. Joel dashed to the window. "It's that guy who said he was from the motel. He and some others have captured Earl!"

Lights flashed as military vehicles poured into the parking lot of the motel. They could hear a heavy thudding in the distance. Paelen raised his head. "I know that sound. It is soldiers in their flying machines!"

"We're trapped in here!" Emily cried.

Tornado Warning was screaming in his stall and kicking the door. Pegasus's eyes were wild, and he whinnied loudly.

"He says we must flee," Paelen translated. "Emily, get the big door open and we will fly out of here."

Emily nodded and then looked back at Tornado. "We're not leaving him here for them!" Before the others could protest, she dashed to the back of the trailer and opened Tornado's stall door.

The racehorse's eyes were wide and frightened, but he let Emily lead him forward to stand beside Pegasus. The stallions' eyes met, but neither made a move against the other, as though they both realized the bigger danger.

Emily climbed up onto Pegasus. "Everyone get ready. I'm going to burn it open. Joel, get on Chrysaor." She looked at the Sphinx. "Can you fly? Or should you ride with me on Pegasus?"

"I am sufficiently healed," Alexis said. "Use your powers—get us out of here!"

Emily looked at her friends. "The moment that ramp goes down, I want you all to fly out. Pegasus, Tornado, and I will follow you. Get up into the sky. Head to Vegas. We'll meet up at the top of that tall black tower we saw on the way in."

When everyone nodded, Emily raised her hands. "Ready?"

Her fear fed the power of the Flame. In an instant, a huge burst of blinding light flew from her hands and hit the sealed trailer ramp. On impact the ramp exploded and blew out. The debris hit several soldiers charging toward the trailer.

"Go!" Emily cried.

Chrysaor was first to move. The winged boar squealed and charged through the burning opening, Joel clinging on to his back, screaming. Paelen followed, running and ordering his sandals to take him up into the sky. As he flew over the heads of the gathering soldiers, he kicked the nearest two men. "Leave us alone!"

"Alexis, go!" Emily shouted as Pegasus moved

beneath her. She looked over to Tornado. "Come on, boy, come with us. Use your wings and fly!"

Like his brother, Chrysaor, Pegasus charged out of the burning trailer, screaming. He opened his wings and leaped confidently into the air.

Emily's eyes went wide at the sight of countless military vehicles pulling into the parking area. Men were pouring out with their weapons raised. Popping sounds filled the air as they opened fire. She felt stings on her arms and back and realized they were using tranquilizer darts, just like when the CRU were after them in New York on the 59th Street Bridge. Only this time, they had no effect other than to make her angry.

She held up her hand and released the laserlike flame at the nearest military vehicle. It exploded in a brilliant blast. A second, third, and fourth vehicle followed the first as the air around them glowed with the light of the burning trucks.

Emily's eyes sought Earl. She looked back and saw him being held down on the ground by several armed men. Earl was shouting at her, but she couldn't hear what he was saying.

"Pegs, we've got to go back for Earl!"

"Emily, no," Alexis said, swooping close. "You are the Flame; you must remain free. Earl knows this. He would not wish you to risk yourself."

Emily looked down on Earl. He had done so much for them, and all they had ever given back was trouble.

As Pegasus climbed into the sky, Tornado Warning screamed. He was still on the ground and running with amazing speed to keep up with her and Pegasus. Military jeeps were chasing him, and men were tossing ropes to catch him.

"Fly, Tornado!" Emily cried. "Use your wings and fly!" But the stallion did not know how. Instead he turned his fear into rage. He stopped, spun around, and charged the soldiers who were trying to capture him. He may not have known how to fly, but Tornado Warning knew how to fight. He instinctively used his wings as weapons. He flapped them and struck the men who were trying to catch him. Others were kicked by his lethal hooves.

As more men swarmed forward, Emily watched the winged racehorse finally brought down by the countless tranquilizer darts being shot into him. Her

187

last sight of the stallion was him collapsing to the ground.

Emily couldn't watch anymore. She looked ahead and saw that they were far from out of danger. A squadron of military helicopters was cresting the mountains surrounding Area 51 and heading straight for them.

Joel, Chrysaor, and Paelen were ahead of them in the dark sky. Emily noticed that Paelen was flying oddly, very close to Chrysaor. Then she saw why.

"Joel!" she gasped. She saw his limp body being held up by Paelen. "Pegasus, look! Joel's been shot!"

Paelen was struggling to stop him from falling off the winged boar's back.

"Paelen!" Emily cried. She pointed at the approaching helicopters. "Get Joel to Las Vegas. Pegasus and I will slow them down!"

Without waiting for a reply, Emily and Pegasus turned in the direction of the approaching military helicopters. "If they want to fight," she called to the stallion, "we'll give them a fight they'll never forget!"

"Emily, do not do this!" Alexis called, flying closely beside Pegasus. "We must flee!"

"We can't! Paelen and Chrysaor can't carry Joel very fast while he's unconscious. We've got to help them get away."

She felt the full power of the Flame rumbling through her entire body. Despite the danger she faced, Emily felt strangely calm. "Are you ready, Pegs?"

Beneath her, Pegasus put on more speed and screamed into the night sky. He was glowing brilliant white like a blazing beacon as he flew at the helicopters. Emily focused her eyes on the closest helicopter. "This is for Joel, Earl, Tornado Warning, and Agent T!" she cried. Emily raised her hands and unleashed the Flame.

14

PAELEN STRUGGLED TO KEEP JOEL FROM FALL-
ing. Unconscious, he was slumped across Chrysaor's
back and at risk of sliding off. But trying to keep his
large friend steady while flying with winged sandals
was proving very difficult.

Over to his right, Paelen saw the glow of Emily
and Pegasus charging through the dark sky toward
the approaching helicopters. He couldn't bear to
watch, but couldn't draw his eyes away either.

Emily and Pegasus looked so small and vulnerable
going up against the deadly flying machines. Yet as
Paelen watched, he saw his best friend use her powers
to bring down the metal monsters.

Paelen saw endless flashes in the sky from the

machine's weapons as they fired at Pegasus and Emily. It brought back terrifying memories of the night Cupid was shot down by similar machines.

But Cupid didn't have Emily's power or determination. Paelen watched machine after machine exploding brilliantly in the sky over the dark desert.

Their burning hulks crashed violently to the ground and set the dry scrub grass and plants alight. Before long, the desert floor was littered with glowing and burning debris.

Paelen shook his head in wonder. Emily was proving to be the better fighter and yet they kept coming, hoping to cut her and Pegasus down out of the sky.

He was so engrossed watching the fight that he failed to notice Joel was slipping. Suddenly Chrysaor screamed.

"Joel!" Paelen cried as his friend tumbled away from Chrysaor and free-fell into the darkness below.

"Sandals, get me to Joel!" Paelen cried in a panic.

The winged sandals reacted instantly. Paelen entered a dive as he chased after Joel. Chrysaor continued to squeal as he turned in the sky and dived down to stop Joel from crashing to the ground.

Both Paelen and Chrysaor reached Joel just a few meters before he hit the ground. Paelen caught hold of Joel's silver arm and slowed his fall just long enough for Chrysaor to fly beneath him and let Joel land on his back.

"Take us down!" Paelen panted as he and his sandals fought to support Joel's weight.

The landing wasn't neat or graceful. As Chrysaor's feet touched down on the desert floor, the unconscious Joel lunged forward on his back. Despite Paelen's best efforts, Joel's silver arm slipped free of his grasp, and Joel was thrown off the boar's back. He crashed to the ground several meters away. Paelen cringed when he realized his best friend had just landed in a cactus patch.

Paelen split his attention between Joel and the fight raging in the sky. He could no longer see Emily or Pegasus, but he did see her laser streams of Flame cutting across the dark sky. He noticed that the remaining helicopters were flying away from where they landed and realized that Emily was leading them away from him, Joel, and Chrysaor.

Be safe, Emily, he silently prayed as the fight faded into the distance.

Paelen reluctantly drew his eyes away from the sky to concentrate on Joel. He quickly discovered that Joel wasn't in just any cactus patch—it had to be the biggest and meanest cactus patch in the desert. As he entered it and tried to get near his friend, sharp needles scratched his feet between the sandal's leather straps and stuck painfully into his ankles and legs.

Paelen cried out in pain and retreated from the patch. Beside him, Chrysaor squealed and offered suggestions.

"You try walking in there, then," Paelen snapped back at the boar. "Your tough hide should be fine with those needles. But they are cutting me to pieces!"

After several more squeals, Paelen looked at Chrysaor. "Oh, I see what you mean," he said. "Good idea."

He looked down at his feet. "Sandals, lift me up in the air and flip me upside down."

The tiny wings on the sandals gave their quick flutter of understanding and then lifted him off the ground. They hovered in the air and then flipped. Paelen yelped as he was tossed upside down.

"Now take me to Joel over the patch." They moved over the cactus needles.

"Easy," Paelen said. "Just a bit more. . . . Good! Stop there!"

Paelen reached for one of Joel's hands and grabbed it securely. "Sandals, lift me up."

Paelen cried out as his hands brushed against a cactus pad that was filled with sharp, stabbing needles. His friend had been lying on that plant. Joel would be in a lot of pain once he woke up.

Paelen carried Joel over to Chrysaor. Even in the dark, they could see the thousands of tiny needles poking into his clothing.

Using his sharp teeth, Chrysaor started to pull the needles out one at a time.

"This is going to take us all night," Paelen said as he joined in.

Chrysaor squealed. "Yes," Paelen agreed, "we did pass a lake on the way here." He looked down at the tiny swollen points of blood on Joel's bare skin where the cactus needles had been removed. He looked over to Chrysaor. "Good idea. We should get him there before he wakes."

The journey to the lake was relatively short. Paelen kept a sharp eye out for more military vehicles. But after the big fight and Emily leading them away, Paelen realized they were completely alone.

They'd landed in a completely different environment. They were still in the middle of the desert, but the lake was lined with trees and lush grass. The air was cooler and fresher.

After removing the remaining cactus needles, they carried Joel into the chilly water. On contact, Joel started to stir. He moaned softly and passed out again.

Paelen remained in the water with Joel until the sun was well up. As Joel started to stir, Paelen carried him out of the lake and settled him gently on the grass beneath a large tree. The heat of the day was already pressing heavily down on them.

Joel opened his eyes, then frowned. "Where are we?" he asked groggily. "What happened?"

"You are all right," Paelen answered. "But you had a rather difficult night. First you were shot with tranquilizer darts by the CRU, then almost crash-landed into the ground, and then had a fight with a cactus plant—and lost."

"You call that difficult? I hurt all over!" Paelen

nodded. "Yes, but at least you are alive." Joel lifted his head and looked around. "Where's Emily? Is she all right?"

"I do not know," Paelen said. "The last we saw, she was leading the machines away from us. I am certain she is fine." Even Paelen didn't believe his own words. There were too many machines against Emily and Pegasus. It was unlikely that they could have escaped unharmed.

"We've got to find them." Joel panicked as he struggled to rise. But there was still tranquilizer residue in his system, and he collapsed.

"We cannot leave here," Paelen said as he stopped Joel from trying to rise again. "Look around you. It is full daylight, and we are in the middle of nowhere. We cannot leave the safe cover of this place until dark."

Chrysaor put a small hoof lightly on Joel's chest and squealed softly.

"Chrysaor agrees. We must not be seen flying during the day. It is too dangerous for all of us."

"But what about Emily?" Joel cried. "I've got to find her."

"Yes we do," Paelen agreed. "But we will not do Emily, Pegasus, or Alexis any good if we are captured. You are still weak from the drugs and the cactus needles. Take today to recover. We will leave here the moment it is dark. Then we can meet up with the others at the black tower."

Paelen could see Joel's thoughts flying like a storm. Like Paelen, Joel was devoted to Emily and hated the thought of her being out there alone. Though Pegasus and the Sphinx were with her, there was still a chance one or more of them might have been hurt in the firefight.

"What if she's dead?" Joel asked.

Paelen shook his head. "Emily is the Flame; she is strong. But we have all been without ambrosia and nectar for days. It is Pegasus and Alexis I worry most for. I hope they are all right. But for now, all we can do is wait."

15

"WHERE ARE THEY?"

Emily paced anxiously along the top wall of the tall black building. She looked out over Las Vegas, searching the cloudless skies for signs of Joel, Paelen, and Chrysaor. The sun was up but there was no sign of her friends.

"They will come," Alexis called softly. She and Pegasus were hiding inside a construction shed that remained on the roof. The building was unfinished, but by the looks of things, construction work had stopped some time ago. There was still an unused crane on the roof and a lot of tools. Over the side, there were several black windows missing, and on the ground, scaffolding rose high up against the side. The construction site was surrounded by a tall wooden fence.

When Emily walked back into the shed, she was more exhausted than she'd ever thought possible. Even after all the training Vesta had given her, she was still unprepared for her encounter with the military.

It had taken a lot out of her. The Flame within had done everything she commanded. But that didn't stop her other powers from surfacing. When she had opened fire on three heavily armed helicopters, instead of flame issuing from her hands, the flying vehicles vanished. But where had they gone?

She sat down against the shed's wall and took a deep breath. Her eyes landed on the Sphinx. Alexis was weeping.

"Are you all right?"

Alexis dropped her head as more tears trickled down her smooth cheeks. "I warned him," she wept softly. "I told him it was a bad idea, but he insisted."

"Agent T?" Emily asked.

Alexis nodded. "After you all went to bed, he came to me. He said getting into Area 51 was a suicide mission. Tom was frightened for everyone, but especially

you. He knew what would happen if the CRU ever got their hands on you and said he could never let that happen."

Emily felt a lump form in her throat. Agent T had never shown a trace of caring. Had he been hiding it?

"Why didn't he wait for us? We could have helped."

"He could not," Alexis wept. "Emily, Tom recognized the man who checked up on us in the trailer. He was from the CRU. He was certain the man had recognized him, too. Tom asked me to take him to the facility before they made a move against us. He was hoping he could reason with them. Tell them what would happen if they did not stop cloning New Olympians."

"Did they listen?"

Alexis shook her head. "Even before we arrived, they must have known we were coming. The moment we touched down, their lights came alive and we were surrounded. I was wearing Pluto's helmet, but they still knew I was there."

The Sphinx's voice broke as she looked tearfully at Emily. "When he realized we were captured, Tom told me to get you all away from here. But then a Nirad guard came at me. . . ."

"What!"

Alexis nodded. "They have Nirads there. We knew they would, but these were not prisoners. Those Nirads were working alongside the CRU. The gray Nirads were CRU soldiers. They were the ones who attacked me and nearly tore off my wings."

Emily's hand shot to her mouth. "This is so bad."

"It is worse," Alexis said. "While I fought the Nirad soldiers, I saw more coming from an open door, so I flew at the door and entered a world of horror." Alexis couldn't continue as her sobs increased.

Emily put her arms around her. "I'm so sorry, Alexis," she soothed, holding the shaking Sphinx. "But you must tell me. What did you see in there?"

"They have Diana clones locked in cages. I also saw Paelens and Cupids. I did not see the Pegasus clones, but I could hear them and feel their fear."

"Cupids?" Emily repeated. "How is that possible? He was never a prisoner of the CRU."

The Sphinx did her best to shrug. "I do not know, but they were there. They were suffering. But I could not help them. It took all my cunning just to escape and get back to you."

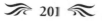

Emily shook her head and whispered, "This is worse than I imagined. It's gone too far for us to do anything. We must tell Jupiter what's happening here and beg him not to destroy this world."

Alexis shook her head. "Please, no, we cannot do that."

Emily was confused. "But you were the one who wanted us to tell Jupiter."

"Yes, I was," Alexis said shakily. "You are so very young and may not understand this. But I cared a great deal for Tom. In the short time we were together, we discovered we had much in common and . . ." Alexis paused and lifted her eyes to Emily. "And how alone we both were."

"Really?"

The Sphinx nodded. "Tom made me laugh. He treated me like a person. Not the Sphinx and not an Olympian guardian, but a person."

And suddenly Emily saw that the great and powerful Sphinx was very lonely, and Agent T had ended that loneliness. "I'm so sorry, Alexis."

Alexis dropped her head. "Before we left for the CRU facility, Tom begged me to help him save this world. It was the only thing he had left to care about." She paused and looked at Emily with her tearful green eyes. "How could I refuse him?"

Emily looked away. "That doesn't sound like the Agent T I know."

"Tom was a very tragic man," Alexis continued. "He deeply regretted many of the things he has done. He joined the CRU to help serve and protect his country. Instead he lost himself. Only at the end did he realize his mistake and want to make amends for it. He told me to tell you and Pegasus he was sorry."

Tears filled Emily's eyes. She reached for her green handkerchief and carefully gathered them before they could fall and explode. "I wish he had told me," she whispered.

The sound of approaching helicopters pulled Emily back to the present. She stood and peered out of the door to the shed. "It's just a tourist helicopter," she explained. "We're safe for the moment."

Leaving Alexis to her tears, Emily stepped out into the midday heat. It was almost unbearable. The tarmac beneath her feet was soft and starting to melt. Approaching the edge, she looked over Las Vegas.

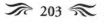

Brightly colored casinos lined the famous strip, and thousands of people were moving around below. None of them were aware of the danger they faced. It sounded as if the CRU had created an army of Nirad soldiers. With fighters like that, they could easily take over the world. Why else would they want to clone Nirads? Emily realized that the CRU posed almost as much danger to this world as Jupiter did.

What genetic engineering had they done to create the Nirad clones? True Nirads had telepathic links to each other. Would Queen Segan or Prince Toban be able to communicate with these new Nirads, like they did with the rest of their people?

A thought entered Emily's mind. She went back into the shed.

"Alexis, did the gray Nirad soldiers seem like the Nirads we're familiar with? Or were they different, like Tornado was different from Pegasus?"

"They appeared the same," Alexis answered. "They had four arms, black stringy hair, and three large black eyes. Their skin was marble like that of all other Nirads. But something felt different about them. I am certain they are not all Nirad but mixed with something else."

"But are they Nirad enough to be like the ones we know?" Emily mused aloud. She went over to the stallion. "Pegs, do you think Queen Segan or Prince Toban would help us? If they could communicate with those military Nirads, maybe we could turn them against the CRU."

Alexis rose to her feet and padded over to Emily. "You are not proposing we bring the Nirad queen to this world?"

"Not the queen," Emily responded. "Segan must remain on her world, but what about Prince Toban? He can speak with his people using his mind, can't he?"

Pegasus neighed softly and pawed the floor of the shed.

"He says it would be very dangerous to bring the prince here. I agree with him. If the prince were captured . . ."

Emily shook her head. "What could the CRU do to him? Nirads are practically indestructible. Only Olympian gold, Pegasus's golden hooves, and my powers can harm them. Nothing on Earth seemed to stop them last time they were here. The CRU has no Olympian gold, and I doubt they'd even know that

was the Nirads' weakness. Prince Toban would be perfectly safe."

"I do not think this is a good idea," Alexis said.

"I don't like it either. But they should be told what's happening here. Those are Nirad clones—part of their people. They should know what the CRU have done. It's only fair."

Alexis looked at Pegasus. The stallion shook his head and snorted. He pressed his head closer to Emily as the Sphinx focused on her. "Pegasus believes this might work. I can think of no other reasonable solution. This seems to be the only course of action. However, there is still the issue of Joel, Paelen, and Chrysaor's absence to consider."

Worry for her friends pressed heavily down on Emily. "I will stay here and wait for them, while you and Pegasus go to the Nirad world to speak to Prince Toban."

Pegasus protested loudly, and Alexis shook her head. "You will not remain here unguarded."

"Then you stay and wait for the others, and Pegs and I can go."

Alexis shook her head. "That is also unacceptable. We will all go."

"But what about Joel and Paelen? Someone should stay here for them. You are the best one to do that."

"I am sworn to protect you, Emily. I go wherever you go."

"But—"

Alexis narrowed her eyes. "I will ask you a riddle. If you answer correctly, I will remain here. If not, we all go."

Emily groaned. They didn't have time for one of Alexis's riddles. But at the same time, she knew the Sphinx needed to do this to help get her back on even footing. "Go ahead."

"Riddle me this . . .

I am the unreachable boundary,
Yet the place you wish to go,
I run away as you approach.
But I am always there.
What am I?"

Emily repeated the riddle to herself. An unreachable boundary that runs away when you approach? She tried to think of something that she might want but could never reach. She looked out of the shed, hoping to find an answer. With the sun high in the sky, there were very few shadows or shelter from the unforgiving heat. Suddenly a thought came to her. Shadows. Like Peter Pan, you can never catch your shadow!

"You are a shadow," she said triumphantly.

As always, Emily was wrong and did not receive the correct answer from Alexis. Instead the Sphinx nodded smugly and walked back to the corner. "We shall all leave at sunset. As we have nothing to eat, drink, or do, I suggest we take this time to rest. It has been an awful night, and I am greatly fatigued."

Emily stroked Pegasus and watched Alexis curl up in the corner. She looked even more like a giant house cat with her wings pulled tight to her body and her tail wrapped around her. "Do you think we're doing the right thing bringing Prince Toban here, Pegs?"

The stallion nudged Emily and invited her to stroke him. It was the best answer he could give.

Emily sighed. "I just hope this doesn't make things worse."

16

PAELEN AND CHRYSAOR LOUNGED UNDER A
shady tree while Joel spent most of the day in the lake.
His body ached and stung from the cactus patch. Only
the cool water seemed to calm his inflamed skin.

Throughout the long day, tourists had come to
visit the unique lake in the middle of the desert.
Picnic tables were scattered along the banks, and on
more than one occasion people had waved at Joel and
called greetings. When they approached, Joel ducked
low in the water to hide his silver arm and shoulder.

When the sun started to set, Joel emerged from
the water. Paelen stifled a laugh as he watched his
friend walk up the bank. Joel was covered all over in
tiny red pinpricks.

He pulled on his sweatshirt and immediately cried out in pain and pulled it off again. He threw it to the ground. "It's still full of cactus needles!"

"I have no doubt your jeans are the same," Paelen commented. "I would suggest you avoid those also."

"What am I supposed to wear now? I can't walk around naked."

"Sure you can," Paelen laughed wickedly. "I'm sure Alexis and Emily will love it!"

"It's not funny!" Joel cried. "Look at me. My arm is exposed."

"That is not all that is exposed!" Paelen roared. Rolling around on the ground, he was lost in fits of laughter. Even Chrysaor's eyes sparkled, and he snorted happily.

"When we get to the black tower, perhaps we can find you some more clothing."

"You're enjoying this way too much," Joel muttered as he sat down to wait.

When darkness fell, Joel climbed on Chrysaor and they took off into the sky. The only words spoken were those of Joel complaining about Chrysaor's coarse hair scratching his bare skin. Paelen found it difficult to fly straight as his laughter continued.

But as they got closer to Las Vegas, Paelen's laughter tapered off, and he started to worry. Had Emily, Pegasus, and Alexis made it to the black building? Were the others waiting for them?

Soon they were flying over the bright city. Paelen looked down in wonder at all the colorful lights. He could never have imagined a place like this. Not even New York lit up like Las Vegas.

"There it is," Joel called as Chrysaor flew high above the Las Vegas strip.

The tall black building loomed directly ahead of them at the far end of the strip. There were no lights shining from within, and in the dark, it was a strangely imposing sight among all the brightness around it.

They touched down on the roof of the unfinished building. After a quick search, they realized Emily and the others weren't there.

"Where are they?" Joel asked as he walked to the edge and peered over Las Vegas. "They should have been here by now!"

"Perhaps they did not make it," Paelen offered.

"How are we going to find them?" Joel asked.

"I know," Paelen said. He had been hesitant to use his sandals, for fear of discovering some awful truth. But now there was no choice. He looked at Joel and Chrysaor. "Remain here. I will be right back."

Paelen looked down at his sandals. "Take me to Emily!"

The sandals flapped acknowledgment and then shot him up straight up the air. Faster and faster the sandals carried Paelen away from Las Vegas, until he realized they were gaining speed to enter the Solar Stream. But when they entered the blindingly bright Stream, the sandals paused and seemed uncertain of where to go.

Paelen felt the drawing whoosh of the Solar Stream all around him, and he could also feel the sandals struggling to keep him still. Dark shapes of travelers sped past him, but they were moving too quickly for him to identify anyone.

"Enough," Paelen called over the roaring power of the Solar Stream. "Take me back to Joel."

The sandals obeyed immediately, and Paelen was

carried back to Las Vegas. He touched back down on the roof of the black building.

"That was fast," Joel said. "Where is she?"

Paelen shook his head. "The sandals do not know. Emily has entered the Solar Stream, but that was as far as they could take me. They cannot track her through it."

"That means she's alive!" Joel celebrated. "And Pegasus is too if he was carrying her!"

"It may have been Alexis carrying her," Paelen offered. "We must consider that Pegasus may have been hurt and captured by the CRU. Emily would do anything to protect him. Including telling Jupiter what has happened."

"Emily wouldn't do that," Joel insisted. "Not even for Pegasus! She knows what Jupiter would do if he found out."

"Perhaps she did not have a choice."

Chrysaor remained silent for most of the conversation. Suddenly the boar squealed and charged across the roof. He ran into a small construction shed. High-pitched screams filled the air.

They found Chrysaor cornering a young boy in

the shed. He looked only nine or ten years old, was dressed in filthy clothing, and had a dirty face. His eyes were bright and terrified.

"Don't eat me!" he screamed.

Paelen frowned. "Why would we eat you?"

He entered the shed, and the boy screamed even louder.

"Please stop doing that!" Paelen cried, putting his hand over his ears.

"It's all right." Joel held up his hands. "We're not going to hurt you. I promise."

"You're lying. You're going to eat me!" the boy wailed.

"No, we are not," Paelen insisted, "though I might throw you off the roof if you scream again."

"That's not helping, Paelen!" Joel knelt down beside Chrysaor and faced the boy. He offered his silver hand. "I promise you, we aren't going to hurt you. This is Chrysaor, that's Paelen, and I'm Joel. Come out of there and tell me your name."

The boy looked at Joel's hand fearfully. "You're an alien robot!"

Joel shook his head. "No, I'm not. But my arm is

made of metal. My real arm was wrecked, and now I have this."

The boy hesitantly took Joel's silver hand. "It's so cold."

"Yes, it is," Joel agreed. "What's your name?"

"Frankie," the little boy said as he walked around Chrysaor and followed Joel out of the shed.

"What are you doing here, Frankie?"

"I live here."

Joel looked around the roof. "Here?"

The boy nodded. "I live on the floor beneath this one."

"But I thought this building was abandoned," Joel said. "It's unfinished."

"It is abandoned. But I live here anyway."

"With your parents?" Paelen asked. He searched for signs of others.

Frankie shook his head. "No, they're gone."

"Gone where?"

"Just gone," Frankie said flatly. He looked back at Chrysaor. "Are you the ones the girl with the flying horse and lion-lady were looking for?"

"You have seen Emily?" Paelen demanded.

Frankie nodded.

"Where?" Joel demanded. "When?"

"Here, today."

"Where are they now?" Paelen asked.

The young boy shrugged.

"You're not big on answers, are you?" Joel said in irritation. He knelt down before the boy. "It's really important that we find our friends. Please, tell us what you know."

Again Frankie shrugged. "They were here all day and left when it got dark."

"Did you speak with them?" Paelen asked.

Frankie shook his head. "No way! I was too scared—that lion-lady would have eaten me! So I stayed hidden over there." He pointed to a large pile of building debris and rubbish.

"You seem convinced everyone is going to eat you," Paelen observed.

"'Cause that's what aliens do: they eat people," Frankie said. "Everyone knows that."

"We're not aliens," Joel insisted, "and we're not going to eat you. Did you hear what the others were talking about?"

"The lion-lady was really sad. She was crying." Frankie's eyes lingered on Chrysaor. "Can I pet your flying pig?"

"He's a boar," Joel corrected. "I don't think he'd like that."

Chrysaor stepped closer to Frankie and invited a pat. The little boy stroked his wings and the coarse hair on his snout. "It feels funny," he giggled.

"Why was the lion-lady crying?" Paelen asked. "Was she hurt?"

Frankie shrugged. "Don't know."

"What *do* you know?" Paelen said impatiently. "What were they talking about?"

"They were talking about nerds."

"Nerds," Joel repeated. "Are you sure about that?"

"I think so. I couldn't hear too good. But it sounded like nerds. They were going to get a nerd prince."

Joel sucked in his breath in understanding. "Not nerds, they were talking about Nirads! They've gone to get Prince Toban."

"What?" Paelen concentrated on Frankie. "Are you sure you heard them correctly? Did they say Nirads?"

Frankie nodded. "It sounded like that. They were

saying they needed the nerd prince to control the crew nerd soldiers."

Joel frowned and tried to decipher Frankie's words. Finally it registered, and he snapped his fingers. He looked at Paelen. "CRU—Nirad soldiers! The CRU have created Nirad clones that are serving as soldiers."

"And Emily has gone to the Nirad world to get the prince," Paelen finished. "Of course—it all makes sense now. She would not go to Jupiter if there was still a chance of saving this world. Now all we need to do is go there to join her."

Chrysaor squealed softly and then nudged Frankie to pet him some more.

"What did he say?" Joel asked.

"That we should wait here. We may miss them in the Solar Stream and lose more precious time. Entering the Solar Stream again may draw Jupiter's attention. Chrysaor believes it is safer to wait here, as they know this tower is our meeting place."

Joel looked incredulous. "You want us to sit here and wait while the CRU create more clones?"

Chrysaor squealed and grunted. Paelen sighed and nodded. "Chrysaor is correct. We are hungry and

getting weaker without ambrosia. We must eat first."

"And you really should wear some clothes," Frankie added. "On my planet, we don't walk around naked."

Joel realized he was still undressed. "This *is* my planet! But my clothes were ruined."

"I've got some," Frankie offered. "But they might be too small. You're really big." He paused and tilted his head to the side. "Are you sure you're not an alien robot here to invade our planet?"

"I'm not a robot!" Joel shouted

Frankie didn't look convinced. "You sure look like one. And your friends look exactly like aliens, especially him." He pointed at Paelen.

"Why is it always me?" Paelen shot angrily. "Why am I always the alien?"

They followed Frankie down a flight of stairs and arrived on the top floor of the black building. It was still unfinished—just one big open space with no walls and a lot of exposed steel girders and wiring. In one corner, they discovered the home that Frankie had made for himself. He had scrounged crates and boxes and created crude furniture. There was a pile of old blankets and

tinned food. Frankie had blacked out all the windows so no one would see the lights he had wired up.

Frankie's housekeeping skills needed a lot of work, but he obviously knew his way around computers and the Internet. He had set up what looked like a control center with at least four working computers. There were others in the process of being built. Off to one side were extra screens and parts neatly laid out and ready to be used.

"This is my headquarters," he said proudly, showing off his computers. "I'm using these to look for aliens."

Joel and Paelen admired the boy's handiwork. He had managed to build all this from scrap he'd picked up on the street. "Wow, this is really cool," Joel said. "Have you ever looked for aliens at Area 51? Can you show us how to get in there?"

Frankie shook his head. "I look all the time, but I can't get into their system. I don't think they're on the Internet. They must be using an internal intranet system instead. I tracked down a few pictures taken from satellites. But I never saw aliens until you got here today."

"We're not aliens!" Joel protested.

"If you say so," Frankie said dubiously. He continued to show Joel his work at trying to hack into Area 51's systems.

Paelen did not understand a word Frankie was saying, but Joel was nodding his head. They looked at the photos Frankie had downloaded from Area 51. They showed the open desert, the dry Groom Lake bed, and two long landing strips with several dark, squat buildings. None of the photos showed any activity or signs of Nirads or other clones.

"Hey, that's great work," Joel said. "How old are you?"

"I'm nearly ten," Frankie answered proudly. "But I'm really smart." He stopped to pat Chrysaor again. "But I don't go to school now. I just like to play with my computers."

"And you live here alone?" Paelen asked.

Frankie shook his head and pointed at the pile of blankets. "No, my friend John lives with me."

They all concentrated on the pile that they'd thought was rags. It was breathing.

"Don't worry about John," Frankie said. "He's

drunk most of the time. But he does help me live. He's taught me how to scrounge stuff and sneak into places. Without John, I don't know what I would have done."

"What about your family?" Joel pressed.

"I told you, they're gone," Frankie said quickly. "I live here with John."

"So it is just the two of you in this building?" Paelen asked.

Frankie shook his head. "No, there are others. But they're on the lower floors. Everyone knows John and I live up here. We help get them money, so they leave us alone."

"Money?" Paelen said as his interest was piqued. "How do you get money? Do you steal it?"

"Not really," Frankie said hesitantly. "I'm really good with numbers, so we go to casinos and I count cards for John. I can tell him what's coming. But we can only do it in the really small casinos. The big ones have rules and won't let kids in—but some of the smaller ones do as long as they're with adults."

Paelen frowned. "What is counting cards?"

Joel explained. "It's a way of cheating. Some

people can look at multiple decks of cards and calculate what cards are coming next. Then they know if they should bet or not. Casinos don't like it and stop card counters."

"But they don't stop me," Frankie said, "'cause they don't think I can do it. But I can."

In the light, Paelen was able to get a good look at Frankie. He was very small and very round, and appeared to be young, with bright-red curly hair. He had huge brown eyes and a freckled face. There was something about him that reminded Paelen of himself when he was younger. Perhaps it was how the kid had been living off his wits outside of society, just as Paelen had on Olympus.

Frankie walked over to a box of clothing. "This is John's stuff. I don't think he'd mind if you borrowed some." He rifled through the box and managed to find a clean but badly mismatched polyester checked suit. "This is John's best suit. He's saving it for a special occasion."

Joel looked at the hideous outfit and shook his head. He could only fit his silver arm through a bold-patterned short-sleeved shirt that clashed badly with the checked suit trousers. He used a T-shirt to fashion a crude sling to help hide his arm. "Well?" he asked. "How do I look?"

Paelen fought to keep back laughter, but failed. "Fine!" he struggled to say before bursting out laughing. "Though I would not let anyone from Olympus see you in that. Not if you hope to live there again!"

Joel looked down at himself and groaned. "I look like a used-car salesman!"

Frankie smiled brightly. "It's better than being naked."

"I guess so," Joel sighed. "Hey, do you have any money?"

Frankie hesitated and then nodded. "John and me split our winnings even Steven. He buys drink with his, but I buy computer parts. I've got all I need now and was saving my money for emergencies."

Paelen looked around and wondered what the boy thought an emergency was. He had no family and he was living wild in Las Vegas with a devotee of Bacchus. How much worse could it get?

"Frankie," Joel said softly, "we haven't eaten in a very long time, and we're really hungry. Look at poor

Chrysaor: He's starving. Can we borrow some money? I promise we'll pay you back."

Frankie stroked Chrysaor's wings again and nodded.

He walked over to a pile of construction debris. After checking to see that John was still sleeping, he put his small hand in and withdrew a used mayonnaise jar filled with money. "Take it. Get food for . . ." He struggled with Chrysaor's name. "Get food for Chrysler."

The winged boar came up to Frankie and gently licked his hand.

"Thanks, Frankie," Joel said. He counted out fifty dollars. "That will get us started."

17

THE JOURNEY THROUGH THE SOLAR STREAM seemed to go on forever as Emily impatiently waited to get to the Nirad world. She hated leaving Las Vegas without knowing what had happened to her friends. But with Alexis refusing to wait for them on the rooftop, her plan was to get there, convince the prince to join them, and get right back to Vegas before the sunrise.

They emerged from the Solar Stream into a dark cave. This was the entrance to the Nirad world. Since the fight with the gorgons, Emily hadn't returned, although she had been invited many times. But the memory was still too fresh and the pain of losing her Nirad friend, Tange, too great.

They emerged from the cave into daylight. Or what passed for daylight in the Nirad world. The sky was still filled with dark, scudding storm clouds, but the air was dry and arid. The black ground was dusty and swirled around their feet in the light, warm wind.

Outside the cave, they approached lilac guards at the entrance. When the guards spotted Emily and Pegasus, they roared excitedly and bowed. Emily slid off Pegasus's back and greeted them.

As the Nirads were a telepathic race, it wasn't long before others arrived. The ground rumbled as the heavy marblelike people gathered around to greet the heroes of their world.

From the back of the gathering, Emily heard a high-pitched, familiar roar. The crowds parted and bowed as a figure approached.

"Segan!" Emily cried as she ran forward to greet the Nirad queen. It hadn't been that long since Emily had seen her on Olympus, but Segan had grown taller and looked older. Yet for her Nirad size, she still remained delicate and elegant in her long pink gown.

Segan called out a sound that was as close to Emily's name as her mouth and tongue would allow.

She ran forward and scooped Emily up in her four arms. As the two friends embraced, Pegasus neighed excitedly.

Emily took one of Segan's hands and directed her over to Alexis.

The Sphinx bowed deeply. "Your Majesty, it is a great honor to finally meet you."

Queen Segan knelt before Alexis and touched the Sphinx's shoulder. She made several soft growls. The smile on Alexis's face told Emily that the queen had made her welcome.

Segan rose and turned to her people. She raised her four hands high in the air and made a long series of growls.

Alexis moved closer to Emily. "They are going to prepare a great banquet in honor of us to celebrate your return to the Nirad world."

Emily shook her head. "But we don't have time. We've got to get Prince Toban and go. We have to find Joel, Paelen, and Chrysaor."

Alexis narrowed her eyes. "I have met your father, Emily, and I know he raised you better than this. This is your first visit back to the Nirad world after the gorgon defeat. Their queen has ordered a banquet and celebration in your honor. You will attend the banquet and you will show your gratitude."

"But—"

Pegasus nickered softly beside her.

"Pegasus agrees," Alexis continued. "We are going to ask them to help us with a very dangerous situation. The least we could do is accept their hospitality. We will attend their banquet, and then approach Queen Segan and Prince Toban and seek their assistance."

Emily looked over to her host. Queen Segan's face was beaming.

She patted Pegasus's neck. "I'm sorry. You're both right. I'm just so worried about the others, and we don't have much time to spare."

"I am certain the others are fine," Alexis said. "Paelen is clever and crafty, and Joel knows your world well. They will find somewhere to hide until we return. Right now, we must concentrate on how much to tell the Nirads."

They sat around a huge banquet table filled with equal amounts of ambrosia and Nirad moss. Since the union of the two worlds, Nirads had acquired a taste for the Olympian food and always had plenty around. As they dined, Emily, Pegasus, and Alexis watched Nirad musicians beat large drums as dancers performed for the group. Emily never knew they could dance. But despite their massive size, the performers moved with a light foot and graceful movement. Emily did notice that it was only lilac and orange Nirads who danced. The grays sat at their tables, clapping their four hands and growling loudly.

Alexis sighed sadly. "I wish Tom could have seen this. He would have enjoyed himself greatly."

Emily studied the Sphinx but remained silent. She knew Alexis was grieving more than she let on. Had the Olympian Sphinx really fallen in love with an ex–CRU agent?

As the evening progressed, Emily felt more and more anxious. They shouldn't be celebrating when so much was at stake on her world. Worry for her friends only added to her stress level, and she was desperate to get moving.

Just before the celebration ended, Emily noticed

that Alexis had slipped silently away from the banquet table. She stood and spotted the Sphinx speaking with Queen Segan and Prince Toban.

"I am sorry that I could not wait for you," the Sphinx said when Emily and Pegasus approached. "But I heard that Prince Toban was planning to leave for Olympus shortly. I had to stop him."

The queen reached for Emily's hands and motioned her to sit down and join them.

"How much did you tell them?" Emily asked.

"Everything," Alexis said. "They know all about the clones. Though they do not understand fully what they are, they do understand how important this is, and what it could mean for your world if Jupiter were to find out. They will help us."

Prince Toban started to growl softly.

"He says he will come with us to rescue the children of Nirads."

"But they're not children," Emily frowned. "They are big, fully grown gray Nirads."

"He understands," Alexis said. "But there is no word in their language for clone. The closest is child or children."

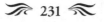

"I am so sorry this has happened to your people," Emily said sincerely. "I promise we will do all we can to stop the CRU from creating more."

Prince Toban made a long series of sounds.

"The prince says he will go with you and gather the children together. He will bring them home where they belong. The children will be made welcome and cared for."

"Thank you, Toban," Emily said. "But I have to warn you. I don't know what the clones—I mean children—will be like. They could be very dangerous. They come from gray Nirads only. The child of Pegasus was wild and deadly. They may not know you as their prince and may try to hurt you."

Once again Prince Toban made a series of sounds.

"They will know him," Alexis said. "He is convinced. He also said not to fear for his safety. He will not be coming alone."

An orange Nirad approached. Emily immediately recognized him as the goalkeeper from Joel's soccer team. Tirk bowed formally to the queen before moving to stand behind the prince.

"Tirk is coming with us?" Emily said, looking at

the huge Nirad. Up close he was even bigger than Tange and twice as strong. His arm muscles seemed to pulse with barely contained strength.

The prince nodded and spoke softly.

Alexis translated. "Tirk will be Toban's royal guard. The prince will not go without him."

A royal guard would definitely help. If he was anything like Tange, he alone should be able to control the gray Nirads. "That's great," Emily said. She stood up and prepared to leave. "Can we go now, please?"

Alexis shook her head. "That would not be wise. We are all tired from the day's events and must rest. We will leave in the morning."

"But what about Joel, Paelen, and Chrysaor? We've got to get back to them!"

"Yes, we do," Alexis agreed. "In the morning. Now I will hear no more about it." The Sphinx stood and nodded respectfully to the queen and prince before trotting away.

18

BACK AT THE BLACK TOWER, JOEL, PAELEN, AND Chrysaor settled down for their first meal in a long time.

Frankie took a sip of his drink and held the can out to Joel. "Do you drink soda on your planet?"

"This *is* my planet!" Joel insisted. "How many times do I have to tell you that? I'm human, just like you!"

Frankie shook his head. "Nah-uh, humans don't have arms like yours. They can't fly with shoes, and their pet pigs don't have wings."

"He's a boar," Joel corrected. "And he's not my pet. He's my friend."

"Do you think he could be my friend?" Frankie asked as he stroked Chrysaor's wings.

"Ask him yourself," Joel said irritably. "I'm going

up to the roof to wait for Emily." He stormed out of the area and made his way to the stairs.

"Why is Joel mad at me?"

Paelen looked at the little boy. Little Frankie seemed so lost and alone. "He is not mad at you. He is just very worried about our other friends."

Frankie nodded and continued to pet Chrysaor.

"Where is your family?" Paelen pressed. "Do you not wish to go home?"

Frankie remained silent a very long time before looking up at Paelen. Tears rimmed his eyes. "This is my home. I never had a dad, and my mom ran away. Now it's just me and John."

Paelen looked over to the pile of rags. The person under that pile hadn't stirred since they arrived. It appeared that Frankie did more for the man than he did for the boy.

"How long have you two been together?"

Frankie shrugged. "I'm not sure—longer than a year. John found me on the street when I was looking for my mom. He tried to help me find her, but we couldn't. Then we moved in here. He says when we make enough money with gambling, we're going to buy a real house. But . . ."

"But what?" Paelen asked.

"But John keeps drinking, so we can't go out to gamble much."

Paelen looked around at the home of the young boy. He felt great sympathy for him. His life was so much harder than Paelen's had ever been. Harder even than Joel's after his parents had died.

"Perhaps we can help you."

Paelen heard himself make the comment and shivered. Had he really just offered to help a human boy? He'd spent too much time with Emily and Joel. He would never have offered to help before. He had always lived only for himself. Now he was offering help to a stranger?

He stood up and stepped over to Chrysaor. "I am going up to check on Joel. Would you keep an eye on things here?"

Chrysaor grunted and remained with Frankie.

Paelen found Joel standing at the edge of the roof, looking up into the sky. "Are you all right?"

Joel shrugged. "I'm worried about Em, and what's going to happen when she gets back. What are we supposed to do? That facility is the most guarded of all of

them. We can't exactly sneak in like we did last time."

"I do not know," Paelen agreed. His eyes looked out over the strip. The ground below was teeming with people despite the late hour. "But until they get back here, I suggest you and I go down there and see what is happening."

"You want to go out tonight?"

Paelen nodded. "Why not? It could be a few days before Emily returns. We don't know what horrors we will face with the CRU. This might be our last opportunity to have some fun."

Joel shook his head. "But won't she be back soon?"

"Time moves differently along the Solar Stream. A day there could be several here. We could be sitting up here for some time waiting for Emily to return. And I for one do not want to miss this chance to go exploring this strange and amazing place. Especially if it's about to be destroyed. I want to see as much of it as I can before that happens."

Joel looked longingly back down to the strip. "Well, I've never been to Las Vegas before."

"Exactly! We will not be out for long, so what can go wrong?"

19

IT WAS EARLY THE NEXT MORNING IN THE Nirad world. After another large meal of ambrosia, nectar, and black Nirad moss, extra supplies were packed up for the other Olympians on Earth. Soon a crowd gathered outside the cave of the Solar Stream. The crowd had no idea where their prince was going or the danger he faced. They just knew he was leaving, and offered their farewells and good wishes.

Emily watched the masses of Nirad people in amazement. For all their size and fierceness, they were a gentle and caring race, bound together by Queen Segan and Prince Toban. She worried what would happen to these people if something were to go wrong and they lost Toban. Perhaps this wasn't such a good idea after all. These people needed their prince.

As if reading her mind, Alexis padded up to Emily. "It will be all right. Tirk will not let anything happen to Toban." The Sphinx looked at the young prince and his sister as they embraced and said their good-byes. "Even if we changed our minds about him coming, we could not stop him. He is bound by blood to protect his people, even if they are just clones."

After the two royals parted, Emily approached the queen. "I promise to use all my powers to protect your brother. I know what he means to you and your people. I won't let anyone hurt him or Tirk."

Small dark tears were forming in the young queen's eyes. She growled softly and embraced Emily. She then stroked Pegasus and kissed him softly on the muzzle. Emily didn't need an interpreter to understand the messages between the two.

20

THE NIGHT AIR WAS COOL AS FRANKIE LED Joel and Paelen on a tour of Las Vegas. Despite his young age, Frankie was very familiar with Las Vegas at night and knew all the interesting places to visit.

As they walked along the famous strip, Paelen's eyes were bright and his mouth hung open as he tried to take in all the sights and sounds around him.

"That's Circus Circus," Frankie explained as he pointed at the large red casino across the street. "They allow kids in there. But John and me never go in."

Joel added, "I've seen it on TV. Let's go in."

Paelen put his hand on Joel's arm. "Not there."

"Why?"

Paelen looked up to the black building beside them.

"It is too close to where we are staying. You never steal where you are living. It may lead people back to you. Trust me. I know what I am talking about."

Joel frowned. "What do you mean, steal? I thought we were playing tourist tonight."

"We are," Paelen agreed. "But we also need money for food." He looked down at little Frankie beside them. "And we promised to return what we took from you. I never break a promise." He glanced back to Joel. "To get money, we will need to steal it."

"We could always find another bank machine."

Paelen shook his head wildly. "I did that once— never again! Those machines eat people. I will not be their next meal! No, we will find some other way."

As they continued, Paelen felt his thief 's senses taking over. He hadn't used them much since he met Emily and Joel. But now he needed them more than ever. Down the strip they walked, past casino after casino. The road was jammed with slow-moving traffic, and the pavement was crowded with people. Men handed out discount vouchers offering cheap tickets to shows, while casino doormen tried to attract the attention of passersby and invite them inside.

A man handed a voucher to Paelen and said, "Cool shoes, dude!"

Paelen frowned. "They are sandals, but thank you," he corrected the man as they continued walking. He looked at the voucher in his hand. On it were several showgirls in brightly colored, glittering costumes with tall feather headdresses. Paelen raised his eyebrows in appreciation. "Look at this!"

Joel studied the card and smiled brightly. "Welcome to Las Vegas! I'd love to see a show."

"Then we will," Paelen agreed.

Joel shook his head. "We can't. One, we need money to get in, and two, we are all underage."

Paelen laughed and put his arm around his tall friend. "Joel, do you forget who you are with? There is not a door, wall, or lock that can stop me. If you wish to see a show, we shall all see a show."

They continued strolling along the strip and came upon a free outdoor show.

"See." Paelen directed them toward the entrance. "I never break a promise."

They found seats and watched a husband-and-wife team working with their performing parrots.

The intelligent birds did tricks and talked to the glamorous wife. Frankie was the youngest person in the audience. When the wife spied him, she called him up to the stage to help with a trick. Paelen smiled as their young friend participated in the bird show.

At the end of the trick, the audience applauded and a beaming Frankie returned to his seat. "This is the best night ever! Did you see me with that big red bird? It was awesome!"

At the end of the show, the woman offered to take a free photograph of Frankie with the birds. Frankie insisted that Paelen and Joel joined him. Frankie proudly clutched the souvenir photograph of the three of them and the parrots as they walked away.

They continued down the strip and came upon a huge, dominating hotel casino. They couldn't help but stop and stare in awe, taking in its grandeur. Its white marble facade glowed against the dark night sky, oozing glamour and luxury and a promise of excitement within. At its entrance they spotted several familiar figures lit up under bright spotlights.

"Joel, look, it is Alexis!"

Before them was a set of Olympian Sphinxes cast

in bronze. They looked remarkably like Alexis, with a human torso, wings, and lion body.

"This is Caesar's Palace," Frankie explained. "There's lots of statues inside. There's even a big fountain with flying horses just like Emily's horse. Want to see?"

Paelen grinned at Joel. "Well, if they have flying horses, we must go in!"

When they entered the casino, Paelen's attention was captured by more beautiful statues, all familiar faces from Olympus. They encountered a giant griffin near the staircases, and deeper in the casino, Frankie led them to the magnificent fountain where a marble Pegasus flew out of each side. At the very top of the fountain stood Jupiter. Holding his lightning bolts in hand, he looked powerful and majestic as he gazed down at the crowds below. A Diana statue with a hawk on one arm and her bow in the other stood at one side of the fountain, as did Neptune with his large trident.

"Jupiter would love this," Paelen said, admiring the large fountain.

"But let's hope he never sees it," Joel finished.

When they entered the main casino, they were immediately struck by the sights and sounds. Frankie warned Paelen and Joel to keep a watch for security. If they were spotted, they could be ordered to leave.

Everywhere they looked, people were sitting at slot machines pressing buttons. Their faces were grim as they concentrated on their games.

"Is this supposed to be fun?" Paelen asked.

Joel nodded. "That's what they say. But it doesn't look like much fun to me."

As they moved deeper into the casino and entered a different area, the slot machines were replaced by gaming tables surrounded by groups of seated people. There was a soft murmur in the air as they played cards. Paelen stopped and watched a woman behind one of the tables dealing the cards.

Frankie leaned closer to Paelen. "They're playing blackjack. That's the game that John and I play. The aim is to get cards adding up to twenty-one. When you do, you win."

Paelen continued to watch the dealer. When she flipped her own cards, she said, "Twenty." The other people around the table shook their heads. Their cards and chips in front of them were taken away. "Does everyone count cards?"

245

Frankie shook his head. "No, and the casinos don't like people doing it. If John and me were caught, we'd be banned from the casino."

Farther along was a long rectangular table with tall sides and rounded corners. There were number markings on the table's soft covered surface. At the end a man was shaking dice in his hands. He threw the dice along the table.

"I know this game," Paelen said excitedly. "We play something like this in Olympus."

They watched the players put down their chips on numbers before the dice were thrown. When the dice stopped, some of the people earned more chips, while others had their chips taken away.

"What are those strange coins they are putting on the numbers?" Paelen asked.

"Chips," Joel explained. "They're like money. The numbers on them are their value. So if you have the number twenty on a chip, it is worth twenty dollars."

"You mean, all around us, those little pieces are worth money?" Paelen asked in shock.

"Yep," Joel said.

"But look how much that man has over there!"

Joel followed Paelen's eyes to a card dealer. There were countless piles of chips in front of him.

"That's the dealer," Joel explained. "They always have a lot of chips."

"And that means they have a lot of money?"

"I guess you could say that," Joel said.

"And the same with that man?" Paelen pointed to a player sitting at the roulette wheel. Before him were several large stacks of chips.

"That's right," Joel said. "Why?"

Paelen felt his heart fluttering with excitement. His fingers itched the way they always did when he was on the hunt. "Joel, you and Frankie wait for me over there." He pointed to a group of slot machines several meters away.

"Paelen, what are you planning to do?" Joel asked nervously.

"What I do best!" Paelen grinned.

Paelen turned on all his thieving skills. He could see, hear, smell, and taste everything going on around him. It was as though the world had slowed to a standstill, and he was the only one moving. His keen Olympian eyes scanned the gambling tables. He looked for

weaknesses in either the dealers or players, someone who wasn't concentrating as sharply as they should.

Then his eyes found their mark. There! He saw a drunk player who spent more time chatting up a waitress than concentrating on the game or his many stacks of chips. Taking a deep breath, Paelen made his move.

With the stealth of a lifetime spent living only by his senses, Paelen walked soundlessly toward the player. Without changing the expression on his face, he stretched out the bones in his right arm to extend it and walked smoothly past the drunk player. His long arm flashed out so quickly, no one saw the long fingers wrap around a stack of chips and pull away instantly.

Paelen moved on to his next victim. And then another. And then another! No one noticed a thing. He walked back to Joel and Frankie and without pausing, whispered, "Follow me."

When they'd reached the other side of the casino, Paelen stopped and burst out laughing. "That was just too easy! I must do it again!"

Joel was frowning. "Paelen, I was watching you. You didn't do anything."

Paelen laughed harder and held out his right hand. Opening his fingers, he showed Joel the stack of fifty- and one-hundred-dollar chips resting inside.

"Wow!" Frankie cried. "You're rich!"

Joel's eyes went wide as he counted the chips. "There's over a thousand dollars here. How did you do it? I didn't see a thing."

"That is because I am not just a thief, I am a very *good* thief!"

"But you told Diana you weren't a thief anymore."

"I lied!" Paelen's eyes were bright as his mind raced with the things he could achieve in this strange and wondrous place. His eyes scanned the crowds of the casino. Nothing had changed. No one had noticed a thing. "Wait here. I will go and get more."

Joel caught him by the arm. "No. We have more than we need right now. Let's not be greedy. We can cash them in and get going."

Paelen wasn't happy, but he agreed. The three walked through the casino toward the secured coun- ter, where chips were cashed into money.

"This is where we're going to have trouble," Joel said.

"Why?"

"Because we're underage. You're not allowed to gamble until you're twenty-one."

Paelen frowned. "I did not gamble. I stole these chips. And I am well over twenty-one, especially if measured in the years of your world."

"How old are you?" Frankie asked.

Paelen shrugged. "Actually, I do not know. But I do know I am very old."

Joel nodded. "Maybe, but you don't look it. I look older than you, but not old enough to play here. We have to find someone to cash them in for us."

"Let me try," Frankie offered. "I do this all the time when John is too drunk. Give me the chips."

Joel looked doubtful but handed the chips over to little Frankie.

"Follow me, but stay way back," Frankie instructed. He walked away and started to study the players at the slot machines. He stopped before a man whose shaking hand was feeding money into a machine. He was in his thirties, and his rumpled clothing suggested he hadn't changed in a few days. The expression on his face was desperate.

Frankie went into his act. His eyes grew large and

round and his face sorrowful. He showed the man his chips and pointed to the cashier counter.

"The kid is good," Joel muttered as they followed Frankie and the man to the counter.

Minutes later, Frankie returned with a fistful of cash. He handed it over to Joel.

"There's only seven hundred dollars here," Joel said, counting the cash and frowning. "Where's the rest?"

Frankie shrugged. "I gave it to the man. He was out of money and couldn't pay his hotel bill. We have plenty."

"But we need more," Paelen complained.

"He needed it," Frankie insisted.

"Then I shall go get us more," Paelen offered.

Joel grabbed Paelen. "Don't. Frankie's right. We have more than we need. Hopefully Emily will be here soon, and we'll be leaving anyway. We don't need more."

Disappointed, Paelen surrendered to his friends. "Well, what do you want to do now?"

"I know!" Frankie jumped up and down excitedly. "Let's go to the Fremont Street Experience!"

"What is that?" Paelen asked.

"You'll see. It will be great. I love it there, but John doesn't let me go very often."

Joel shook his head. "I think we should head back and wait for Emily. She could be here any moment, and we still have to plan our next move."

"Would you relax!" Paelen insisted. "We have plenty of time before Emily returns. I told you, this may be our last opportunity to see this place. I for one do not want to miss a thing. We can go just for a while. Please?"

Joel looked from Paelen to Frankie's hopeful face. He shook his head and started to chuckle. "All right, you win. But if we find Emily has been waiting for us, you're going to be the one to tell her why, not me."

"Agreed!" Paelen said. He turned to Frankie. "Lead on."

The Fremont Street Experience was like nothing Joel or Paelen had ever seen before. It was an outdoor pedestrian mall covered with a long, tall barrel canopy that was alive with a brilliant light show that filled the entire area with blazing colors. Loud music blasted from an act on the open-air stage as well as from speakers that coordinated with the light show above.

Thousands of people filled the street, which was lined with more casinos and shops than Paelen could count. No cars were allowed along Fremont, so the road itself teemed with tourists. Countless performers in costume invited the crowds to have pictures taken with them.

"This is insane!" Joel said as his wide eyes tried to take it all in.

They gazed around in absolute wonder.

"I wouldn't mind one of those." Joel pointed to a red Ferrari raised on a platform. It was surrounded by more flashy sports cars, and people were having their photos taken with the luxury vehicles.

"I agree," Paelen said, eyeing the car. He then pointed at a DeLorean with its gull-wing doors open. "Or that one! It looks like it can fly."

As they admired the cars, they suddenly heard screaming from directly above them. A tourist was sliding along a zip-cord cable suspended high above the crowds. The cable ran the whole length of Fremont Street.

"I should like to try that," Paelen said excitedly to Joel.

"Me too," Frankie agreed. "I've always wanted to do it. But John says it's too expensive."

"That is not a problem for us," Paelen boasted.

"So can we try it later?" Frankie asked.

Paelen grinned. "Why not?"

Paelen, Joel, and Frankie paid little attention to where they were going as they toured along the bright street through the dense crowds. The sights around them were crazy and exciting. Sounds and lights overwhelmed their senses. Time itself seemed to stop as they visited one casino after another, each more exciting and extravagant than the one before.

"I really hope Jupiter does not destroy this place," Paelen said as they stood and watched a street performer doing magic tricks. "That would be a tragedy."

"It would," Joel agreed.

As the magician finished his act and the crowds dispersed, Paelen became aware of a group of young men staring at them and moving closer. Something about their expressions and manner disturbed him.

"Come, Frankie," Paelen said quickly, catching Frankie by the arm. "Let us keep moving."

"Not so fast, Runt!" one of the men called as he and his men ran to surround them. "The boss wants to talk to you."

"Hey," Joel shot as he was shoved closer to Paelen. "Back off!"

The dense crowds around them were completely unaware of what was happening as the men pulled out weapons and shoved them into Paelen's and Joel's backs.

"Keep it cool and no one gets hurt," the greasy-haired leader of the group said discreetly. "Just come this way. The boss is waiting for you."

"What boss?" Paelen demanded. "We do not know any boss, and we are not going anywhere with you." He tensed to fight, but then saw one of the men press the barrel of his gun deep into Frankie's back.

"Paelen," Frankie whimpered softly, "they've got guns."

"We ain't foolin' around here, Runt. Now get moving!"

Paelen looked over to Joel. His friend was also

preparing to fight. "No!" He indicated the weapon on Frankie. "Let us go with them and see what they want."

Putting his arm around Frankie, Paelen faced the greasy-haired man. "Release this boy. He is only a child and must have nothing to do with this."

The leader shook his head. "The boss said bring all of ya, and that's what we're gonna do. Now, move it."

They were led to a narrow street running off Fremont. It was much darker, and there were no crowds. The fronts of buildings were filthy. Desperate, homeless people slept in doorways.

Paelen looked around for a way out of the situation. But with the four armed men, it was too dangerous to make a move just yet. The only option was to wait to see what they wanted.

"In here," the greasy-haired man ordered.

They were escorted into a building and taken up to the second floor, where they were ordered into a sparsely furnished apartment. Inside were three more large, thuggish-looking men and one shorter one, who seemed to be in charge. The man was in his late thirties and had tattoos on every part of his exposed skin, including his bald head. Their expressions were anything but friendly. There was a thick, pungent aroma of danger in the air.

The greasy-haired man went up to the short, bald man and pointed at Paelen. "That's him, ain't it? That's the Runt you've been looking for?"

"That's him, all right," the man said gruffly.

Joel found his voice. "What's going on here? Who are you people and what do you want?"

"Shut up!" the greasy-haired man ordered as he shoved Joel.

Paelen felt a rush of anger. "You are making a grave mistake," he warned. "Release us now or there will be trouble."

"Yeah," Frankie added, puffing himself up to his full, tiny height and trying to be brave. "These guys are aliens. You put your guns away or they'll eat you!"

"Shut up, kid!" the tattooed man barked. He approached Paelen. "And don't you go making threats you can't back up, Runt. You might have beaten me and my boys last month, but we're ready for you now. It's time for payback."

Paelen looked around the room. There were eight

men altogether. With his Olympian strength and Joel's silver arm they could easily overpower them. But the thugs had weapons, and Joel and Frankie were human. They could be hurt or even killed.

"I believe you must have us confused with someone else," Paelen said flatly. "We have only just arrived in this city. Now, if you do not mind, we will be leaving."

Paelen tried to pull Frankie closer and head toward the door.

"You ain't going nowhere, Runt," the tattooed man said. "I never forget a face—especially one that disrespects me and breaks my nose!"

"Disrespects you?" Joel said. "How? We've never met you before. How could Paelen break your nose?"

"Shut it!" the tattooed man said, pointing a finger in Joel's face. "This don't concern you." He concentrated on Paelen. "Now, Runt, what do you gotta say for yourself?"

"First, that I am not a runt," Paelen said. "And second, I have no idea what you are talking about."

The tattooed man punched Paelen in the stomach. "I told you before what I'd do if I caught you again.

But you're too stupid to listen. You just go on disrespecting me and invading my territory. That ain't cool. My boys tell me you were on Fremont Street again."

It took all of Paelen's willpower to contain his temper. "I have no idea what you are talking about. We have never met before!"

"Wrong answer!" the tattooed man said. "I know it was you. Same scrawny body and same dumb expression on your face. It was you all right, and I ain't about to forgive you."

Paelen suddenly understood. He held up his hands. "Wait, please. I assure you that was not me. The CRU have created a clone of me. It was him who attacked you!"

"Clones?" the tattooed man cried, starting to laugh. He looked at his men, who were also laughing. Then his face went serious. "Just how stupid do you think I am, Runt? Clones? Give me a break!"

"It's true!" Joel insisted. "Listen to us. The government has created clones. If we don't stop them—"

"Enough!" the tattooed man shouted. He looked at his men. "I've had it with these punks. Kill 'em all!"

Paelen shoved Frankie to the floor as he and Joel moved. Joel pulled his silver arm free of his sling and started to fight. One man after another went down as he struck them with his heavy silver arm. Beside him, Paelen launched a powerful attack on the others. A shot went off and hit Joel's arm, but the bullet ricocheted off the silver and hit one of the men.

Paelen was on the shooter in an instant. His superior Olympian strength was overwhelming. One blow had the man flying across the room. He hit the far wall and fell to the floor, unconscious. And although Joel was mostly human, working in Vulcan's armory had given him amazing strength. He was able to fight off another man before he could pull the trigger of his weapon. That man crashed to the floor.

"Paelen, behind you!" Frankie screeched.

Paelen turned. His eyes went wide as he saw the tattooed man holding a gun up to his head.

"Say nighty-night, Runt!" He pulled the trigger.

The bullet knocked Paelen backward. He felt a searing pain in the center of his forehead. It was almost like the time Agent O had shot him in the grocery store, but much, much worse.

"Paelen!" Joel charged the shooter. He smashed down on his gun arm before he could fire again. The tattooed man cried out as the bones in his arm shattered under the impact of Joel's silver arm. He collapsed to the floor, crying and clutching his broken arm. Joel kicked his gun away.

"Paelen, are you okay?" Frankie cried as he crawled closer.

With Joel and Frankie's help, Paelen climbed unsteadily to his feet. "I am so fed up with being shot in the head!" He turned his fury on the tattooed man and kicked him viciously in the leg. "If one more person shoots me—just one—I swear I will turn the Solar Stream on Earth myself!"

Paelen swayed on his feet as his head pounded mercilessly. "I need to sit down."

Frankie pulled over a chair and helped him sit.

"Just relax," Joel said. "Let me take a look." He gently prodded Paelen's bleeding wound. "Yee-ish, that's gotta hurt!"

"Really, Joel, do you think so?" Paelen said sarcastically. "Of course it hurts! I have been shot in the head!"

Paelen saw the fear in Frankie's young eyes, and his voice softened. "I am all right, Frankie. You need not be frightened."

The boy's eyes were as wide as saucers and filling with tears. "You've got red blood just like humans. But you're not human. "Cause humans couldn't survive being shot."

"No, I am not human," Paelen admitted.

"What are you?" the tattooed man demanded. He was still on the floor in a heap, clutching his broken arm. His eyes lingered on Paelen. "You should be dead. I shot you point-blank in the head!"

"No kidding," Joel said angrily. He put his silver hand around the man's throat and hoisted him up in the air. As the tattooed man squirmed and tried to break free, Joel slammed him hard against the wall. "You're lucky I don't break your neck for what you've done to my friend. Now tell me, when did you last see Paelen's clone? Where was he?"

The man shook his head. "There's no such thing as clones."

"Of course there is!" Paelen cried as he stood up. But the pain and dizziness forced him down again.

"It's all right, Paelen," Frankie said softly. "Don't move or you'll start bleeding again."

Joel gave the man's throat a squeeze. "I think I should warn you. You see this silver arm? I haven't got any feeling in it. So I can't tell when I am squeezing too hard. So you'd better start talking, or I might accidentally squeeze the life right out of you. When did you see the clone?"

"Last month!" the man shot. "Working Fremont Street. Me and my boys tried to stop him. He didn't say a word, but beat the stuffing outta all of us."

"What do you mean, 'working Fremont Street'?" Paelen asked as he clutched his pounding head. "What was he doing?"

"Working," the man repeated. "You know, stealing and robbing without my permission and without giving me a share. I run this area; everyone works for me. But you've been running wild around here for months, giving me nothing but headaches." He focused fully on Paelen. "You're sloppy. You'll bring down the heat on all of us."

"I told you it was not me. It was the clone!" Paelen cried, then clasped his head and swayed.

"Paelen, calm down," Joel warned. He released the tattooed man. As he slipped to the floor, Joel pointed a threatening finger at him. "Don't move or I swear it will be the last thing you ever do!"

He approached Paelen and untied his sling and tore it into thin strips. Working with Frankie, he bandaged Paelen's bleeding head. "The bullet is still in there," Joel warned. "We really need Emily."

"What I need is to get off this world and never come back!" Paelen muttered.

The tattooed man clutched his broken arm, but leaned forward and studied Paelen closely. "You really ain't the Runt, are you?"

"Of course he's not!" Joel shot back.

The tattooed man leaned back. "How is that possible? The Runt looks just like you but he's wild and crazy. He don't talk and don't respect no one."

"That's because he's a clone!" Joel said. He concentrated on Paelen. "And by the sound of things, he's still here in Las Vegas."

21

PAELEN, JOEL, AND FRANKIE TIED UP THE unconscious men. They restrained the tattooed man and warned him what would happen if his men went after them again. It didn't take much to convince the criminal leader that they meant business.

When they made it back to the insanity of Fremont Street, Joel looked up and down the busy pedestrian mall. His silver arm was now fully exposed, as he'd used the sling to bandage Paelen's head. But with so many odd sights, no one gave him or Paelen, with his blood-covered clothing, a second glance.

"That was so awesome," Frankie was saying excitedly to Paelen. He was bouncing up and down and reenacting the fight. "The way you both bashed those guys, they didn't stand a chance against you."

"They did manage to shoot me," Paelen said. "So I hardly think we did that well."

"Yeah, but you won," Frankie cheered.

Joel stopped to look around. His concerned eyes landed on Paelen. "We need to get you some sugar. It's not ambrosia, but it will help you heal until Emily gets back."

"He is out here," Paelen mused distractedly. "My clone is somewhere very near. I can feel him. We must find him."

"Are you insane?" Joel said. "You heard that guy. He said the Runt is wild and crazy. He can't talk and is really strong. Paelen, you are hurt and weak from lack of ambrosia. It would be stupid for us to try to find him. Remember what happened between Pegasus and Tornado Warning."

"That was different," Paelen said.

"How? Pegasus is as intelligent as you. But the moment he saw Tornado, he snapped. They both tried to kill each other."

"I do not wish to kill my clone. Simply to see him."

Joel shook his head. "Right now, Paelen, what you

need is sugar. After that, we can argue about your clone."

It was late into the long night as the three sat down in one of Fremont Street's all-night diners. They settled in a booth beside the window and ordered pancakes and chocolate milkshakes. When their drinks arrived, Joel topped up one of the drinks with all the sugar on the table and half the bottle of pancake syrup.

"Gross," Frankie said as he watched Joel. "Are you really going to drink that?"

Joel shook his head. "Not me." He shoved the glass over to Paelen. "He is. Paelen, drink it all."

Paelen's head was pounding mercilessly, and he could hardly see straight. The last time he'd been shot, Agent O was standing several meters away, and the bullets hadn't done much damage. The tattooed man had been right beside him when he pulled the trigger.

"You okay?" Joel asked, peering closer. "You look really pale."

"I have felt better," Paelen admitted as he took a long drink of the sugar-charged milkshake.

"Well, just try to eat as much as you can. I'm sure it'll help. Emily should be back any minute now and will heal you right up."

When their food arrived, Paelen wasn't the least bit hungry. But Frankie tore into his like he hadn't eaten a decent meal in days. He grinned as he shoved a whole pancake into his mouth. He looked at Joel. "Do you have pancakes in your world?"

"This *is* my world!" Joel muttered angrily.

"If you say so," Frankie finished doubtfully, forcing a second pancake into his full mouth.

Watching Frankie devour his meal was making Paelen feel worse. He picked at his food, unable to eat.

But the look of concern on Joel's face forced him to take a small bite. He gazed out the window at the crowds along the street. It wasn't as interesting as it had been earlier.

The light show was starting on the overhead canopy again. The bright colors hurt Paelen's eyes and forced him to look away. "I wish we were back in Olympus."

"Me too," Joel said. "And I really wish Steve and

Diana had never brought those newspapers back with them. Then we'd never know about the clones."

Paelen nodded, but it caused his head to pound harder. "But then the CRU would have built an army of Nirads with no one to stop them."

"Paelen, in case you didn't notice, we haven't exactly done a lot to stop them so far," Joel said. "All we've managed to do is get ourselves into trouble and you shot in the head."

They sat in silence, eating their meal. Each swallow made Paelen feel worse. He pushed his plate away, unable to take another bite, and wondered how things could have gone so wrong. With so much at stake with the CRU, it was foolish to have gone out. They should have stayed at the black building to await Emily's return with the Nirads. Instead his desire to see Las Vegas had turned into a disaster.

As the minutes ticked by, a strange feeling came over Paelen. He knew something was seriously wrong. He was now certain he was in big trouble.

Suddenly there was a loud screech and pounding on the window beside them. Both Joel and Frankie turned and stared into the face of a wild teen. His eyes were wide and enraged. His hair was dirty and matted, and he was dressed in rags. His mouth was open and seemed to be snarling at Paelen.

"Hey, Paelen," Frankie observed, "he looks just like you—"

"It's the clone!" Joel cried. But as he turned to his friend, he saw the same expression on Paelen's face. His eyes matched the clone's in wildness, and his face contorted in fury as he moved to confront his clone.

"Paelen, no. Stop!"

Paelen had never reacted this way in his life. It was like an irresistible command. Every instinct in his body cried out in rage, demanding he destroy the unnatural "thing."

His confused thoughts came together with one solid realization. The sickening weakness he felt was not caused by the gunshot wound, but by the proximity of the clone. The closer his clone was to him, the worse Paelen felt and the stronger his desire was to kill the creature.

Paelen rose to his feet. He could barely hear Joel telling him to stop. He had to destroy the clone.

He smashed through the diner door and turned

on the clone. It screeched and roared and charged at him with murderous fury in its eyes.

The reaction of the Olympian meeting the clone was explosive. The clone lifted Paelen in the air and threw him through the plate-glass window of the diner, right where he'd just been sitting.

Paelen landed on the table but was back on his feet in an instant. He charged through the broken window and out onto the street. He lunged forward and attacked the clone with all his strength. He lifted him high in the air and threw him at the Ferrari up on the display platform opposite.

The side of the expensive car caved from the impact of the clone and was knocked off its platform. All around them, people panicked and ran to get out of the way of the two superstrong beings.

Paelen ran forward and caught hold of the clone. He wrapped his arms around the other boy, and they started to wrestle.

"Paelen, stop!" Joel cried as he tried to wrench the two apart.

"Joel, get back!" Paelen warned. But it was too late. The clone struck out at Joel with a brutal blow that threw him several meters in the air. Joel landed on the roof of a seller's pushcart and slipped down to the ground, badly winded.

"Joel!" Paelen cried as his fury revved up a notch. "You hurt Joel!"

The very last thing Paelen saw before losing all control was Frankie running over to Joel. But then he lost himself in uncontrolled rage. Nothing compared to the burning fire of fury he felt at the moment. He released every ounce of power he had at the clone. He tore up a streetlight from the pavement and used the pole like a bat, smashing the clone into a tall, brightly lit casino sign. Lightbulbs burst and sparked as debris poured down into the street.

But Paelen had met his match. The clone rose up and charged after him again.

It caught hold of his arm and started spinning him madly around, faster and faster, until it roared in rage and released him into the air. Paelen screamed and cartwheeled high above the crowd. He smashed into the lighted canopy almost thirty meters above the street. The lights exploded and the framework buckled as electrical sparks and fire filled the air.

Thousands of tiny glass shards and debris rained down on the panicking crowd below. On the ground, the computer console controlling the light show burst into flame from the overwhelming power surge. The electrical fire spread quickly as a sudden inferno engulfed part of Fremont Street. Within minutes, the front of a nearby casino had caught fire and burned brightly.

Heedless of the raging fire, Paelen untangled himself from the canopy and commanded his sandals to fly at the clone. He lunged down and picked it up in the air. Using all his remaining strength, Paelen hurled the clone at the biggest, heaviest thing he could find—the lighted front wall of a casino.

The casino's sign exploded with the impact, and the wall crumbled. As the clone fell to the ground, part of the lighted sign collapsed and fell on top of it.

Panting, hurt, and exhausted, Paelen could barely stand upright. But as he staggered over to Joel, he saw little red-haired Frankie trying to half drag and half carry the stunned Joel away from the spreading fire.

The sound of sirens filled the air and made Paelen's

head pound worse. Bright flashing lights blinded him as police cars screeched to a halt before him.

"Police! Stop where you are!" a loudspeaker announced.

Blood was seeping into Paelen's eyes from his wounds. He was dizzy and sick. After a few more staggered steps, he saw a police officer kneeling on the ground and raising a weapon. It didn't look like a normal gun. It was bright yellow.

"Stop!" the officer warned. "I have a Taser and will use it."

"Paelen, stop!" Joel called. "Please stop!"

There was no real sound as the weapon was fired. But Paelen felt it immediately. Electrical current tore through him. He lost control of his muscles and collapsed to the ground, convulsing. The pain was intense, and he couldn't move. Finally darkness descended, and he passed out.

22

EMILY WAS WORRIED ABOUT WHAT THEY would find on the other end of the Solar Stream. Had Joel, Paelen, and Chrysaor made it to the black building?

As they emerged from the Stream into the sky above the desert, Emily was disappointed to see they had arrived in daylight. There was no way they could fly into Las Vegas without being seen.

She was seated on Alexis, with Prince Toban behind her. Ahead of them, Pegasus was straining to fly with the heavy Nirad Tirk on his back. Despite his best efforts, Pegasus was losing height in the sky.

Emily leaned forward on Alexis. "Can you fly us closer to Pegasus? I have an idea. I think we should land."

Alexis looked back at her. "If we land now, it is doubtful Pegasus will be able to lift Tirk again. You can see he is struggling."

"I know," Emily said. "Look down. We aren't that far from Area 51. We don't want to be seen by them in daylight."

"Agreed," Alexis said. She flapped her wings harder and soon gained on Pegasus and Tirk. She called to the stallion and told him to find a place to land. Soon they were gliding lower to the ground until Pegasus found a spot in a small canyon. It wasn't far from a strange and beautiful lake in the middle of the desert. They touched down on lush green grass instead of the hard desert floor.

Emily and Toban helped Tirk get down from Pegasus. When the huge orange Nirad stepped away from the stallion, Emily saw the foaming sweat on Pegasus's back and neck. She had never seen him like that before.

"Are you okay, Pegs?" she asked worriedly, stroking his quivering neck. Pegasus's head was down and his wings were drooping.

"He is exhausted," Alexis said. "Tirk is a particularly large and heavy Nirad. Emily, get Pegasus some ambrosia. He needs to eat and rest."

They found shelter in a small cluster of trees. Tirk didn't look much better than Pegasus. He sat down heavily and leaned against a tree. If Emily didn't know better, she could have sworn the Nirad was about to be sick.

Using the sack they carried their food in, Emily started to brush Pegasus down. "Just relax, Pegs. We can't leave here till dark." Finally the stallion settled under the shade of a tree. He soon dozed off.

The group lounged under the trees as the sun blazed high above their heads. Despite the shade, the temperature continued to climb. Emily had never felt it so blisteringly hot in her life. New York City could get warm in the summer, but it was nothing like the Nevada desert.

Even Alexis, who never showed any kind of discomfort, appeared to be feeling the heat. She couldn't settle and was constantly flapping her wings to create a breeze. Prince Toban and Tirk were not much better as they tried to get comfortable while the temperature soared.

With nothing more to do but wait for darkness, Emily settled down beside Pegasus. She was too hot and worried to sleep. They were facing the fight of their lives at Area 51. As the heat rose, she wondered what Joel, Paelen, and Chrysaor were up to in Las Vegas. Whatever they were doing at the moment, it had to be better than this.

23

PAELEN MOANED. HIS HEAD THROBBED, AND
he ached all over. He was lying on a hard surface and,
when he tried to move, discovered that his hands
were chained to his sides.

"Paelen," a voice softly called. "Wake up."

He opened his eyes and looked up into the concerned face of Joel. They were in a small, brightly lit
room. Like him, Joel had his hands chained to his
waist. There was one door to the room with a thick
glass window. The walls on either side of the door
were also made of thick, hardened glass. Across the
room he saw an empty bench. There was a short wall
beside it, and behind that was a toilet.

Paelen struggled to sit up. He still felt like he was about to be sick. "Where are we?"

Shouts came from the hall outside, and they watched several large policemen struggling to contain a chained prisoner. One police officer looked in at them as they led their prisoner down the hall to another holding cell.

"We've been arrested," Joel quickly explained. "We're in jail. When I wouldn't tell them our names or cooperate, they put us in here. They've had someone look at your head and put fresh bandages on it, but I don't think they realize you've been shot. I couldn't stop them from taking our fingerprints, though. Since I've got a police record, it won't be long before they know who I am."

Most of what Joel said made no sense to Paelen. But the fear in his friend's face was clear enough. They were in trouble. "Where is Frankie?"

Joel sighed. "Safe, I hope. I told him to run back to the black building to tell Emily what happened. When the police used the Taser on you, I kind of lost it and attacked them. Hopefully he got away."

"You attacked the police?"

Joel nodded. "You were hurt, but they used the Taser anyway. I tried to stop them."

"You could have been wounded!" Paelen said.

Joel shrugged. "No one shoots my friends and gets away with it. Not that I helped. We still got arrested."

They sat together and looked around the tiny cell. Paelen looked down at his bare feet. "Where are my sandals?"

"They took them. They took my shoes too." Joel showed his own bare feet. He leaned closer. "How are you feeling?"

"Dreadful." Paelen staggered over to the glass window in the door and peered down the hall. "The Runt is here too. He is close. When he is near, I feel ill." He looked back at Joel. "Right now, I feel very ill."

Joel shook his head, "You can't start fighting again, Paelen. Not here. We're in enough trouble already."

Paelen crossed back to Joel and sat down tiredly on the hard wooden bench. "Do not worry. I have neither the strength nor the energy to fight again. I also cannot remember much. What happened?"

"What happened?" Joel repeated. "Are you serious? Your clone found us at the diner and you went ballistic! The two of you pretty much destroyed Fremont Street."

It all came rushing back to him in strange flashing images. "Now I understand how Pegasus felt when he saw Tornado. Joel, I could not control myself. It was like I had no will of my own. When I saw the clone, I had to destroy it."

"That *is* just like Pegasus," Joel agreed. "I wonder if the same applies to all Olympians when they meet their clones. Would Diana want to kill her clones?"

Paelen nodded. "You know me. I do not like to fight if it can be avoided. But I could not contain myself. Diana loves a good fight. She would be unstoppable if she came here and encountered her clones."

"We can't let that happen," Joel said.

A key was inserted in the lock, and their cell door opened.

"Sleeping Beauty wakes! Just stay seated where you are," a large, burly officer said, entering the cell. He concentrated on Joel. "You may not have wanted to talk, but your fingerprints said plenty, Joel DeSilva. You're a long way from home, aren't you, boy?"

Joel said nothing.

"We know you're a runaway from foster care in New York City. Normally we'd be sending you to the Juvenile Center, but after you assaulted a police officer, you're staying right here with us."

A second officer drew near and studied Joel's exposed silver arm with great curiosity. "What is that? I've seen artificial limbs before—heck, my brother came back from Iraq with one. But I've never seen anything like that. Where'd you get it?"

Joel remained silent as the police officer stepped even closer. "I can't see any joints at the wrist or fingers, but you can move it. How does it work?" He reached out to touch the silver arm.

"Don't!" Joel warned as he slid down the bench away from the officer.

"So he does speak," the first officer said. "What happened at Fremont?"

Joel glared at the officer but said nothing further.

"Fine," he said. The officer concentrated on Paelen. "Just what kind of drugs are you on, kid? From what I've heard, you and your twin brother all but destroyed Fremont Street. There are crazy stories going on about how you tossed each other around like rag dolls and destroyed a hundred-thousand-dollar sports car."

"That Runt is not my brother," Paelen said indignantly. "And I will thank you to return my sandals."

The police officer raised his eyebrows. "You will thank me, eh? How about I thank you to answer our questions? What happened at Fremont Street? How did you do all that damage?"

This was too familiar to Paelen. Back on Governors Island, Agents J and O had asked a lot of questions that he did not want to answer. Paelen avoided the question. "Why do you not ask the Runt?"

The police officer laughed, but there was no humor in it. "I've had more than my share of dealings with that freaky little punk. We'll keep him chained up and leave him alone till the folks from the psych ward at the hospital come to collect him. But you, I am interested in. Who are you?"

Paelen straightened up the best his injured body would allow. "I am Paelen the Magnificent," he said proudly. "You would do well to release Joel and me before I lose my temper."

"Oh really," the officer said, smiling. "Well, how

about we give you more time to cool off and coop-erate."

A serious-looking police officer arrived and called the others outside. They closed and locked the door behind them.

Paelen strained to listen. "We are in deep trouble. I heard that man say there is a special warrant out for us. We are considered dangerous and they should not approach us."

Out in the hall, the officers looked back at them, but moved quickly away from the cell.

Joel's eyes grew large. "It's the CRU. They could come for us any minute. Paelen, you've got to get out of here." Joel rose and crossed to the door and checked to see if the hall was clear. He looked down at his silver hand. Curling it in, he used its strength to break the handcuff binding it to his waist chain. Then he reached over to his left hand and freed that as well. With his hands free, he pushed the food flap in the door—but it was locked.

"I will not leave you," Paelen said flatly. He crossed to the door. "With my strength and your arm, we can force open this door. We will both go."

Joel shook his head. "No, we can't. This is a jail. We'd never make it to the end of the hall, let alone out of the building. But you can."

"I told you, I will not leave you."

"You've got to," Joel insisted. "You must get back to Emily. Tell her what's happening."

"But—"

"You can't stay. Not if the CRU have been alerted."

Paelen and Joel looked around the tiny cell. There was only the one door and no windows. There were two air vents in the white ceiling high above their heads.

"You can fit through there," Joel offered. "Just stretch out of your chains and I'll boost you up."

Paelen saw the grim determination on Joel's face. But how could he leave his best friend to face the CRU alone? He remembered what had happened to Joel at Governors Island and how he had been drugged and tortured.

"It's the only way," Joel insisted. "Get help. If the CRU do come for us, we'll disappear and no one will ever know what happened. You are Olympian. We can't let them get hold of you again."

Paelen shook his head. "I cannot leave you. If they take you to Area 51, they will cut off your arm to see how it works. Remember how Agent T was interested in it. He told you what would happen if they caught you."

Fear rose in Joel's face as he looked at his mechanical arm. It had been a part of him for so long that it was as if he'd been born with it. "If they cut it off me, you'll just have to come and get me so Vulcan can put it back on. Now go!"

Joel was right, but it didn't make it any easier for Paelen to abandon him. "Listen at the door. Let me know if anyone is coming."

Joel stood by the door as Paelen concentrated. He was still aching badly from his fight with the clone, and his head continued to pound from the bullet.

First, Paelen extended his hands until they pulled free of the cuffs chaining him to his waist. Then his whole body started to pop, snap, and stretch until he slipped out of his clothes and he was free of the chain around his waist.

"I am ready," he said in a high, reedy voice. "Help me climb up."

Joel laced his fingers together to make a stirrup and gave the snakelike Paelen a leg up.

Clutching his clothing in one hand, Paelen reached up with his free hand and pulled the vent cover away from the opening. He shoved his clothes through the hole and stretched out his body until he was thin enough to slip up into the narrow vent.

Paelen winced in pain as he felt the bullet shift in his elongated head.

He was grateful to find the ventilation shaft was wider than he'd expected. His mind kept replaying the first time he had traveled through the vent at Governors. But then he had had the sandals to help. This time he was alone.

Paelen turned and looked back down into the small cell. He saw Joel looking hopefully up at him. His large friend suddenly looked very small and vulnerable.

"I'll be fine," Joel said. "Just go and find Emily and Pegasus. Tell her what's happened."

"I will," Paelen promised as he pulled the vent cover back into position. His last sight of his best friend was Joel sitting down on the bench, all alone.

...

Paelen wasn't sure how long he'd spent in the ventilation system of the Las Vegas jail. But as he crawled along a course that took him away from the holding cells, he felt the passage of time as acutely as he felt the bullet lodged in his head.

Looking through the vents along the shaft system, he soon found he was over an empty office. A desk was directly below him. Peering sideways, Paelen could see the frame of a window. If it wasn't too high off the ground, he could jump out of it.

Paelen pushed down on the vent and peeked through. He used his thief senses to listen and feel for danger. There was no one in the hall outside the closed office door. For the moment, he was safe.

He winced as he extended his body to slip through the narrow opening. Pushing his clothes ahead of him, he poured himself into the room and landed with a heavy and painful thump on the top of the desk.

Grateful to return to his normal shape, Paelen dressed quickly and crossed to the window. It was daytime, and he realized they'd been in jail longer than he'd expected. He hoped that Emily and Pegasus would be back at the black building, waiting for them.

Looking down, he saw he was at least four, perhaps five stories off the ground. Normally that wouldn't bother him. But he was weak from lack of food, and wounded. Sighing heavily, Paelen knew he had no choice. He forced open the sealed window. Checking to see that no one was below, he climbed out on the ledge and jumped.

Paelen had leaped from greater heights many times before. But that was when he was healthy. When he hit the pavement, his right ankle gave way and twisted with a loud snap. It took all his will not to cry out.

As pain pulsed and shot all the way up his leg, Paelen looked back at the tall, brown building that was the jail.

He couldn't see anyone at the windows and hoped he'd gotten away without being noticed. Paelen limped away from the jail and Joel.

24

WHILE PEGASUS, ALEXIS, AND THE NIRADS rested under the trees waiting for the safe cover of darkness, Emily could not relax. She stood and started to pace. Looking back, she saw Prince Toban seated beside Tirk. Their arms were crossed over their chests, and their eyes were closed as they wilted in the oppressive desert heat. Tirk's orange, marblelike skin glistened with sweat, and he was panting softly in blistering temperatures he had never known before.

Emily worried that it had been a bad idea to bring them here. They belonged on the Nirad world, where they were safe. Not out in the middle of the open desert where dangers surrounded them. As it was, she was reconsidering her plan to take them to the black building. Two Nirads in Las Vegas? Now, that would be really stupid.

But leaving them behind would be equally dangerous and stupid. Emily cursed herself for not thinking ahead. Her thoughts spun wildly out of control as anxieties pressed down on her. She still had no idea how to get into Area 51, let alone get back out again. How would the Nirad clones react to the prince? Could he reach them telepathically? Or was she leading Toban and Tirk into disaster?

The more she thought about it, the more muddled she became. There seemed no solution to the problem. No clear plan of action. Emily ached to speak with Joel and Paelen. Maybe once everyone was together again, they could come up with a decent strategy that would solve the clone problem before Jupiter found out.

Emily returned to Pegasus and sat beside the stallion, resigned to the fact that they couldn't do anything for the moment. Until everyone was reunited, all she could do was wait and worry.

25

PAELEN WAS AN OLYMPIAN LOST AND ALONE in Las Vegas. There was a large white bandage wrapped around his head, and his clothes were tattered and covered with blood. He knew he would not receive any help from the strangers he passed, looking as he did.

"Sandals, where are you when I need you?" he muttered softly as he made his way along a quiet street.

The full heat of the day pressed down on him. The sun was high and unforgiving in the blue, cloudless sky. Paelen felt weak from his wounds and lack of food. If he didn't eat some ambrosia soon, he feared he might collapse.

Over to his left he recognized the remains of Fremont

Street. The area still smoldered and was blocked off by police tape. Fire trucks remained in the area, and men wearing white protective gear sifted through the rubble.

There was no way the damage could not attract the attention of the CRU. Fighting the clone had been a terrible mistake and had put his best friend in danger.

Paelen kept to the quieter streets as he tried to find his way back to the tall black building. But Las Vegas in daylight looked nothing like it did at night. Not to mention they had traveled to Fremont Street by taxi. There was no telling how long it would take him to walk back, especially with a broken ankle.

Paelen needed help. He approached a homeless man lying in a doorway.

"And I thought I had it bad." The homeless man smiled a toothless grin.

"Please, I need your help. I am badly lost. Do you know where Circus Circus is?"

Paelen's instincts wouldn't allow him to mention the black building. Instead he remembered the name Joel had used the previous night.

The homeless man shook his head. "Boy, you sure are lost. You're walking in the wrong direction. You want the strip." The man sat up and pointed down the street and gave Paelen a series of directions. "But on that foot, it'll take you all day."

"I have no choice," Paelen said grimly. Thanking the man, he slowly limped away.

As the homeless man had warned, it took Paelen the better part of the day, but he finally made it back to the tall black building, sunburned and with heat exhaustion. Half limping and half staggering to the elevator, he took it up to the top floor. Chrysaor was waiting for him when the doors opened.

"Emily . . . ," Paelen called out, and then crumpled to the ground.

26

PEGASUS PROTESTED LOUDLY AS EMILY PRO-
posed her latest idea. The sun was setting and the heat
of the day finally fading—but not by much. Within
the small cluster of trees, everyone was on their feet.

"Pegs, I've thought about it all day. This is the only
way," Emily insisted.

The stallion snorted and pawed the grass beneath
his golden hoof.

"I don't want to leave them either, but Tirk is way too
heavy for you to carry. After we get the others, we'll come
right back. Toban and Tirk won't be alone for long."

Prince Toban was standing beside Emily and nodding his pink head. He let out a long series of growls
and strange sounds.

Emily looked to Alexis to translate. "The prince agrees with you," she said. The Sphinx approached Pegasus. "Emily is correct. Tirk is too heavy for you to carry for a long distance. We are closer to Area 51 than we are Las Vegas. It would be wise to leave them here for a short time, collect the others, and then gather our forces before we make our move on the CRU."

Pegasus was still arguing when the prince started to stroke the stallion. He growled a few soft words. Pegasus bowed. Again Emily looked to Alexis to translate, but the Sphinx shook her head. "That is between the two of them," she whispered.

Finally Pegasus snorted and raised his head, but his ears were twitching. Emily knew him well enough to know he was going to go along with the plan, but wasn't happy about it.

"It is agreed," Alexis said. She turned to the prince. "Your Highness, we shall only be a short while. Please remain here and wait for us. Should any human come along, please try to keep hidden."

Toban nodded. He and Tirk returned to the trees to sit down and wait.

27

PAELEN AWOKE TO THE SOUNDS OF CHRYSAOR squealing and a man's loud, terrified screams. When he opened his eyes, he discovered he was lying on a smelly pile of rags. His head was screaming, the skin on his face and arms was on fire, and his ankle pounded like his foot was about to fall off.

Chrysaor had cornered a man against a wall.

Paelen's thoughts were sluggish as he finally recalled what had happened to get him to this place. He lifted his head, his eyes seeking Emily and Pegasus. When he didn't see them, he called weakly, "Has Emily returned?"

Before Chrysaor could answer, the frightened man called, "Help me! Call the police, call the FBI! Call the zoo! This freaky pig won't let me move."

Chrysaor squealed with anger and trod on the man's foot, causing him to yelp in pain.

Paelen's eyes drifted over to the piles of rags where Frankie's friend John had been sleeping. The lump was gone.

"Are you John?" he asked as he tried to climb to his feet.

"Who are you?" the filthy man demanded. "How do you know my name? And why have you brought this pig to my home? What have you done with Frankie?"

"Frankie is not here?"

"No, he's not here!" John shouted angrily. "I woke up and found this creature here instead. What the hell are you?"

Chrysaor jumped on the man's foot again.

The pounding pain in Paelen's head was unbearable as he made it to his feet. But when he tried to put weight on his broken ankle, he cried in pain and fell down. Lying in the stack of smelly rags, all he wanted to do now was sleep. It was calling to him, beckoning him and promising to take him away from the pain.

Chrysaor left the man and trotted over to Paelen.

He squealed softly, then sniffed the wound on Paelen's head.

"It has all gone wrong," Paelen muttered. "Joel is in jail and the CRU are coming for him."

Chrysaor continued to sniff along Paelen's wounded body. He snorted and squealed in deep concern.

"We cannot go back to Olympus," Paelen panted. "I know I am hurt badly. But we must wait for Emily and Pegasus. The police have Joel. He is counting on me to get him out. I must not let him down."

But Chrysaor squealed again. The high pitch of his voice bored into Paelen's head like a drill. Paelen tried to beg him to stop, but his voice was gone. Soon the world around him started to spin, and darkness approached.

Paelen welcomed the coming darkness, the end of pain. But as he started to surrender himself to it, he felt overcome with a familiar nauseous feeling. The same sickness he felt in the presence of his clone. The clone was nearby, Paelen was sure of it. The clone must have escaped the police and followed him back here.

Fighting back to consciousness, Paelen heard screaming from the stairwell and then something charged toward him. Chrysaor was the first to react. The winged boar squealed and ran toward the clone. He opened his wings and tried to knock him away. But the clone was fast and agile. He leaped high into the air and soared over Chrysaor's head. He landed a short distance from Paelen.

With the drive to fight rising in the pit of his stomach, Paelen climbed up to stand on one foot. But he was too weak to fend off the clone. It caught hold of him and, screaming in rage, lifted him high above its head.

Snarling with uncontrolled hatred, it hurled Paelen at the painted window. The hardened glass shattered with the impact and sent Paelen out into the open air, sixty-nine stories above the ground. Without his winged sandals to save him, Paelen started to fall.

28

PEGASUS, EMILY, AND ALEXIS FLEW HIGH above Las Vegas. As they started to descend, they saw bright flashing lights from fire trucks lining a street well away from the strip. The acrid smell of freshly extinguished fire rose up to meet them.

"I wonder what's going on down there," Emily called.

Pegasus nickered and whinnied, and Emily wished she could understand the stallion's language. What Pegasus said sounded important. In the distance, she saw the black building rising dark and silent.

When they landed on the roof, Emily's heart sank to discover that Joel, Paelen, and Chrysaor were not there. She climbed down from Pegasus.

"Wait!" Alexis warned. "Something is very wrong. I can feel it."

Emily stopped and watched the Sphinx lifting her head and sniffing the air. The hair on the hackles along her back was high and her wings were fluttering. Her tail whipped the air.

"Get back on Pegasus," she ordered. "Now!"

Just as Emily settled on the stallion's back, the Sphinx hissed and drew her claws.

The door to the roof was flung open. A little boy of nine or ten came running forward. His clothing was in tatters, and his eyes were filled with terror. He ran at Pegasus and waved his hands in the air. "Emily, it's a trap! Fly away before they get you!"

Alexis rose on her hind legs and roared, "Men are here. Pegasus, get the Flame away!"

The Sphinx's eyes went black, her jaw unhinged, and teeth came out. As she charged the stairwell door, she looked back at Pegasus and screamed, "Go now!"

Pegasus reacted immediately. The stallion lunged forward and caught the little boy's shirt in his sharp teeth. Lifting him off the ground, without a second's pause, he galloped to the edge of the roof and leaped off. Flapping his powerful wings, he carried them high in the air.

On the roof Alexis roared as armed men poured through the door. Their screams filled the air as they were greeted by the enraged Olympian Sphinx.

"Alexis!" Emily screamed. "Leave them, come on!"

Pegasus was flying too high and too fast for Emily to see what was happening on the roof. The sound of gunfire filled the air. But were the men shooting at them or Alexis?

The little boy was screaming in terror as he hung only by his shirt from Pegasus's mouth, suspended high over Las Vegas.

A few minutes later, Pegasus landed on the roof of a casino farther down the strip. Emily slid off his back and ran to the roof edge, searching the skies for Alexis. "Come on," she cried. "Alexis, where are you?"

"Emily?" the little boy said as he carefully approached her.

His eyes were huge as he looked at her and Pegasus. "They got the lion-lady."

"Who?" Emily demanded, turning on him. "Who was it?"

"The soldiers." He started to sob. "They shot my friend John."

There was so much pain in the little boy's face. Emily put her arm around him. "Please tell us, what soldiers?" she asked softly. "Who are you and how do you know my name?"

"I'm Frankie." The little boy sniffed. He wiped his running nose on his dirty sleeve. "Joel and Paelen are my friends. So is Chrysler the pig."

Emily's heart was pounding in her chest, and it was hard to take everything in. She knelt before the boy and took both his hands. "Where are Joel and Paelen? Can you tell me?"

Tears rushed to Frankie's eyes and trailed through the grime on his face. "Paelen is dead," he wept. "He got shot in the head, and then the wild Paelen threw him out the window and he fell. Joel is in jail. Chrysler flew away and I don't know where he is."

"What?" Emily cried. "Paelen is dead?"

Frankie sniffed and nodded.

"My Paelen?" Emily cried in panic. "No, it's not possible. He had his winged sandals. They would have stopped him. He could have flown away."

"He didn't have his sandals. John says Paelen was half-dead when the wild Paelen beat him up really bad, and then threw him out the window."

Emily sat back in shock. It wasn't possible. Paelen couldn't be dead. Not after all they'd been through, all they had suffered together. She pulled out her green handkerchief to catch her uncontrollable tears.

Emily was hardly aware of Alexis's arrival. It was only when Frankie screeched in terror and begged the Sphinx not to eat him that she realized Alexis had returned.

"Emily, what is wrong?" Alexis demanded, coming closer. "Are you hurt?"

Pegasus neighed softly to explain. "The boy is mistaken." Alexis put her paw on Emily's back. "Paelen is far too resourceful to allow this to happen."

But Emily could not speak and could hardly breathe as sobs tore through her.

"You, boy," Alexis demanded. "Tell me what happened to Paelen and Joel."

Frankie filled them in on everything that happened over the last two days.

"Wait." Emily sniffed. "You didn't see Paelen die?"

Frankie shook his head. "My friend John told me what happened. He swore he would never drink again because he was seeing too many crazy things. When I asked him what, he told me what happened. John still thinks it was the drink. But I saw the broken window. When I told him that Paelen could fly with his shoes, John said he was barefoot with a broken ankle. Chrysler followed him out the window, but John didn't see Chrysler catch him."

"Then it is likely that Chrysaor reached Paelen in time," Alexis said calmly. She concentrated on Emily. "There is no evidence that Paelen is dead—just the word of this boy's friend. You must keep your hope alive."

Emily clung to Alexis's words. Chrysaor would not let Paelen fall. He just wouldn't. "You said a wild Paelen attacked our Paelen?"

The boy nodded. "At the diner. Joel said it was the clone. But when the real Paelen met the wild one, they both went crazy and wanted to kill each other."

Alexis looked up to Pegasus. "Just like you with Tornado Warning."

Pegasus snorted at the name and pawed the roof.

Alexis concentrated on Frankie again. "Who were those men on the roof?"

"Soldiers," Frankie said. "People must have seen Paelen go out the window and called the police. John tried to protect me, but they shot him." Frankie started to cry again. He lifted tearful eyes to Emily. "I've been hiding and waiting for you."

Alexis narrowed her green eyes and concentrated on the boy. "You waited for us? Knowing you were in danger by doing so? Why would you do that?"

Frankie looked at Alexis fearfully and stepped closer to Emily. "Because Joel and Paelen and Chrysler are my friends. They told me they were waiting for you to come back. I couldn't let the soldiers get you."

Alexis tilted her head approvingly. "That was very brave of you."

"I don't think so," Frankie said. "I cried when they chased me."

"I would have done the same," Alexis said gently. She winked knowingly at Pegasus.

Frankie lifted his hopeful eyes to Emily. "Do you really think Chrysler saved Paelen?"

Emily nodded. "I'm sure he would have. They are very good friends."

She could see the relief washing over the young boy as he wiped his filthy cheeks. She just prayed it was true.

"Good. I really like him," Frankie said.

"Me too," Emily agreed, drying her own eyes.

Behind her, Pegasus nickered.

"We must get moving," Alexis said. "We must not leave Prince Toban and Tirk alone for long."

Emily shook her head. "First we've got to get Joel." She concentrated on Frankie. "You said he was in jail?"

The little boy nodded. "Near Fremont Street. That's where the two Paelens fought. They caused a really big fire."

Emily recalled all the fire trucks and the smell when they'd first arrived. "Can you show me where it is?"

Pegasus stepped forward and nickered again.

"This will be the hardest thing Pegasus has ever asked you to do," Alexis translated, "but he said we must leave Joel where he is. Prince Toban and Tirk are our first priority."

309

Emily looked at the stallion in shock. "No way! We've got to rescue Joel before they find out who he is and call the CRU."

Alexis sighed heavily. "It is highly likely the CRU already know, which is why Paelen would have left him. He was sent to warn us, but was wounded instead."

Emily was shaking her head. She couldn't believe they were suggesting leaving Joel to the mercy of the CRU.

"Think about it," Alexis pressed. "The chances of Joel still being in their jail are remote. We must not waste precious time on an uncertainty. Prince Toban and Tirk do not belong in this world. We must return to them and get the others away from Area 51 as quickly as possible."

"But if Joel is still in their jail, I have to get him out." Emily panicked. "You don't understand. I—"

"You love him," Alexis finished gently. "Yes, I know. We all do. But we must not let our emotions rule us."

"But—"

Alexis shook her head. "I am sorry, Emily. But we

have no choice. If you really want to help him, you will leave him where he is. If he is still in their jail, he is much safer there than at Area 51. But if the CRU have been alerted, they will no doubt deliver him to Area 51 anyway."

Emily looked at Pegasus and then gazed out over Las Vegas. Was Joel out there, just a short reach from where she was? Or had he been taken to Area 51? Every instinct in her body screamed to go to the jail to see for herself. It tore at her heart to know that there was a greater need. Prince Toban and Tirk were alone and in more danger.

She stepped up to Pegasus and pressed her forehead to him. "I know we've got to go, Pegs. But what if Joel is still in jail? How can I abandon him?"

Pegasus neighed softly. There was little he could say or do to ease Emily's pain. Finally she pulled away. She climbed onto his back without a word.

"What about me?" Frankie said. "I'm coming too. I want to help with the nerds."

Alexis padded closer to him. "I am sorry, child, but you are safer here."

Frankie shook his head. "Nah-uh, I'm not. Those

men are looking for me. What if they find me? They'll take me to Area 51 with all the other aliens. They shot John and wrecked my home. I have nowhere to go."

Alexis stole a look at Emily before turning to Frankie. "All right, child. I will ask you a riddle. If you answer correctly, you may come with us and I will carry you myself. But if you get the answer wrong, you must remain here."

Frankie's eyes trailed from Emily, to Pegasus, and finally to Alexis. "Okay."

Alexis sat down before the little boy. "Riddle me this . . .

At night I come without being fetched
And by day I am lost without being stolen.
I am like a diamond,
But I am no jewel.
What am I?"

Emily watched little Frankie chew on his lower lip as he struggled with the riddle. She realized that the ferocious and deadly Sphinx of Olympus had given the boy a very easy one. Even she knew the answer.

Finally Frankie looked up to the night sky and pointed. "I know!" he cried. "It's the stars."

Alexis smiled and stroked his head with her large paw. "There is only one other person in history who has ever answered one of my riddles. You are in very good company. Your answer is correct. You may join us."

Alexis stood and offered her back to the boy.

"I hope I'm not too heavy," Frankie said earnestly as he climbed on.

The Sphinx looked up at him. "I have carried heavier." Her eyes trailed over to Emily. "Are you ready?"

Emily inhaled deeply. She gazed out over Las Vegas in the direction of Fremont Street. "Forgive me, Joel," she said softly as she looked back at Alexis. "Let's go."

29

EMILY'S HEART WAS SITTING HEAVY IN HER chest as Pegasus carried her away from Las Vegas and deeper into the dark desert. Joel would never have abandoned her. Would he ever forgive her?

As they approached the area where they had left the Nirads, Emily saw a glow rising from the ground. Fear knotted her stomach. Nirads didn't use fire. The closer they got to the glow, the bigger and brighter it became. Pegasus tilted his wings and glided lower in the sky.

On the ground beneath them they saw the burning debris of two destroyed military helicopters scattered around the cluster of trees where they had left the two Nirads. One of the trees was ablaze while the grass smoldered and burned. Pegasus circled the area a few times searching for activity from below. They saw nothing. He landed a few meters from the trees.

"Toban!" Emily cried as she slid off the stallion's back and started to search the area. "Tirk! Are you here?"

Alexis joined in, but after a few minutes of calling and searching, they received no answer. Emily approached the tree where she had last seen the Nirads and found a dark stain on the ground. Her heart dropped.

Emily bent down and summoned the Flame to her hand. Lowering it down to the ground, she discovered that the liquid was bright red. It was blood. Human blood. Not far from the stain, she saw a large piece of desert camouflage fabric.

"Pegasus, Alexis, over here!" Emily pointed at the ground and held up the fabric. "That's human blood, and this is part of a uniform. Those are military helicopters."

Alexis surveyed the area. "There must have been a ferocious battle here if the Nirads could bring down two of those machines. I pray neither of them was wounded."

Emily straightened and looked at the burning helicopters. "The soldiers must have attacked them right after we left. But how did they find them?"

Frankie was still seated on Alexis's back. "They have radar," he answered softly. "I've read about it on my computer. This whole area has big radars. This is all part of the Nellis Air Force Base. They track anyone who comes here—on the ground or in the air. I bet they're tracking us, too."

As Frankie's words sank in, Emily realized the truth. "We led them into a trap!" She looked at Pegasus. "We've just handed Prince Toban and Tirk over to the CRU."

Pegasus reared up in rage and screamed into the night, while Alexis cursed and started pacing. As the full ramifications hit Emily, she felt the power of the Flame rising uncontrolled within her. Turning away from the others, she held up her hands and released the pent-up power.

Wild flames shot from both her hands and rose for hundreds of meters into the air. Emily threw back her head and howled in fury, "I have had it with the CRU!"

Emily charged over to Pegasus. "That's it! This is

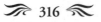

war! Pegasus, ever since you first came to my world, the CRU have been hounding us and doing all they can to destroy us. They've captured us, tortured us, and taken my father away. They've created clones that just may get this world destroyed, and they killed Agent T when he was trying to warn them. No more. If they want a fight, they've got it!"

"Calm down," Alexis ordered. "You must think before you act."

"No," Emily cried, turning back to the Sphinx. "We have been thinking all along, and look where it's gotten us! They've just captured the Nirad prince. I promised Queen Segan that I would keep him safe. But I didn't! Why have I got all these powers if not to protect us from the evil that is the CRU?"

"Emily, stop!" Alexis shouted. "Remember your other powers. You have no control when you are angry."

Emily stomped up to Pegasus. "This time they've pushed me too far. You can stay here if you like, but I'm going in and demanding they release Toban and all the other Nirads. And if they don't, they are going to see just what the Flame of Olympus can do!"

∙ ∙ ∙

The journey to the secret CRU facility at Area 51 was short. But even before they made it to the mountain range that surrounded the large base, military helicopters were rising in the air and coming to meet them.

"Emily, you must wait!" Alexis cried. "This is a dangerous approach."

But Emily clung to Pegasus's mane and told the stallion to put on more speed.

"Take Frankie away from here," she called to Alexis. "This fight is between the CRU and me!"

"No, foolish child, it is not," Alexis called. "It is between Olympians and the CRU. I was wrong not going back to Jupiter. We must return to Olympus. The others must be told what has happened here. Jupiter would be furious if he knew I allowed you to do this alone."

Emily called an answer back, but the sound of her voice was drowned out by the heavy rotors of the approaching military helicopters. As they neared, Emily felt the power of the Flame anxious to be freed.

"Be careful, Pegasus!" she called.

Emily tucked in her knees to hold on and raised her hands. The Flame was ready, but she held back on releasing it until she knew what the military intended. Within seconds, she had her answer. Without giving a warning, or the opportunity to surrender, the nearest helicopter fired at them.

There was no time to think, only to react. Emily released the Flame. Against the dark sky it shot white-hot from her hands toward the approaching helicopters. The bullets they fired melted into liquid burning metal and glowed like fireflies as they fell, harmless, to the ground.

Emily never wanted to hurt anyone. But when the helicopters continued firing, she had no choice but to turn her full powers on them. One by one, the helicopters exploded in the air and rained fire down on the dark desert floor.

Soon they were alone in the sky. Within moments, Pegasus was cresting the mountains surrounding Area 51. Up ahead, Emily saw the lights of the two superlong runways burst to life as jet fighters taxied out of their hangars and down the runways.

"Too late!" Emily shouted in a fury. She raised her

hands again and let the Flame go. Instead of hitting the jets, her target was the two long tarmac runways. When the heat of the Flame struck them, the tarmac melted instantly and burst into flames. The jets on the ground scattered and were forced onto the desert floor.

"Emily, be careful!" Alexis warned.

Emily looked over and saw Frankie clinging to the back of the Sphinx. Both his hands were gripped around Alexis's wings where they emerged from her back. His head was tucked down, and he wasn't watching the fight.

Down on the ground, all the lights of Area 51 burst to life. The place was massive! Agent T had said only part of it was the CRU facility. But what was the rest of it? There were multiple large, squat buildings with flat, corrugated-steel roofs. She could see a parking area filled with cars. There were the two large hangars the jets had emerged from and three full-size airliners parked at the side. Farther along she spied several other military helicopters still on the ground. She hoped they stayed there.

As Pegasus flew closer, she saw the white chalk bed

of the dry Groom Lake. Agent T wasn't kidding. It had once been a huge lake. Suddenly her eyes caught movement. Soldiers were emerging from the squat buildings. As she approached lower, Emily got a closer look at them and sucked in her breath. Nirads! They were wearing the desert camouflage uniforms of the military and carrying rifles. It was true. The CRU had created a Nirad army

"Pegasus, look," she cried. "Nirad soldiers!"

Alexis swooped closer. "Why are you not firing? Look, they all have weapons!"

The easy solution would have been to burn Area 51 off the face of the Earth. But despite her fury, Emily couldn't do that. Prince Toban and Tirk could be down there somewhere.

"I can't! Not until we get the others away. Stay behind us!" Emily concentrated on Pegasus. "Take us down, Pegs, right in the middle of them. If they fire at us, I'll shoot back."

The soldiers crouched down on the ground and trained their weapons at the group. But they did not open fire.

"Don't shoot!" Emily called. "Please, don't shoot!"

Pegasus stopped flapping his large white wings and glided silently over their heads. He landed on the ground and trotted to a stop near the large group of soldiers.

"Put your hands in the air!" a human soldier demanded.

"Listen to me," Emily cried. "Earth is in terrible danger. I must speak with your commander right away!"

As she slid off Pegasus, she heard the urgent clicking sounds of soldiers preparing their weapons. Emily held up her hands. "Please, don't fire. We need to speak with your commander!"

The soldier held up his weapon. "Get down on the ground. Now!"

"You don't understand!" Emily took a step closer. "Jupiter is going to destroy this world. You can stop it!"

"Stop!" the soldier cried. "Don't move another step!"

"Please, listen to me," Emily begged, holding her hands up. "We don't want to fight. We're here to warn you."

Behind her, Pegasus was pounding the ground

and snorting. His wings fluttered. Alexis let out a soft growl. She folded her wings to cover little Frankie and warned him to keep his head down.

"Foolish humans," Alexis spat as she concentrated on the soldiers. "Listen to the child. She speaks the truth! Jupiter of Olympus will destroy this world if you do not stop creating these clones."

As the Sphinx took a step closer to Emily, one of the human soldiers panicked. He raised his weapon and fired. His reaction caused the others to do the same. Nirad soldiers roared and charged forward. They dropped their rifles and opened their four arms. Their bead-black eyes were wide and their mouths hung open, showing rows of sharp, pointed teeth.

Pegasus shoved Emily forcefully in the back and knocked her to the ground. He reared up, spread his wings, and whinnied angrily. He struck one of the Nirads in the chest with a golden hoof.

The Nirad soldier howled in pain and collapsed instantly to the ground as the gold of Pegasus's hoof poisoned it. Suddenly more Nirad soldiers ran at them. The frightened human soldiers lost control and fired their weapons.

Emily reacted instantly. She rose to her feet and summoned the Flame. As it flowed down to her hands, she turned them on the soldiers. But before she could release the Flame fully, she felt her body exploding in pain as several bullets found their mark. Thrown backward, she hit her head on the ground with an explosive impact.

Her thoughts flew at light speed. The soldiers were firing. Pegasus and Alexis were in danger. She had to save them! She sat up and raised her hands to release the Flame, but she was hit with more bullets and knocked backward just as her powers let go. There was a blinding flash and a tremendous peal of thunder.

And then they were gone.

Alexis and Pegasus had vanished!

It took Emily a moment to realize what had happened. Her hands must have been aimed toward Alexis and Pegasus when she released her powers.

"Pegasus!" she cried. "Pegasus, no!"

More bullets tore into her, and Emily howled as she realized what she had done. Suddenly her body burst into flame. She glowed brilliantly and melted the bullets within her, healing the damage done by the soldiers.

Emily's heart blazed in agony, but not from the flames.

Pegasus was *gone*!

Overwhelmed by grief, Emily welcomed the approaching darkness that always accompanied self-healing. She no longer cared what happened to her. She had destroyed the very best thing in her life. Now all she wanted, all she deserved, was death. She prayed it would come with the darkness. The CRU could do whatever they wanted to her now.

Without Pegasus, there was nothing.

30

"COME ON, SON, DRINK IT ALL UP."

Paelen awoke in terrible pain, cradled in strong arms and with a cup being pressed to his lips. He tasted the blissful sweetness of nectar and started to gulp down the healing drink. He opened his eyes to see Steve Jacobs pulling the cup away. He was lying in his bed at Jupiter's palace. Through the open windows he could smell the sweet, warm Olympian breeze.

He tried to focus on the figures standing around his bed. Diana and Apollo were standing at his left. Pluto was at the foot of the bed, his face a picture of anger. And then his eyes moved to his right and landed on Jupiter. Paelen's heart started to pound in fear. The eyes of Olympus's leader were like thunder, and his mouth was held in a thin, tight line.

Chrysaor was crouched on the ground beside Jupiter, looking downcast and defeated. The boar was terrified and wouldn't meet his gaze.

Jupiter stepped closer. His expression was dark and threatening. "Chrysaor caught you as you fell from the window. He brought you back to Olympus. But by the time I am finished with you, you will wish he had not done either."

Paelen dropped his eyes. "Forgive me, Jupiter. I deserve everything you will do to me. But before you do, I must go back to Earth. Joel is in jail, and I fear that Emily, Pegasus, and Alexis are about to take on the CRU by themselves."

There was a sharp intake of breath from everyone in the room. As Paelen devoured ambrosia and drank several more goblets of nectar, he started to speak. He told them everything that had happened, starting with the arrival on Earth to the moment his clone threw him out of the window of the tall black building.

"So you do not know where Emily is?" Jupiter

demanded incredulously. "The Flame of Olympus is on Earth and facing down the CRU alone?"

Paelen felt the furious intensity of Jupiter's stare. "She is not alone," he stammered. "Pegasus, Alexis, and—I believe—Prince Toban are with her!"

"What?" Jupiter cried. "Are you telling me the prince of the Nirad world has left the safety of his people to join this insane quest?"

When Paelen nodded, Jupiter was furious. He walked over to the window and released a lightning bolt and peal of thunder that shook Olympus to its core. "Deliver me!" he howled as he released more lightning and thunder.

With his fury spent, Jupiter returned to the bed. "How many of these creatures, these . . ." He looked to Emily's father for the word.

"Clones."

"Yes, clones," Jupiter repeated. "How many are there?"

Paelen shrugged. "I do not know for certain. But there is a Diana clone on the loose with a Nirad clone. They have killed many people. There is my clone as well, and Tornado Warning was a clone of Pegasus.

We believe there are many more, but only Alexis has been to Area 51 to see for herself. I have not seen her since the CRU attacked us outside their facility."

The leader of Olympus turned furious eyes on his daughter. "Diana, you knew of this and did not tell me?"

Diana dropped her head. "Forgive me, Father. But we only suspected. We had no proof of the clones. That Tornado Warning looked identical to Pegasus was not enough. Emily and Pegasus were determined to return to Earth to see for themselves. We sent Alexis with them for protection."

"Why did you not come to me?" Jupiter demanded. He turned on Pluto. "And you, my own brother! You did not think to tell me?"

Pluto shook his head. "Not until we knew for certain. You have a temper, brother. Emily feared you would destroy her world if you knew they were creating New Olympians."

Jupiter's eyes went black with barely contained rage. "She was right to fear for her world," he shot back. He advanced furiously on his brother. "Summon Neptune! Prepare for war. Once we have collected Emily, we will turn the Solar Stream on Earth!"

31

FOR A BLISSFUL INSTANT, EMILY FORGOT
what had happened. She awoke fully from the healing sleep and looked around but couldn't see the stallion. "Pegs?"

Then it all crashed back on her. There was no
Pegs. Pegasus, the magnificent stallion of Olympus,
had disappeared forever. And it was all her fault.

Suddenly Emily couldn't breathe. She sat up,
gulping air as she tried desperately to deny the truth.
"Pegs?" she gasped.

She looked around as the full memories of the
awful night returned. Pegasus was dead, and she had
been captured by the CRU. Tears rushed to her eyes.
Emily was so used to having her green handkerchief

with her, and automatically collecting the tears, that she was stunned to discover it was gone. Instead she used the crisp white sheets from her bed to collect her tears. And if they blew up because of the power they contained, she hoped she would blow up with them.

Emily curled into a tight ball. She sobbed openly for the loss of her beloved Pegasus. Alexis and little Frankie were gone also. But it was the death of the stallion that crippled her most.

"Forgive me," she wept. "Pegs, please forgive me. . . ."

Alexis had warned her about her powers. But in her fury at the CRU, she hadn't listened. Why hadn't she listened? Why had she done it? It was all her fault! Pegasus and Alexis would be alive now if she had only listened to the Sphinx. Why hadn't she?

It seemed a lifetime ago that the gorgons had tried to get her to use her powers against Jupiter. But she wouldn't do it. Pegasus had been there and given her strength to do the right thing. Now it was those same powers that had destroyed him.

Emily didn't hear the door in her room open. It was only when a voice called her name that she become aware of someone entering.

A man was standing at the side of her bed. Two large gray Nirad soldiers in uniform stood behind him.

"Emily Jacobs," the man repeated, "I am Agent PS. I am here to speak with you."

He appeared to be in his thirties, with cropped reddish hair and eyes the color of a peat bog. He had a neatly trimmed beard, but his eyes looked tired and drawn, as though he hadn't slept.

"Go away," Emily wept.

"No," the man said coldly. "You have a lot to answer for, young lady. Do you have any idea what you have done?"

Emily's grief turned into anger. "Yes, I know what I've done. I've killed Pegasus!"

"You've done a lot more than that," he said. "Shall I tell you?"

Emily felt the Flame inside her rumbling with anger. This CRU agent was doing his best to provoke her. "I'd go away if I were you," she warned. "You don't know what I can do when I'm upset. Pegasus is gone, and I am *very* upset!"

The agent didn't seem the least bit concerned. "I

know full well what you can do, Emily. I have made it my business to learn all about you and your amazing powers. I need to talk to you about them, to understand them. You were born in New York to two very human parents. You lived an ordinary life until last year. What changed? How do you have these powers? Where do they come from?"

"You're wrong if you think I'm going to tell you anything," Emily spat.

"Why do you want to make this so difficult?" Agent PS asked "We are on the same side. Who knows, perhaps one day you will use those powers to work with us instead of against us."

"Work with the CRU?" Emily said incredulously.

She sat up. "Are you crazy? Do you have any idea what you have done by creating clones? We came here to warn you! Jupiter is going to destroy this world if you don't stop."

The man sighed. "I know all the myths, Emily. Never has it been suggested that Zeus—or Jupiter as you prefer—has the power to destroy the world."

"You're wrong," Emily said. "He does. And he doesn't even have to come here to do it. All he has to do is turn the Solar Stream on Earth and it will be destroyed in an instant."

The comment made Agent PS pause. But only for a moment. "He wouldn't do that with you here." He smiled slyly. "We have seen your powers, Emily. We know how valuable you are to him."

"I am nothing without Pegasus," she said softly. "I don't care what Jupiter does now. If he destroys the Earth, I hope he destroys me, too."

"What about the other Pegasi we have here? Surely you could find another Pegasus among them? I know you have spent a lot of time with Tornado Warning. He is here waiting for you, along with all the others."

Emily sniffed. "Pegasi? What are you talking about?"

"Pegasus may have been the original, but we have all his clones here. Collectively we call them the Pegasi."

Hearing the pluralized name made Emily explode.

"There was only one Pegasus, and he's dead! All you've got are flying horses. There is no such thing as Pegasi. Don't you dare call them that! What do you call your Diana clones? Diani?"

The agent nodded. "Exactly."

"You're sick!" she replied as her temper flared even more. The bed started to rumble and shake. Behind the agent, the two gray Nirads stepped closer.

"Call them back," Emily threatened. She raised her hand and it burst into flame, snapping and crackling the air around her. "Not a lot can kill a Nirad, but I can!"

Emily was stunned to see the two Nirads step back by themselves. Their eyes were clearly focused on her and seemed to have intelligence. "Can you understand me?"

"Of course they can understand you," the agent said. "What did you think they are? Mindless monsters?"

"But they're clones of the gray Nirads," Emily insisted. "They're not the smart ones. I don't understand. Tornado Warning was wild. So was the Paelen clone. Why aren't these?"

The agent smiled smugly as he patted one of the clone's arms. "Nirad DNA works much better when mixed with Olympian. These two were our first successes, but there have been many more. However, it's taken us much longer to perfect Olympians."

"They're not Olympians!" Emily shot.

"Of course they are," the agent said. "Would you care to meet some of them?"

"No, I don't want to meet them. Just go away and leave me alone to die."

The agent chuckled. "Well, we both know that's not going to happen, is it? You can't die."

"Yes, I can," Emily shot. "When Jupiter turns the Solar Stream on Earth, we'll all burn up."

"All right," he agreed, almost teasingly. "Don't you want to see Joel before you die?"

"Joel?"

"Yes, he's here too. He is recovering. His surgery went well."

Was Agent PS baiting her? But if they had done anything to Joel, she had to know. "What surgery?"

"You'll have to come with me if you want to find out," the agent said. At that moment, another man entered the room.

"Agent PS, the boy is waking."

"Perfect timing," Agent PS said. He turned back to Emily. "If you want to see Joel before we start our interrogation, you'd better say so."

A desperate need to see Joel rose within her. She needed him more than ever. And if the CRU really had him, he needed her, too. Should she call their bluff?

"Joel isn't here. He's in Las Vegas," she tested.

"Not anymore."

"You're not going to touch him," she threatened.

"Who's going to stop us?"

Emily sat up and slid her legs over the side. She was wearing a hospital gown, but her silver leg brace was gone. "I am," she challenged. "Where's my brace?"

"In the lab, being analyzed," Agent PS said. "You can use these instead." He collected a pair of crutches and handed them to Emily. "Or"—he indicated the Nirad soldiers—"one of these big fellows can carry you. It's your choice."

Was this a trick? She looked around the small white room. It was similar to her room at Governors Island, but there was no lock on the door, and it was kept open. Emily reached for the crutches and followed the men to the door. She paused. "No locks?"

The agent stopped. "Could any locked door ever contain you? We all know you could leave here any time you wanted and we couldn't stop you. But it is

my hope that when you see what we've accomplished here, you won't want to go."

"Don't bet on it," Emily said furiously. "Just take me to Joel."

The agent chuckled as Emily followed him out of the room. The corridor was bright and spacious and filled with people in lab coats. There were other uniformed Nirad soldiers walking down the hall beside humans. As she walked past, the Nirads paused to watch her.

She turned and looked back at her Nirad escorts. They were both staring at her intently. There was something in their eyes.

"This way," Agent PS said as he turned down a second corridor. He approached a set of double doors. "We have a couple of patients in here. I think you know them both."

The two Nirads held the door open for Emily and Agent PS. As she walked past the Nirad on the left, she felt the huge clone pat her gently on the shoulder. When she looked up at him, she was convinced he was trying to tell her something.

But then Emily got the shock of her life. There

were two curtained-off areas in the room. One had the curtain drawn around it, but in the other open area was a bed with an occupant hooked up to a breathing machine and lots of tubes.

"Agent T!" Emily cried as she hopped over to the side of the bed.

The ex–CRU agent was awake and looking at her. The breathing tube in his mouth meant he couldn't speak. But as she leaned over him, tears formed in the corners of his blue eyes and trailed silently down his cheeks.

"You're alive!"

"If you call that living," Agent PS said casually. "He was shot when he and that winged cat woman attacked us. One of the bullets severed his spine. He can't move, eat, or even breathe on his own. But in time he may be able to speak. We do have a lot of questions for this traitor."

"He's not a traitor," Emily responded angrily. "He worked with us to try to warn you about Jupiter to save this world. He's a hero."

"Not to us."

Emily stroked Agent T's cheek. She wiped away

his tears. A part of her had hoped that her powers would heal him. But he was human and had never eaten ambrosia. It wouldn't work.

"I'm so sorry," Emily said, brushing back his hair from his face. "I failed all of us."

Agent T blinked his eyes slowly. He looked so weak and vulnerable lying in the bed, hooked up to all the machines. Emily leaned forward and kissed him gently on the forehead.

"Em?" a weak voice called.

"Joel?"

Emily struggled over to the long curtain that separated each treatment area. When she pushed back the curtain, she was met with an awful sight.

The crutches fell from her arms as she hopped over to the bed. "What have they done to you?" She trembled as she looked at Joel. His silver arm was gone, and his side and shoulder were covered in thick bandages. He was deathly pale.

The roller-coaster ride of emotions took another dip as fury rose to the surface. She turned on Agent PS and pointed an accusing finger at him. "You did this!"

Suddenly the CRU agent was thrown violently

across the room. He crashed against the back wall and crumpled to the ground, unconscious. Orderlies looked at Emily fearfully but ran over to the agent. They lifted him up and carried him from the room.

But Emily could only concentrate on Joel. She stroked his pale forehead and felt her powers working. His time in Olympus and all the ambrosia and nectar he'd consumed meant Joel was now more Olympian than human and her powers could heal his wounds.

She watched in relief as the color in Joel's face returned and he was fully awake. "They took my arm!" He sat up angrily. "Vulcan is going to be furious!" Then he looked at the pained expression on Emily's face.

"What's happened? How did they catch you? Where are Pegasus and Alexis? Are they here too?" Then his eyes fell on the other bed. "Agent T!"

Joel sprang up from his bed to get closer to Agent T. "Em, can't you heal him?"

Seeing Joel without his arm and Agent T lying destroyed in the bed, Emily felt herself breaking. "No. All I can do is kill."

She looked at Joel. He was going to hate her for

what she had done, but she had to tell him. "I killed Pegasus. Alexis and Frankie, too."

"What?" Joel cried.

"My powers got away from me. Now they're dead—and it's my fault," she whispered as tears rimmed her eyes.

Joel pulled Emily into a tight embrace and clung to her with his one arm. "Where's your handkerchief?" he asked softly as tears streamed down her cheeks and landed on her hospital gown.

"They took it," she wept. "But I don't care anymore. I hope my tears blow me up!"

Joel held her tighter. "If they blow us up, there's no one I'd rather go to pieces for."

Emily turned tearful eyes up to him and saw he was smiling gently. "It's not funny, Joel." Joel kissed the top of her head. "I know it's not."

Then his voice because serious. "But you listen to me, Emily Jacobs. You did not kill Pegasus. It was an accident. I know for sure Pegasus would not want you blaming yourself."

"But it was me," she said miserably.

Joel lifted her face to him. "No, it was them. The

CRU. If they hadn't created the clones, we'd never have left Olympus."

Emily was inconsolable as her mind replayed the moment of Pegasus's death. She could never forgive herself for losing control. As they clung together, the two Nirad soldiers stepped forward.

"Stay back," Joel warned. "I may only have one arm, but I can make you sorry you tried anything!"

The closest Nirad raised one of his large gray fingers to his thin lips and made a shushing sound. He looked back to the door and grunted a few times. His companion nodded and went to the door and peered out.

The first Nirad reached out and gently stroked Emily's head. His eyes were filled with compassion.

"You can understand us," Joel said in shock, "can't you?"

The Nirad nodded.

Emily removed herself from Joel's embrace. "Do you know where Toban and Tirk are?"

Once again the Nirad nodded. He struggled to form his mouth into words. After a moment, he pointed at his head and in a deep growling voice said, "Hear—our—prince."

Emily and Joel were stunned. This was the first Nirad to ever speak a language they could understand.

"How is this possible?" Joel asked.

Emily carefully wiped her eyes on her hospital gown. She looked at Joel. "He's not pure Nirad. They mixed him with Olympian DNA."

"Can others here speak?" Joel asked.

The Nirad nodded.

"Does the CRU know?"

The Nirad shook his head quickly and put his finger to his lips again. "Shhhhhh."

"This is amazing," Joel continued. "Do you have names?"

The Nirad pointed to his chest. "A-Two." Then he indicated the Nirad by the door. "A-Three."

"And you can hear Prince Toban in your head?" Emily asked.

When the Nirad nodded, she looked at Joel with pain-filled eyes. "The plan worked. Prince Toban can reach the clones. I wish Pegasus could know. He'd have been so happy." She turned back to the Nirad guard. "Do you understand why he came here?"

The Nirad nodded and again formed two words. "Going—home."

"Yes," Joel said. "If you help us, you can go home."

The large gray Nirad nodded and patted Emily again. "We—all—protect—Flame."

Joel looked at the Nirad in shock. "Em, he knows you're the Flame of Olympus!"

"Prince Toban must have told him," Emily said softly.

Joel's face brightened. "This is fantastic! If the Nirads help us, we can get out of here and stop Jupiter from destroying the Earth."

Emily should have felt relieved. But all she could feel was pain. She approached Agent T again and stroked his face. "I'm so sorry. I wish I could heal you."

Joel joined her. "If we can get out of here and get him some ambrosia, I bet it would help him." He looked down on Agent T. "I promise we won't leave you. We'll bring you back to Olympus with us."

Agent T slowly blinked his eyes again.

Joel turned back to A-Two. "Can you take us to the prince?"

The Nirad shook his head. "Not—now," he grumbled. "Night—sleep."

"When everyone is asleep?" Emily asked softly.

Again the Nirad nodded.

At the door, A-Three growled loudly. He approached A-Two and pointed to Joel and then the bed. The message was clear: *They are coming. Get back to bed.*

Joel hesitated before returning to his bed and focused all his attention on Emily. He lifted his hand gently to her chin and tilted her face up to look at him. "It will be all right, Em," he said softly. "I promise. As long as we're together, we'll be fine. I know you don't see any hope right now, but you must find a way to go on. Pegasus wouldn't want you to punish yourself. Deep down inside, you know that. He loved you and would hate to see you suffering."

"How can I go on?" Emily said miserably.

"You go on by remembering what you felt for Pegasus. How you two fought together to protect this world. How he would want you to keep fighting."

"But I can't."

Joel bent down and kissed her gently. "Yes, you can." He held her tight. "You're my Em; you can do anything."

32

EMILY WAS STANDING BESIDE JOEL'S BED
when soldiers and several more CRU agents ran into the
room. Joel was lying back and pretending to be asleep.

The two Nirads were standing by the door, looking like loyal military personnel who were keeping
their prisoner from escaping.

A younger CRU agent approached her with his
hands in the air. "Just calm down, Emily. No one is
going to hurt you. I'm Agent R. Agent PS is recovering. He will be back shortly."

Emily looked at the CRU agent and felt her anger
returning. Joel was right. Pegasus was dead because
of them. "Why did you take Joel's arm? You could
have killed him."

"That wasn't my decision," the agent said, diverting blame away from himself. "But I'm sure you must understand. There are things we could learn from that arm. It would be a revolution in prosthetics. It could bring relief to thousands of people."

"Soldiers, you mean," Emily challenged. "Nothing the CRU does is for the good of the people. All you care about is building an army. Look what you've done to these poor Nirads. You've enslaved them!"

"These Nirads are not slaves," the young agent said indignantly. "They are personnel. Just like me and just like all the human soldiers here."

"Can they leave if they want?" Emily demanded.

The young CRU agent looked at Emily with contempt. "Don't be ridiculous. If the public were ever to see these soldiers, there would be panic in the streets."

"Then why are you creating them?"

"There is a bigger picture here you are incapable of understanding, a larger goal. With an unstoppable army, we can bring order to the world. We will end human suffering and bring peace to every country on this planet. Wouldn't you want that?"

Emily stood in stunned silence as she processed

the agent's words. It was too horrible to consider. "No," she said in a hushed voice. "You're planning to use a Nirad army to take over the world! And if anyone tries to stop you?"

"There are always casualties in any regime change," he said. "But soon everyone will see that our way is the only way."

"You're all insane!" Emily cried. "You can't use these Nirads to make war on anyone who opposes you."

"It's not war, Emily; it is change. And the Nirads aren't the only ones. We have our Olympians and now we have you." He paused and stepped closer to her. "We've taken some of your blood. Before long, you will have many sisters who can do all the things you can do. You won't be alone anymore. And together we can change this world."

Emily shook her head. "I won't let you clone me."

The young agent shook his head. "Technically, you don't have any choice. We are holding Joel and we have your friend Earl as well. And I'm sure you wouldn't want anything to happen to Tornado Warning and the other Pegasus clones we have here.

Especially now that you destroyed the original."

The agent's words cut Emily to the core. "It's wrong," she whispered. "What you are doing is wrong. You can't force other people to think like you do."

"We can and we will," he said. "One world order isn't a bad thing, Emily. There will be no more borders, no more wars. Isn't that what it's like on Olympus? One language, one people, and one country? It will be the same here. The CRU are going to create Olympus on Earth."

"But Jupiter doesn't kill people who oppose him."

"Of course he does. The myths are filled with all the tales of death and destruction caused by Jupiter."

Emily felt her temper flaring. "They're just myths! Stories! They aren't all true! Jupiter is a caring man. He would do anything for his people. And the myths said that the Sphinx was a cold-blooded killer. But Alexis wasn't that way at all. She was a caring person who loved Agent T!"

The beeping heart monitor at Agent T's bed increased as he listened to Emily's words. She stepped over to him. "It's true," she said softly. "Alexis loved you."

"Now, isn't this a lovely scene!" Agent PS said as he

returned to the room. He approached Emily, rubbing the back of his head. "That's some punch you've got there." He regarded the other agent. "Agent R, did you tell her our plan and her part in it?"

The younger agent nodded. "But she's not convinced."

Agent PS smiled, but it chilled Emily to the bone. "Well then, we're just going to have to convince her."

"And this," Agent PS said proudly as they stood in front of a large picture window, "is where we create our new world fighters. It is here that we first spliced Nirad DNA with Olympian DNA. As you know, it's been a resounding success."

Emily was being given a full tour of the CRU facility. She was in a wheelchair that was being pushed by A-Two. Emily had quietly counted almost a hundred different Nirad soldiers. As she was pushed past, they all looked at her with the secret expression in their eyes. They knew who she was and were waiting for the right moment to move against the CRU.

But the expressions on the human faces she encountered was different. The soldiers and scientists all looked delusional with their glazed eyes, as if they were all drugged.

Emily looked through the window down into the lab. The scientists were all dressed in white spacesuits with breathing tubes coming out of their backs. She couldn't tell the men from the women as they worked at their large microscopes, collections of test tubes, and huge freezers that lined the walls. There were countless other large machines inside, and Emily had no idea what they did. But whatever it was, it wasn't good.

Emily was horror-struck at the sight. This was where it all started. That white, sterile laboratory was truly the place of nightmares. Somewhere down there, they were playing with her DNA, trying to create Emily clones.

Farther away from the main lab, they entered another laboratory. This one contained tall, upright tubes. The tubes were filled with thick, pale-green liquid. Emily was shocked to see that each tube held either a Nirad or Olympian clone in the process of development.

"This is where we mature our clones," Agent PS

explained proudly. "They grow exceptionally fast. It only takes a few months to reach maturity. It takes a normal human soldier a heck of a lot longer."

Emily said nothing as she was pushed past the long line of occupied growing tubes. When they stopped, she looked up at Agent PS. "This is so wrong, can't you see that? Please, listen to me. You must shut this down before it's too late. If Jupiter were to see this—"

"Don't you worry about Jupiter," Agent R said. "We are prepared and waiting for him. Can you imagine what we could create with his DNA? An army of Jupiter clones would be unstoppable."

Emily watched the scientists around her playing with Nirad and Olympian DNA as if it were some kind of game. She suddenly realized Joel was right. Despite her crippling grief over the loss of Pegasus, she had to continue the fight. The CRU had to be stopped.

Emily felt the Flame inside her rumbling and begging to be released to melt the clone factory. But this wasn't the time. She had to wait until she understood everything about the place. More than anything, she needed to find Prince Toban and Tirk.

Once they were safe, Emily promised herself she

would free the Flame and turn the lab into ash.

Emily was next taken to another level of the facility. The entire floor was made up of large gymnasiums, training areas, and sleeping dormitories. This was where the real nightmare began. This was where they kept the New Olympians.

Diana after Diana was training at the machines, lifting weights no human could ever hope to even move and running faster than the wind. Along with the Dianas, Emily's eyes landed on several Paelens. Some were practicing manipulating and stretching their bodies the way the real Paelen could, while others trained with equipment and fought each other in mock battles.

Above them flew countless Cupids near the roof of the tall gym. Some carried weapons as they performed midair acrobatics while shooting guns at targets.

"How?" she asked in horror. "Cupid was never your prisoner."

"Sadly, no. But he was wounded," Agent PS said. "We found a large pool of his blood in the snow outside Tuxedo, New York. It was frozen enough for it to still be viable. As you can see, the cloning worked perfectly."

"These are all soldiers?" Emily said.

"Not all," Agent PS responded. "As you can see, some make perfect athletes. We are going to test some of the clones at the next Olympic Games. For the first time ever, the Olympics will have real Olympians competing. It will be the perfect arena to introduce the clones to the world. And when the world sees what our athletes can do, they will realize there is no opposing us."

While they were speaking, they hadn't noticed the change in the large training area. One by one the clones stopped their training, put down the weights and weapons, and started to approach Emily.

"What's going on?" Agent PS demanded, looking around. "All of you, get back to work!"

"Back to work!" Agent R repeated, clapping his hands. "Now!"

The New Olympians ignored the order and pressed forward. The Cupids glided down from the roof and landed on the ground near Emily's wheelchair.

Emily studied them closely and saw they were identical to the real Cupid. Their wings had the same pheasantlike colors, and their faces and bodies were just as stunningly beautiful. But the expressions in their eyes were different. There was none of Cupid's arrogance or intelligence. These Cupids were like very young, innocent children. They cocked their heads to the side and smiled brilliantly at her.

Emily leaned forward in her chair and rose on her one good leg. She hopped over to the first Cupid.

"What's going on here?" Agent PS said in alarm. "What are you doing?"

Emily looked back and shot him a cold expression. "I'm going to meet my people!"

Every clone reached out to touch her, to stroke her head, and to hold her. Soon Emily was swallowed up in the large group of New Olympians. She was embraced by all the Cupids and Paelens.

As Emily looked from face to face, she was shocked by the overwhelming silence. Some grunted and made strange, soft mewing sounds, but no words came out of their mouths.

She recalled what Alexis had told her in the barn about how all the Olympians were drawn to her. They could feel her power and knew it was the source of their strength. Looking around, she realized it was

the same for these New Olympians. They instinctively knew who she was.

A tall Diana came forward and offered Emily her spear. Like the Cupid clones, this Diana was like a beautiful, hopeful child.

"Thank you," Emily said.

The clone grinned broadly.

"Can you talk?" Emily asked. When the clone shook her head, Emily continued, "But you can understand me?"

The Diana clone nodded. So did all the others in the gym. Emily looked back and saw several scientists and the CRU agents watching her intently. Finally Agent PS pushed his way through the group.

"All right, the excitement is over. Everyone get back to your training. Emily will be remaining here with us. You can see her again later."

The New Olympians did as they were told. The Cupids bowed, opened their wings, and returned to the air.

"Why aren't they wild?" Emily asked as she was helped back to her wheelchair. "Tornado Warning and the Paelen clone were wild."

"They were early experiments. It was before we perfected the mix of Olympian to Nirad to alien DNA."

"Alien?" Emily cried.

The CRU agent nodded. "We've had alien bodies here for years. But we've never been able to successfully clone them. Until now. Their DNA combined perfectly with Olympian and Nirad."

Emily didn't think it was possible to be shocked by anything anymore. But with each new revelation, she found herself stunned to the core.

But Agent PS had saved the best for last. Emily was taken down to one of the lower levels of the deep facility. When the elevator doors opened, she immediately smelled straw and heard the sounds of horses' whinnies.

"It seems they know you are here," Agent PS said curiously.

At the end of the hall, the doors were pushed open, and Emily nearly passed out. There were over fifty large stalls. Each stall contained a Pegasus clone.

"You see, Emily," Agent PS said, spreading his hand out before her, "you have no need to grieve over the loss of your Pegasus, because if you join us, all of these are yours."

All the white winged stallions came to the fronts of their stalls, kicking their doors and calling to her. Although they were all nearly identical, there was one particular stallion Emily recognized immediately. Once again she climbed from her wheelchair.

"Careful, Emily," Agent PS warned. "These experiments are our big failure. We can't seem to create calm Pegasi."

Emily cringed at the name. "They are not Pegasi!" she shot back. "There was only one Pegasus. These are just winged horses."

Agent PS straightened his back. The dark expression on his face said more than his words. "If you insist. They are all dangerous monsters. The only reason we've kept them alive is for you."

Emily ignored the warning and hopped over to a stall. "Hi, Tornado," she called softly as she stroked his soft muzzle.

Tornado Warning neighed with excitement and looked at her with his big brown eyes. Emily looked deep into those eyes, but could find no trace of Pegasus. It was true, Tornado was just a beautiful winged stallion who looked like Pegasus, but was nothing like him.

"Pegs is dead," she whispered softly as she laid her head against his warm face. "But I won't let them hurt you." She looked down at all the other stalls. "Any of you. I'm here, you're safe now."

As Emily hopped from stall to stall, each white winged stallion came forward to greet her with no aggression. They knew who she was and wanted to be with her.

Finally she returned to Tornado just as one of the scientists ran into the area. He approached Agent PS and Agent R and handed over several sheets of paper. Soon all eyes turned to Emily.

The expression on Agent PS's face darkened further. "Do you want to know what these are? They are the results of your blood tests. And you know what? They say you don't exist! You have no blood cells, no DNA, and no matter! They say you are made up of nothing!" Agent PS crumpled the pages and threw them away. He stormed over to her. "Okay, the game's over. Who the hell are you? And what did you do with the real Emily Jacobs?"

33

THOUSANDS OF OLYMPIANS OF ALL SHAPES and sizes gathered to watch their leader's departure. There was no joy in their faces, and their heads hung low. It had been eons since the Big Three had turned the Solar Stream on a living world. But this time it was especially painful. They were about to destroy the Flame of Olympus's home world.

Vesta stood at the front of the crowd, weeping softly. Venus and Cupid were beside her. Cupid's wings drooped as he dropped his head in sorrow. Several Nirads in the crowd raised their heads and howled mournfully.

Paelen ran with Emily's father up to Jupiter's chariot. "Please, Jupiter," Steve begged. "You can't do this!"

The Olympus leader's expression was as dark and thundery as the lightning bolts he carried. "I can and I must. The humans must be punished for what they have done to us."

Jupiter's large golden chariot was being drawn by six fiery, winged stallions. They pawed the ground, causing flames to rise up, and chewed at their bits, anxious to get moving.

Beside Jupiter's chariot stood Pluto's own black chariot, made entirely of the bones of the most valiant stallions fallen in battle. Cerberus, the three-headed dog of Hades, was beside the leader of the night world. The chariot was being drawn by a set of six black, skeletal stallions. The stallions had not seen the light of an Olympian day for so long that Pluto had to tie dark rags over the empty eye sockets to calm them.

On the other side of Jupiter waited Neptune, clutching his war trident. His eyes were the color of a stormy sea. Beneath him, his chariot was made of coral, large colorful seashells, and beautiful pearls. It was floating on top of a contained pool of water while six large, fish-tailed sea stallions waited and whinnied, preparing to move.

Behind the Big Three, four other chariots filled with the best Olympian fighters waited to follow their leader into battle. Vulcan was riding with Hercules and was carrying his most powerful shields and weapons.

Diana approached Steve as he continued to plead with Jupiter. She was wearing full battle armor and carrying a spear and shield. Her long dark hair was tied tightly back, and her expression was grim.

"Steve, stop," she said. "Father is correct. We tried to give Emily a chance to save your world, but she has failed. Now Earth must face the consequences of their actions. I have sent Apollo to New York to fetch your sister. Maureen will be saved from destruction and given a new home here in Olympus. But there is nothing that can be done for the others. Please ride with me in my chariot."

He looked at her incredulously. "You expect me to go with you and watch you destroy my world?"

Jupiter shook his head. "No, Steve. You are the Flame's father. Emily will need you now more than ever. You must come with us to be there for her."

That comment stopped Steve's protest. Finally

he walked back to Diana's chariot and reluctantly climbed on with her.

"And you, little thief," Jupiter said darkly to Paelen, "you and my nephew, Chrysaor, will lead us to where they are holding Joel. Then we will collect Emily, Pegasus, and Alexis, and end this once and for all."

Paelen and Chrysaor had also tried to plead with Jupiter, but had received a stark warning. The furious leader had threatened to feed them to Cerberus.

Paelen dropped his head and walked up to the winged boar. He climbed on his back. "Do you think he will ever forgive us?"

Chrysaor squealed softly.

Paelen agreed. "I do not think so either."

Once everyone was gathered, Jupiter raised his fist in the air, and thunder and lightning filled the skies.

"To Earth!" he commanded.

They emerged from the Solar Stream in the middle of the dark night. Beneath them, the colorful lights of Las Vegas were shining brightly. With Chrysaor and Paelen guiding them forward, they headed down.

As they descended, Paelen looked back. The Big

Three led the way. On the left was Pluto's bone chariot, with the skeletal stallions charging forward. Their haunting screams filled the air and struck a chill in Paelen's heart. On the right was Neptune's chariot, with the sea stallions rising on the crest of the huge wave of water Neptune had created around his chariot. Then in the very center was Jupiter's golden chariot, with its flaming stallions filling the night sky with their blazing light. Together they were a terrifying sight.

Jupiter raised his lightning bolts and fired them in the air, announcing the Olympians' arrival in the sky over Las Vegas. They continued down until they were just a few meters above traffic level. Car horns blared at the sight of the flying chariots tearing down the strip, and people on the street panicked and ran for cover.

Jupiter threw back his head and roared in fury as he unleashed more lightning bolts at the unsuspecting city. They struck the tall casinos and exploded with the impact as fire and sparks rained down on the streets.

Neptune raised his trident and commanded the

water hidden deep below the city to rise up and burst through the surface. Streams of fresh water shot high into the air.

Pluto released Cerberus. The three-headed dog sprang from the chariot and ran amok in the stopped traffic. His three heads caught hold of the bumper of an empty tourist bus and lifted it in the air. Cerberus then started to shake it like a dog would shake a toy.

Las Vegas was in an uproar with the arrival of the Olympians. But the chariots did not stop. They continued to follow Paelen through the city streets until they reached the police station and jail where Paelen had been held.

When Chrysaor landed on the top step outside the jail, Jupiter called his stallions to a halt. They hovered in the air several meters off the ground. The leader of Olympus raised a lightning bolt and fired at the police station.

"Bring out Joel!" he commanded as his booming voice filled the canyons of the city. "Now!"

The doors to the station burst open as armed police poured out. Paelen had seen this all before and ducked down into the protection of Chrysaor's wings. Behind him, Jupiter continued to demand Joel's release. But the police weren't listening. They opened fire on the chariots. Unaffected by their bullets, Jupiter returned fire with his lightning bolts. Suddenly the ground beneath the police exploded as Neptune commanded water to come forth.

"My brothers, stop!" Pluto called.

When Jupiter and Neptune paused, Pluto bowed elegantly to them. "Please, allow me."

The leader of the night world stepped down from his skeletal chariot. He was dressed in his long and flowing black robes. He carried no weapon. He didn't need one. Pluto was Death.

With Diana and Hercules moving in behind him, Pluto walked slowly and calmly up the steps of the station. "Surrender now or you will be delivered to me," he called.

The nearest police officer raised his weapon and fired at Pluto. The bullets entered his robes, but had no effect. "Fool!" Pluto said softly as he swept his hand in the air. An instant later, the officer collapsed dead to the ground.

"Who is next?" Pluto demanded as his eyes trailed

over the police officers. "Who will take on Death?" His eyes landed on a young policewoman. "Perhaps you, young woman? Are you ready to end your life early?"

The young policewoman cried in terror and threw down her weapon. She fell to her knees and begged for her life.

"Granted," Pluto said as he breezed past, leaving her untouched.

The other police officers quickly threw down their weapons and fell to the ground.

Diana moved forward. She caught hold of the policewoman and hauled her to her feet. "Tell me— where is the boy, Joel? He has a silver arm and is a prisoner here."

"I swear I don't know who you're talking about," the policewoman wept. "Please, I've only just started working here today!"

Diana's eyes scanned the other officers. "Who here knows Joel?" she demanded. "Answer me now or you will know our wrath!"

"He's not here!" a large police officer called. "They took him."

Hercules trotted over to the man and lifted him high off the ground. "Who took him?" he demanded. "Where is he?"

"The CRU!" the officer cried. "They came for him two days ago. He's not here. The CRU have him!"

Hercules started to shake the man. "Are you certain? Where would they take him?"

"That is enough, Hercules," Diana called. "Put him down."

The hero of Olympus lowered the police officer to the ground. He loomed over the man, almost a foot taller, and his eyes blazed the same color as Jupiter's. "Where did they take him?" he repeated.

"I—I don't know. Maybe Area 51."

Paelen groaned at the mention of the CRU base in the desert. He looked back at Jupiter. "We know where that is. Chrysaor and I will take you there."

"Do it!" Jupiter demanded.

As Diana, Hercules, and Pluto returned to their chariots, the building beside them exploded in fire and flying debris. Above them came the heavy, thudding sound of helicopters.

Paelen groaned a second time. "It is the military!"

he cried to Jupiter. "Those are the machines they use to attack us!"

A second rocket was fired at the Olympians. Jupiter raised his arm, and the rocket shot away from the chariots and tore into the police station. The rocket exploded on impact. All the windows were blown out as the building groaned under the pressure.

Jupiter looked up at the hovering helicopters and fired powerful lightning bolts at them. They burst into flame and crashed down to the street in a heap of burning metal.

"Olympians," Jupiter called in fury, "let us show these people who we are!"

The leader of Olympus commanded his fiery stallions to lift them higher in the air. As they rose above the burning buildings, they saw that the sky was filled with hundreds of military aircraft, heading straight for them. Jets zoomed past and launched a barrage of rockets at them.

With little effort, Jupiter diverted them, and they flew wildly into more buildings. "Father," Diana roared excitedly, "if they wish to fight, let us give them a fight!"

At Jupiter's command, the Olympians launched themselves at the military. Jupiter ordered Paelen and Chrysaor to move away from the battle until it was over, as they had no weapons and no means of protecting themselves. Not waiting to be told twice, they flew away from the fighting and headed to the tall black building. Ducking and dodging between the buildings and helicopters that pursued them, they finally made it back to the relative safety of the roof of the black building. Standing together, they watched the fight raging in Las Vegas.

Not far from their roof, three military helicopters pursued Neptune's chariot on his living wave of water. They fired their guns and launched their rockets at him. But Neptune fought back. He raised his trident in the air. Water spouts rose from the ground and knocked the rockets away. They flew straight at the city's tallest golden tower. With the impact of multiple rockets, the tall tower shuddered. Finally, like a great monster defeated in battle, it tipped over and crashed violently to the ground.

"Chrysaor, look," Paelen said in hushed shock as he pointed farther up the strip. Helicopters and jets were firing at Jupiter's chariot and the one containing Diana and Emily's father. But the weapons did not strike their mark. They were deflected by the Olympians' powers and crashed into a big black pyramid-shaped building. The light at its top went out, the windows exploded, and the building burst into flame.

"The military are destroying their own city in the hopes of stopping us. Can they not see the damage they are doing to their people? The lives they are wrecking? They cannot defeat Jupiter—why are they even trying?"

Paelen couldn't understand any of it. Not everyone in this city was bad, and yet they were being destroyed. Perhaps in the past he might not have cared. But after growing to know and love Emily and Joel, he had learned how good humans could be. Watching this destruction only made it sadder.

Chrysaor squealed in horrified agreement as they stood together watching the destruction of Las Vegas.

34

EMILY SAT ALONE IN HER ROOM. SHE WAS reeling from what the doctors and scientists had said. After the strange blood results, Emily had allowed them to examine her fully. Not only was she not human anymore, she wasn't really "alive." It was true that she had blood. It was red and it was wet. But it didn't have any cells in it. And although she had internal organs and a beating heart, they were not necessary to her survival.

"What am I?" she said aloud. "Pegasus, what happened to me in the Temple of the Flame?"

Emily heard the sounds of a scuffle outside her door. She hopped over just as it was opened by a Nirad. Out in the corridor, A-Two and A-Three were lifting several unconscious human soldiers off the floor. They carried them into her room and deposited them on the bed.

"What happened?" she asked as the Nirads bound the soldiers.

"Prince—frightened—trouble—go!"

"Prince Toban is in trouble?"

A-Two nodded. "Come." Without asking, he scooped her up in two of his arms and carried her into the corridor.

Emily pushed aside her concerns for herself. At the moment her only thought was for Prince Toban. As they entered the stairwell and started down, she tried to ask the Nirads what was happening, but their single-word answers puzzled her.

After several flights, the three Nirads stopped. A-Two dropped Emily. He and the others collapsed to the floor, clutching their heads.

"Hurt—prince!" A-Two cried. "Pain!"

Fear coursed through her. "They're hurting Toban?"

A-Two nodded and howled in agony.

"Please, I know you're hurting. But you must take me to him. I can help!"

Black tears of suffering were streaming down the Nirads' faces as A-Two picked Emily up again. Other collapsed Nirads were howling in the stairwell.

"Come with us," Emily ordered. "We will free Toban!"

A-Two roared at the others. They staggered to their feet and started to follow.

The growing group continued down deeper than Emily thought possible. She realized Agent PS had been very selective in his "tour" of the CRU facility. He'd claimed it only went down a few levels. He'd lied.

At the very bottom, Emily heard growls and roars filling the corridor. She recognized Tirk's voice. But worse than that, she heard Prince Toban screaming in agony.

The closer they got to the screaming, the harder it became for her Nirad escorts to move.

A-Two collapsed to the floor. "Pain!"

Emily crawled from his arms. "I'll stop your pain. Wait here."

Without her leg brace, walking was difficult and running impossible. But then her mind went back to the scientists' horrible words. She wasn't human. She wasn't even alive. Emily pulled up her trouser leg past her knee and looked at her damaged leg. It had been hurt in her first encounter with the Nirads. But as she studied the deep scars and ruined muscles, Emily wondered if the scars were only there because she thought they should be.

Emily concentrated harder than she ever had in her life. "Your leg is whole," she ordered. "There is no damage. It is perfect!"

The screaming of her friends threatened to distract her. But Emily closed her eyes to force it away and concentrate. "Your leg is whole!" she commanded. "There is no damage."

She opened her eyes and slowly looked down. Her bare leg was healed. No more scars and no more damage. She lifted her foot and flexed her muscles. They worked perfectly. Part of her celebrated her success. But deep down, in the darkest recesses of her mind, a part of her cried in despair. It was true. Emily Jacobs was gone. And if she wasn't human or Olympian, what was she?

With two good working legs, Emily ran forward.

She pushed through a set of double doors and entered a room of horrors.

The walls were lined with large steel cages holding what looked like failed clone experiments. She saw a Diana with four Nirad arms and no legs. There were Nirads with grotesque Cupid wings. Some of the creatures had two heads and were lying on the floors of their cages in misery. Others were beyond rational description. From her place at the door, Emily could feel their pain coming at her in waves.

These were the failures Agent PS didn't want her to see. The price they paid for creating a superrace of New Olympians and Nirad fighters.

In the center of the room, Prince Toban was strapped to a table. Gold bands pinned him down and were burning into his bare pink flesh. It was Earth gold, so it wouldn't kill him. But it scalded him until his skin smoldered, opened, and bled. She watched scientists extracting fresh black blood and skin samples from the suffering young prince.

Tirk was pounding his fists against the gold bars of his cage. With each contact, he howled in pain. But his loyalty to his prince kept him at it.

Emily was so stunned she didn't know where to look next.

"What are you doing here?" Agent R demanded furiously. "You are not allowed down here."

He was standing back from the table and holding a medical mask to his face. Around him, other scientists in caps, masks, and white jackets were crowding around the prince. Their gloves were wet with the Nirad's blood.

Watching her friend being tortured was too much to bear. Emily raised her hand and fired her powers. The scientists were tossed away from the prince and landed on the floor several meters away.

Emily ran up to the table. The prince's eyes were shut as he writhed and howled in pain. The tight gold bands were cutting deep into his smoking, opened flesh. Emily saw that the scalpels and tools the scientists were using on him had also been made of gold.

She used the flame like a laser to cut away the straps keeping him pinned down. But then she saw that the entire bed of the table was also made of gold. Every part of his back was being burned.

Emily caught hold of one of the prince's hands and

started to tug. Toban was not a large Nirad, but he was heavy. Too heavy for her to lift. As he continued to howl in pain, Emily focused her powers.

"Lift!" she commanded.

Concentrating on what she needed to do, Emily felt her powers answering. Prince Toban started to rise above the table. She turned to the side and lowered him gently to the floor.

Prince Toban was awake and looking at her in misery. Emily cradled his head in her lap and started to stroke his face. "I'm so sorry, Toban," she said. "I didn't know they knew about gold. It's over now; you're safe."

As she stroked him, Toban's open wounds started to close. It was slow and not complete, but it was enough to save the Nirad's life.

Now that the prince's pain was greatly diminished, the Nirads were released from their agony too. A-Two, A-Three, and all the Nirad soldiers from outside the lab charged in. They knelt down on the floor around their prince. Toban raised his four arms and greeted his new people.

Tirk continued to pound the bars and howl. Emily

burned the lock off the gold cage door. Tirk charged out. He barked furiously and pushed through the others to get to the prince. Finally he lifted Prince Toban in his arms and hugged the young Nirad. Emily saw that his hands were burned raw from pounding the cage. But he didn't notice. All he cared about was his prince.

"Emily, stop—you don't know what you're doing!" Agent R was moving closer.

"Stay back," Emily warned. "It's over. All of this is finished. No more torture, no more clones."

Tirk's eyes flashed with uncontained fury as he looked over at Agent R. He handed the prince over to another Nirad and ran at the CRU agent. Emily turned away as Tirk punished Agent R for his part in the torture of his prince.

Emily looked around the large room at all the clones and worried. What was to become of them now? She approached one of the mutant Dianas' cages. The clone had only one arm and three Nirad legs. Her Nirad black eyes seemed to have no understanding other than the desperate need to touch Emily.

Emily reached in and cradled the creature's face in her hands. "I promise you will be free soon," she said. As her eyes panned over all the cages, her heart—whether she had a real one or not—went out to them. "You will all be free!"

Her temper rose as she charged back to Prince Toban and the Nirads. She concentrated on the Nirad soldiers. "Capture the scientists and bring them." She looked at Agent R as he struggled to rise after being struck by Tirk.

"It's over, Agent R. This all ends now!"

35

SIRENS BLARED AND SOLDIERS ARMED THEM-
selves as Emily stormed through the corridors of the
CRU facility at Area 51. Behind her followed an
army of Nirad soldiers. Prince Toban was being carried in the arms of Tirk as he summoned his people
together.

Soon the number of Nirads joining her outnum-
bered the humans at the facility. Emily looked back
at Prince Toban. With each passing moment, his
strength was returning.

"Would you please ask some of your men to find
Joel and Agent T and guard them? And we need to
locate a man called Earl. He is a friend and is here
somewhere."

"I—go," A-Three said. "Find—Earl." He called several Nirads forward. They ran ahead into the stairwell. Gunfire echoed back, but Emily knew it would not hurt the Nirads.

As they made their way through the huge facility, Emily asked the Nirad soldiers to round up all the humans and get them to the ground level. Emily kept A-Two back to help her find her way to the main lab. Halfway there, she heard a familiar and very welcome voice.

"Em!"

She turned and saw Joel running toward her, escorted by two large gray Nirads.

"You didn't think I was going to let you total Area 51 alone!" Joel grinned.

Emily felt stronger with Joel at her side. "Of course not."

Together they made their way through the chaos to the super-lab where the clones were created. Nirads were capturing scientists and agents, disarming them and leading them up to ground level.

Joel looked through the window of the super-lab and whistled. With the alarms still blaring, the night shift of scientists were busy trying to store away the cloning materials. They looked up in terror when they saw Emily and Joel standing at the large picture window.

"Can you nuke that lab without burning down the whole facility?"

"I can try," Emily said.

The Nirads tore down the secured doors to the lab and poured in. The scientists were rounded up and presented to her.

"Get them to the surface with the others," Emily ordered.

Joel and Emily now walked through the empty lab and began to destroy the equipment. With each passing moment, Emily's confidence with the Flame grew. By the time they had left the lab, Emily could look at a machine and turn it to ash in a matter of seconds.

They moved on to the secondary labs. Emily showed Joel and Prince Toban the tall tubes that contained the clones in various stages of development, from embryonic to nearly fully grown.

"What do we do with these?" Joel said.

"I don't know," Emily admitted. "We can't destroy them; they're alive."

"But we can't leave them here either. The CRU will just build more."

Emily shook her head. "Once everyone is out of here, I'm going to destroy the place."

"And these guys?"

"We're just going to have to find a way to save them. Let's get everyone else out of here first and worry about these guys later."

In another lab they came across Joel's silver arm. It was laid out on a table and had been completely dismantled and was now useless. Paelen's winged sandals were found in the same lab, and they were grateful to discover these were intact. Emily prayed that Paelen was still alive and ready to wear them again. They also found Pluto's helmet.

"Boy, am I glad to see this!" Joel said. "Pluto would have had a fit if he knew we'd lost it."

Emily dropped her head. "No, we didn't lose it. We just lost Pegasus and Alexis instead. I'm sure Pluto won't care about his helmet after that."

Prince Toban growled softly. He closed his eyes

and tilted his head back. When he opened his eyes again, he concentrated on Emily and made several sounds.

"I don't understand," Emily said desperately.

A-Two struggled to say, "Place—all—empty. Ours. No—more—people. All—prisoners. All—above."

Joel approached the prince. "So your soldiers have gathered all the people here and taken them above? There is no one left?"

Prince Toban shook his head and made several more sounds.

"Pegasuses," A-Two said. "They—stay. Children—below."

They understood that all the CRU agents, scientists, and human soldiers had been captured and taken to the surface. The facility now belonged to them.

"All right, we've got to get the New Olympians out of here and the poor clones from down below. And I've got to free all of Pegasus's clones as well."

"You've seen them?" Joel asked.

Emily nodded. "Tornado is here too. But all the

winged stallions are the same. They're as wild and dangerous as Tornado. I'm still the only person who can get near them. I'm going to have to lead them out."

"Then what?" Joel asked. "Em, what are we supposed to do with all these clones? Yes, we can destroy this place, but then where do we take them? And how? Without Pegasus, I don't even know how we're supposed to get back to Olympus or get Prince Toban and his people back to the Nirad world."

Emily hadn't thought that far ahead. Her only concern had been to stop the CRU from creating more clones. But now what? Joel was right. They were stranded on Earth with no way of getting back.

"I don't know," she said softly. "But Dad has got to know something is wrong by now. He and Diana will come for us. And Paelen, I hope. He was hurt, but I'm sure Chrysaor must have taken him back to Olympus. Paelen knows where we are. We just have to get to the surface and wait for them."

Joel didn't sound convinced. "Or wait for the military to launch a full assault on us for destroying their base here."

"We'll just have to risk it," Emily said. "We don't have any choice."

As the long night continued into dawn, Emily, Joel, and the Nirads entered the secured quarters of the New Olympians. They welcomed Emily into their midst and showed no aggression toward Joel or the Nirads.

When Emily explained the situation, the clones were excited at the prospect of going outside. They had never been to the surface before.

The sun was rising on the horizon by the time all the New Olympians emerged to the surface level. They looked at the approaching sunrise in absolute wonder. The Cupids were thrilled to leap into the air and soar in a wide-open sky.

Emily took a moment to watch them with envy. Those sweet, ignorant clones had no idea of the danger and uncertain future they now faced.

There were hundreds, maybe a thousand gathered on the dry Groom Lake bed. The heavily armed Nirad soldiers kept the Area 51 personnel apart from the clones.

"Is that my friend Emily I see?"

Emily turned at the voice and saw Earl approaching. He ran forward and embraced her tightly. "Ain't you a sight for sore eyes! Lord, I thought you'd never get here. These CRU folks ain't nice people!"

Emily clung to Earl, grateful that he was alive. There was a Nirad standing close at his side. Earl turned to introduce him. "This is my friend B-Fifteen. He got me out of my cell."

As Emily greeted the Nirad, there were sounds and cries coming from the crowd. She turned and saw them all pointing up at the sky. The Cupid clones squealed in terror and quickly landed.

Emily and Joel looked up, and their eyes went wide. "Jupiter!"

36

EMILY WATCHED JUPITER'S CHARIOT BLAZE across the dawn sky, with Pluto and Neptune beside him in their own chariots.

A chill ran through her. It took the Big Three to move the Solar Stream. And here they all were.

"That the big fella himself?" Earl asked fearfully, watching the approaching chariots.

Emily nodded. "You'd better get back." Then she turned to Joel. "You too. I said I would fight Jupiter if I have to, and I meant it. He's not going to destroy this world and all these innocent clones without a fight."

"No way," Joel said. "I started this with you. I'm going to end it with you."

Emily's heart swelled at Joel's constant support and loyalty. She reached out and took his hand. Together they walked out onto the dry Groom Lake bed and awaited Jupiter.

As the Olympians drew closer, Emily noticed someone else in the sky. "Joel, look! It's Paelen!"

Leading the Olympians was Chrysaor, carrying Paelen. He was the first to touch down on the ground, just a few meters from them. Paelen jumped off the boar's back and ran to his friends. They embraced like they hadn't seen each other in years. So much had happened since they were last together.

"Las Vegas is destroyed!" Paelen cried. "The military tried to kill us, but we fought back. Now it is all in ruin."

"Las Vegas is destroyed?" Joel repeated.

Paelen nodded and concentrated on Emily. "He is going to do it. Jupiter is going to destroy this world. He's already started with Vegas."

This only strengthened Emily's resolve. "No, he's not," she replied.

"You cannot stop him," Paelen cried. "He is Jupiter, the all-powerful."

"And I am the Flame of Olympus!" Emily shot

back. "If he wants to destroy this world, he'll have to get past me first!"

The screaming of Pluto's skeleton stallions as the chariots landed on the dry lake bed before them cut off further conversation. Emily saw Jupiter's face. It was furious. She had never seen the leader of Olympus so angry.

"Emily!" Jupiter boomed. "What have you done?" The leader of Olympus climbed down from his chariot and stormed up to her. "You have a lot of explaining to do!"

But before she could even think of how to respond, a comforting voice cried out her name.

Emily turned around and watched as her father climbed down from Diana's chariot. He ran past Jupiter and scooped her up in his arms. "Are you all right?"

Emily nodded and fought to keep control of her emotions. She turned to Jupiter. "Pegasus is dead. So is Alexis. My powers got away from me, and I killed them."

A shocked silence halted the Olympians. The only movement came from Neptune, his face a portrait of pain. "My son is dead?"

"Neptune . . ." Emily started to break. "I didn't mean to. . . . We were fighting the CRU. . . . I got shot and lost control."

"They shot you?" her father cried.

Emily nodded again. "I'm okay," she said sadly. "But Pegasus isn't."

Chrysaor started to squeal and howl in pain, breaking Emily's nonexistent heart.

"Please, Jupiter, I beg you," she cried, facing the leader. "There has been too much death already. Don't destroy my world."

The fire was gone from his eyes. But his expression was still full of anger. "The CRU have left me no choice. Their crime cannot be forgiven."

"Then punish them!" Emily's father cried. "But not the whole world!"

"No," Jupiter insisted. "There will be others just like the CRU, ready to rise up and do this again. We must not let that happen. Earth must be destroyed."

Emily stepped away from her father and approached Jupiter. "I understand you are angry," she said, suddenly very calm. "So am I. I have lost Pegasus. I have seen firsthand the horrors these people have done

here. But I cannot let you destroy my world."

Jupiter stared at her and a frown darkened his brow. "Are you challenging me?"

Emily inhaled deeply. This was it. She felt the Flame rumbling inside her, but felt equally sick realizing what she was prepared to do.

"Yes, Jupiter, I am," she finally said.

A hush fell over everyone as Emily and Jupiter faced each other.

"Em, stop," her father cried.

Emily looked back at him but shook her head. She turned back to Jupiter. "You know how I feel about Olympus and how I have fought to protect it. I love you, Jupiter. But I will not allow you to destroy my world."

Pluto's and Neptune's eyes flashed from Emily back to their brother and to Emily again. "Emily, stop," Neptune warned. "You do not want to do this."

"No, I don't," she said, concentrating on him. "But to protect this world, I must." She looked back at Jupiter. "You have taught me so much. Like how to care for others outside my family, my race, and even my species. You have shown me the price you must pay and the sacrifices you have made for leadership. You have taught me to be a better person. How could you teach me all that and then expect me to allow you to destroy this world?"

"This is different," Jupiter said.

"No, it's not," Emily insisted. "Most of the people on this planet are innocent. They have no idea what the CRU have done. Why should they be made to suffer for that?"

"Do you care so much for these people that you are prepared to make war with me?" Jupiter asked incredulously.

Emily stared Jupiter in the eye. She raised both her hands as they burst into brilliant flame. The powers bubbled up from her core as she prepared to fire at the leader of Olympus. "To save Earth? Yes!"

37

EMILY CLOSED HER EYES AND COMMANDED her powers to fly. An instant before they did, a crying whinny shattered the stillness of the air around her. It was a sound she'd never thought she'd hear again. A sound she loved. The Flame in her hands went out. She turned and saw Pegasus tearing through the sky. Alexis was behind him, struggling to keep up.

"Pegasus!" she howled.

Emily ran out onto the dry lake bed. Pegasus landed and galloped toward her. His mane billowed behind him, his nostrils flared, and his golden hooves stirred a wild dust storm in the air. Pegasus was covered in foaming sweat and panting heavily as he whinnied to her.

They met in an explosive reunion.

Emily threw her arms around his neck. She squeezed him as tight as she could, just to prove he was there. "You're alive! You're alive!"

Pegasus neighed excitedly and turned his head back to embrace her as best he could. His wings were fluttering and his tail flashed behind him.

Alexis landed on the ground beside Pegasus. Her face was bright red with exertion, her hair was a matted mess, and she was panting with exhaustion. Frankie was on her back, with a huge grin on his face.

"We're back!" he cheered. He climbed off Alexis and ran over to Joel and Paelen. He threw his arms around them and hugged them tightly. "That was so awesome! We went to another planet! There were lots of big statues and it was a jungle! There were helicopters from here too. The pilots are waiting for us to come get them."

Emily was too emotional to speak. She released Pegasus and collapsed on the ground before Alexis. She hugged the Sphinx tightly. "I'm so sorry." She started to cry.

"It is all right, Emily," Alexis panted softly, patting

her on the back with a large lion's paw. "We are all right."

Neptune and Chrysaor ran over to greet Pegasus. "When Emily told me you were dead, I could not bear it." Neptune's eyes were filled with tears as he embraced his son.

Pegasus greeted his brother, but then stepped closer to Emily. He neighed for her.

She left the Sphinx and kissed his soft muzzle, his face, and finally his eye. "Oh, Pegs, I really thought I'd killed you."

"Hardly," Alexis said. "Though you did cast us to the very end of the Solar Stream."

"She did what?" Jupiter asked as he approached.

"The Flame cast us to the very end of the Solar Stream. The journey lasted the shortest blink of an eye. But it has taken us ages to fly back here." She paused and looked from Emily to Jupiter and then back to Emily again. "It appears we arrived just in time."

The Sphinx climbed stiffly to her feet and padded over to Emily. "Do you know everything you have made disappear was on this beautiful world? There are no people but many kinds of plants and wildlife. There are ancient temples and signs of a great society that must have existed there. But they are gone."

Emily was still holding on to Pegasus to prove he was really alive. "I don't understand. How could I send you there? Why would I do it?"

Alexis smiled gently. "Child, do you not remember? The soldiers were shooting at us. You had been hit. You did the only thing you could to protect us. You sent us away from the danger." The Sphinx paused and smiled. "Though, to be honest, I would have much preferred being returned to Olympus and not across the cosmos."

"I don't understand," Emily stammered. "How did I do it?"

"That is a very good question," Jupiter said as he approached her. "And one that I believe we should investigate. . . ." He stopped, and his eyes concentrated on Emily. "Together."

Emily gazed up into the face of the leader of Olympus. Her hand was wrapped around Pegasus, and she was pressed closely to him. "What about Earth?"

Jupiter dropped his head. "Perhaps I was a bit rash

in ordering its destruction. I never realized how much this world still means to you. I was wrong, and I am not above admitting it."

"So you won't destroy it?"

Jupiter shook his head. "Not this time. But Emily," he warned, "these people must be punished for what they have done."

Emily nodded. "I agree. And if you will allow me, I want to turn Area 51 to dust!"

Jupiter opened a ground-level portal to the Solar Stream. He summoned Olympians to come to Earth to escort the New Olympians back home.

With his two brothers, Jupiter watched the long lines of clones heading into the Solar Stream. Diana was standing among her many clones. The new Dianas looked at the original in awe and sought to touch her. Though she was greatly disturbed by them, Diana felt no urge to fight.

Prince Toban was still covered in cuts and burns, but his strength had returned. Tirk was behind him, keeping a protective watch over him, while other Nirad soldiers kept guard over the Area 51 employees.

As the final clones entered the Solar Stream, Emily turned to Neptune.

"There are lot of winged stallions still inside. They're clones of Pegasus and they're wild and dangerous. But we can't leave them behind. It's not their fault they exist. Would you help me get them to the Solar Stream?"

Neptune looked uncomfortable at the mention of his son's clones, but he agreed. With the Nirads on the surface guarding their prisoners, Emily spoke to Pegasus, asking him to remain with them.

"I don't want you going down there, Pegs." She kissed his muzzle. "There are a lot of clones, and I don't want them hurting you when they're released. I lost you once; I couldn't bear it again."

Pegasus snorted but finally agreed. Emily approached Alexis. "I think you should come too. There is someone you should see."

As they made their way to the facility, Jupiter, Pluto, and a large number of Olympians joined them. "We must all see," Jupiter explained. "I must understand what has happened here."

Emily feared that Jupiter might change his mind

if he actually saw what the CRU had done. But as if reading her mind, he put his arm around her and reassured her. "Your world is safe, Emily," he said. "But I must still see."

The facility was eerily quiet as Emily, her father, and the Olympians journeyed down to the lowest levels, where failed clone experiments were kept. When Jupiter saw what had been done to his daughter's clones, his fury arose.

"This must not be tolerated!" He went up to the nearest cage and tore the door off. The crippled Diana clone cried as she struggled to climb out.

Jupiter knelt down to her level and stroked the clone's misshapen head. "You will come home with me, my child," he said gently. "You are safe."

He commanded the Olympians to collect every last one of the broken, tormented clones. They would all be given a home on Olympus and cared for till the end of their lives.

From there, Emily escorted them to the lab containing the tall tubes. "These are the unfinished clones," she said softly. "I don't know how to save all of them. The younger ones need these machines to develop."

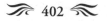

"We cannot save them all," Jupiter said sadly, "but we will do our best to release those ready for the world. Leave it to us."

With a heavy heart, Emily reluctantly left the room to wait for Jupiter and Pluto to do what they must. She knew it was a hard task and grieved for those clones who could not survive. When it was done, she led the Olympians to the level of the Pegasus clones. When she pushed open the door, the clones began kicking their stalls and trying to escape.

Emily led the group to one stall in particular. "This is Tornado Warning."

Jupiter stepped forward. Emily was frightened Tornado might bite or try to attack him, but the stallion was calmed in his presence.

"So, my young friend, you are the one who caused all this mischief."

Tornado neighed softly and invited more attention.

Jupiter and his brothers walked from stall to stall, talking to and touching all the clones. Their touch tamed the wild stallions.

Neptune raised his hands in the air. "Open!"

The stall doors flew open, releasing the winged stallions. Emily was stunned to see there was no fighting among the clones. They all pressed in close to be with her and the Olympians.

The final spot on their tour of the CRU facility was the medical center. Two Nirad guards were keeping watch over their patient.

"Tom!" Alexis sprang over to his bed and leaned over the ex–CRU agent and kissed his face.

Agent T was making strange, excited sounds as his grateful eyes filled with tears at the sight of Alexis.

The Sphinx looked anxiously to Emily. "Heal him!"

Emily felt her throat tighten. "I've tried. It won't work."

"It cannot work," Jupiter explained. "He is a human who has never consumed ambrosia. The Flame's powers cannot touch him."

"Give him some ambrosia," Alexis demanded. "Then Emily can heal him."

Jupiter looked at all the strange devices attached to Agent T. "Do these machines keep him alive?"

Emily nodded. "His spine is destroyed. He is paralyzed and can't breathe or eat on his own."

Jupiter dropped his head and placed his hand on the Sphinx's shoulder. "I am sorry, Alexis. The damage is too great. Ambrosia will not heal him sufficiently. It would only keep him alive but in this state. That would be too cruel."

"Please, Jupiter," Alexis begged. "I have never asked anything of you in all my life. But I ask you this. Please let me have my Tom. I love him."

"But he will not survive the journey to Olympus away from these machines. His life in this form is over."

"Then change his form," Alexis pleaded desperately. "You have the power. Turn him into something that does not require a moving body to survive. A rock, a jewel, a tree? Anything, but let him live."

Jupiter approached the side of the bed. He looked down on Agent T thoughtfully. "I am sorry that I do not have the power to restore your body. But I can change it. I will do this only if you wish me to. It must be your choice."

Alexis was still standing up beside the bed. "Please, Tom, let him do it. You can come back to Olympus with me. We can be together. Tell him you wish this."

Emily watched Agent T blinking his eyes. Jupiter reached forward and placed his hand on the man's forehead. The leader of Olympus closed his eyes. Finally he nodded.

"Alexis, everyone, stand back."

Emily stood back with her father as Jupiter unhooked Agent T from the equipment keeping him alive. When his breathing tube was removed, the agent's eyes flashed open as he started to suffocate.

"Jupiter, please!" Alexis begged.

The leader of Olympus placed both his hands on Agent T's chest. He closed his eyes again and lifted his head. The air around Jupiter snapped and sparkled and seemed to be filled with stars. There was a blinding flash and a loud snap. In a moment it was over, and when the light faded, the bed was empty.

Alexis's frightened eyes looked desperately at Jupiter. "What has happened? Where is my Tom?"

Jupiter looked at the Sphinx and smiled gently. "I suggest you return to Olympus and see for yourself. He is at your home, waiting for you."

"How will I know him?"

Jupiter smiled gently. "You will know him."

Alexis didn't pause to say good-bye. She flashed past Emily and was a blur flying down the empty corridor.

Emily looked at Jupiter. "What did you do to him?"

"I asked the man what he wanted. He told me he wanted to live with Alexis. Then I asked him what he would choose to be if he could not move."

"What did he say?"

Jupiter smiled. "A willow tree. He told me his happiest childhood memories were of a tree house he had in the giant willow in his back garden. The willow is soft and forgiving and moves gently in the breeze."

"Agent T is a willow tree?"

Jupiter nodded. "A very happy one. I am sure when we return to Olympus we will find Alexis sitting quite contentedly in her Tom-tree."

With every last living being out of the facility and on the surface, Jupiter looked at Emily. "This is yours now. Proceed."

Emily stood before the squat buildings. Her mind played back all the horrors that had occurred in this facility. Suddenly Agent PS darted away from the guards and ran up to her. "Please, Emily, don't do it. Don't destroy all that knowledge!"

Emily looked at him and felt her anger growing. "Knowledge? Is that what you call this?"

"Yes, knowledge," the agent said. "There must always be some casualties in human development. But we could achieve something amazing here. We could change the world."

"Ah, yes," Jupiter said as he cast his eyes on the CRU agent. "Everything is permissible if it is for human development. Is that what you are telling me?"

The agent suddenly realized to whom he was talking. But instead of offering respect, he straightened his back and let his arrogance show. "Yes, Jupiter, human development! The only reason you're here is because you're frightened that one day we'll be as powerful as you—and you hate that."

Jupiter shook his head sadly. "No, we are here because you stole something precious from us, and we have now taken it back." He sighed. "I have not been back to your world for a very long time. It saddens me greatly to see that your knowledge has far exceeded your wisdom to use it wisely. You are as hard and unforgiving as a Prometheus Oak."

Suddenly a sparkle came into his eyes. "Prometheus Oak. Of course, how fitting." He concentrated on Emily. "Flame, let loose your power."

Everyone but Pegasus moved back from Emily as she raised her hands in the air. She closed her eyes and summoned not only the power of the Flame, but all her other powers as well. She envisioned every room and every corridor of every level of the wretched facility. She thought of the unfortunates who had suffered and died there in the name of science. She grieved for the clones left in the tubes that they could not save.

When she was ready, Emily unleashed her full powers. Laserlike flames rushed from her hands and burned their way into the buildings. But they did not stop. From deep beneath the ground came rumblings and loud explosions. Emily felt the power of her collected tears on her hospital gown and sheets explode and add to the firestorm.

The ground started to shake like a powerful earthquake. The sounds of the groaning and crumbling

facility filled the air and grew in intensity until they became almost unbearable. In one final push, Emily envisioned it all gone!

An instant later the sounds stopped. The dust settled, and where once stood the CRU facility was nothing but an impossibly large crater.

"Well done!" Jupiter cheered as he and his brothers clapped their hands.

Pegasus nickered beside her and pressed his face to hers.

"It's over, Pegs," Emily sighed tiredly as she pressed her head to his.

"Not quite," Jupiter said. "Pegasus, if you look around us, you will see the remnants of a dead lake. I believe it is time for water and life to return to it. Would you oblige me?"

Emily looked at Pegasus and frowned. "What does he mean?"

Pegasus whinnied excitedly. He reared slightly and flapped his wings. The stallion galloped away from the group until he was a safe distance away.

"Watch this," Paelen said, coming up to her. "I have not seen Pegasus do this in a very long time."

"Do what?" Joel asked.

"Use his powers," Paelen explained.

"Pegasus has powers?" Emily asked.

"Just watch," Paelen said.

Far from where they stood, Pegasus opened his wings fully. He glowed so bright, Emily could barely see his outline in the blazing light. The stallion reared up as high as he could and came crashing back down to earth with a mighty blow.

Once again the ground rumbled and quaked. Pegasus moved farther away and repeated the action. He did this several more times around the lake bed before he returned to Emily. They stood together and watched as the cracked, dry surface of the dead lake suddenly burst open and fresh water started to rise.

It filled the whole of Groom Lake and seeped into the crater Emily had created with the destruction of the CRU facility.

Over the roar of the rushing water, Jupiter caught hold of Agent PS by the scruff of the neck and hauled him over to the edge. "What lake would be complete without shady trees?"

He released the CRU agent and pointed his hands at him. "Prometheus Oak!"

Agent PS started to run from Jupiter, but just a few steps away he slowed down. He turned back and looked at Emily. His eyes were filled with defiant hatred as his body changed and stretched out. He started to scream. Suddenly his black suit tore away and branches sprang from his body.

Emily watched in shock as Agent PS was turned into a giant oak tree.

"Ouch!" Paelen said. "Jupiter really is angry."

"What do you mean?" Joel asked. "Being turned into a tree is letting him off easy. He did the same to Agent T. He's now a willow tree."

Paelen shook his head. "They are not the same at all. Agent T will never feel pain but can still experience joy. He can think, speak, and live a long and happy life with Alexis. But not Agent PS. Being turned into a Prometheus Oak is living torture. He will remain fully conscious and aware of his previous life. He will feel everything. A snapped branch will cause him to bleed. His bark is like breaking bones, and when the wind blows through his leaves, you will hear him screaming. There is no worse punishment than that."

Emily looked back at the tree that had once been Agent PS. Yet she could feel no pity for him.

Moments later Jupiter approached the gathered scientists, military personnel, and CRU agents. "You have offended all Olympus with your actions here. But I will not kill you. Instead I will give you a thousand years to consider your actions."

Once again the leader of Olympus raised his hands in the air and shouted, "Prometheus Oak!"

Agent R and the other people of Area 51 scattered and tried to run away from the punishment raining down on them. But all they succeeded in doing was spreading out enough to create the most beautiful leafy forest around the shores of the new Groom Lake.

38

EMILY AND PEGASUS STOOD IN THE COOL shade of the tree formerly known as Agent PS. Those she cared for most were with her, including Prince Toban and Tirk. They gathered together to watch the last of the Nirad soldiers enter the Solar Stream and head first to Olympus and then on to the Nirad world. Before they entered the Solar Stream A-Two and A-Three paused and waved excitedly at them. "See—you—soon!"

When they were gone, Jupiter sealed the entrance to the portal as if it had never been there.

Frankie was standing beside Joel with a big grin still painted on his face. "That was totally awesome. I knew you were aliens!"

"We're not aliens!" Joel cried. But then he looked into the boy's hopeful face. "Okay, maybe we are."

"What now?" Earl said. "Tom is gone, now you guys are going. What am I supposed to do?"

Emily frowned. She thought it was understood. "What do you mean? You're coming with us."

"Really?" Earl cried, excited. "I can finally see Olympus for myself!"

Emily's father, Diana, and Jupiter came forward. "Of course you may return with us to Olympus. It is not safe to leave you here in this desert. But you may come only for a visit," Jupiter said. "After everything the CRU have done here, I must ask if you would return to Earth to keep watch for us. We will ensure your safe return, and you will have more wealth than you could ever spend. I promise you, no one will ever find you. But we need you here working for us."

"You betcha!" Earl said excitedly. "I always wanted to see Olympus, but this is still my home. I could never leave it for long. I'd be happy to keep an eye open for y'all." His eyes settled on little Frankie, and he held out his hand. "How 'bout it, short stuff?

You fancy being an Olympian spy with me?"

Frankie grinned. "Awesome!" he said, and took Earl's outstretched hand. He turned and looked back at Jupiter. "Can I still visit Paelen, Joel, and Chrysler?"

Jupiter nodded. "Of course."

The leader of Olympus mopped his brow. "I had forgotten how hot this world can be. I think it is time we headed back."

Diana had removed most of her armor and stood in a light tunic. "Indeed, Father. I should like a nice long swim when we get back to Olympus."

"I'm with you," Emily's father agreed.

In the distance, Pluto and Neptune were climbing into their chariots. They waved at Jupiter and then launched into the air. In moments they entered the Solar Stream and were gone.

Jupiter offered a ride in his chariot to Prince Toban and Tirk. As the two Nirads approached him, he looked at little Frankie. "Would you like to ride with me?"

The boy's eyes were huge. "Cool!"

Little Frankie bounced away with Jupiter and the Nirads.

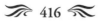 416

"There's room in our chariot for you," Emily's father said to Earl.

"You don't gotta ask me twice," Earl responded.

Diana and Steve stepped up to Emily, Joel, and Paelen.

"Well, you did it," Emily's father said. "I am so proud of you!"

Emily embraced him. "I'm just glad it's over."

She clung to him and put her head against his chest, listening to the strong beating of his heart. He was alive. He was human and he was wonderful. But after everything she'd learned about herself, Emily grieved to know she was not. The Emily who had been his daughter was gone. Somehow, she was just an echo of her former self. She still felt the same, but deep inside, she knew she wasn't. It would take time to figure out exactly what she was and to learn to accept it. But as long as she had her father, Joel, Pegasus, and Paelen to help her, she knew she would be all right. Whatever she was, Emily was still Emily.

"I'm proud of all of you." Steve looked over to Joel and Paelen when he released Emily. "C'mon, everyone, let's go home."

Emily stood with her best friends as her father and Diana made their way back to their chariot. She felt Joel slip his hand into hers. He smiled at her, and his brown eyes sparkled. "I don't know about you, but I could sure use a swim about now."

Emily grinned up at Joel and then over at Paelen. He was wearing his winged sandals again. "Me too," she agreed. "Last one to Olympus is a rotten egg!"

As Joel dashed over to Chrysaor, Emily climbed up on Pegasus. Paelen launched into the air first, with Joel and Chrysaor close behind.

Emily was in no hurry. She leaned forward and hugged the stallion's neck. It terrified her to think she'd almost lost him.

"I love you, Pegs," she said softly as she held him and gazed out over the beautiful new lake surrounded by tall, leafy trees. There was no hint of the facility that had once stood there. No runways, no buildings. Area 51 was truly gone.

Pegasus looked back at her and neighed softly, sensing the change in her. "It's a long story," she said. "Just promise you'll never leave me, no matter what."

Pegasus nodded and snorted. He entered into a

trot and then a full gallop as he launched himself into the sky. In the distance, they could see squadrons of jet fighters heading their way. The CRU was going to fight back.

"It's over," she said to them. She clung to Pegasus as the winged stallion gained more speed and entered the Solar Stream.

ACKNOWLEDGMENTS

I know I always say it, but it is still true. Books are a collaborative effort—created by a bunch of people, both seen and unseen. There are my amazing agents V and Laura, and then my fabulous editors Anne and Naomi. But then there are loads of people involved with the birth of this book that I offer my heartfelt thanks to—even if I can't name you all here.

In the case of *The New Olympians*, I would also like to offer my personal thanks to my dearest friends Debbie and Mark Obarka for introducing me to the Fremont Street Experience in Las Vegas. Many thanks also to Janine McCullough of the Golden Eagle Farm in Ramona, California, who showed me how an ethical horse farm should be run. Then, of course, there are the kind folks at the Little A'Le'Inn outside the real Area 51 in the Nevada desert, who helped so much, even if they'll never know how. Thank you and Nanoo, Nanoo!

Beyond my family, who are the support I need to keep Pegasus flying, I would also like to thank Monica Percy and Laura O'Brian for writing such great riddles for this book. You guys are the best!

And finally, I would like to thank you, my dearest reader, for taking Pegasus into your hearts and for showing me that you love him as much as I do. I am putting all my hopes on you to create a better future for horses and animals than my generation has done. Please show them you care.

Q&A WITH KATE O'HEARN

Q) When did you first get the idea to write about Pegasus?

A) The idea came to me a couple of years ago, and all by accident. A friend asked me if I would ever write a book about horses. I responded, "No, not unless it was Pegasus, as he's my favorite stallion in the world." After that, the idea just spread like wildfire until it became *The Flame of Olympus*. I think I owe that friend a big thank-you! (And maybe a huge box of chocolates.)

Q) In this book, Emily and Joel are very normal teens who become heroes. Do you believe that ordinary people can make a difference?

A) Absolutely! I have always believed that it is the ordinary people who make all the difference in the world! They are the best heroes. How often have we heard stories of ordinary people doing extraordinary things? Most of the time they don't even want thanks. They are just everyday, generous, and wonderful people. So I believe that each and every person—you, me, anyone—can make a phenomenal difference to this world if we try.

Q) Was it a challenge to mix mythology and the modern world?

A) It was amazing and so much fun. I grew up with the myths and have always loved them. Even before I started writing the book, I felt I already knew the characters so well—it was like revisiting old friends. But what really excited me was to put those great Olympians in our modern world and imagine how hard it would be for them to fit in. I mean, hiding Pegasus in the middle of New York City? It doesn't get better than that!

Q) The Flame of Olympus was compared to the Percy Jackson books by Rick Riordan. Have you ever met Rick Riordan, and has he influenced you?

A) I haven't met Rick Riordan, but I really want to! I have read the Percy Jackson books and love how he mixes the myths with reality. We are so different in our approach to our stories, but I can tell he cares for the myths just as much as I do! I'm such a big fan of his. I can just imagine the fun we would have debating the difference between the Greek and Roman myths! I hope that one day I may have the opportunity to meet him and personally thank him for writing such fantastic books and for being so generous in writing his great review of my book.

DID YOU SOLVE ALEXIS'S RIDDLES?
ANSWERS ARE BELOW:

1) *My shallow hills are the faces of kings / My horizon is always near*
My music sends men to the grave / My absence sends men to work.
What am I?

Answer:
A coin/money

2) *Riddle me, riddle me ranty ro / My father gave me seeds to sow.*
The seed was black and the ground was white
If you riddle me that / You'll escape my bite.

Answer:
A story told on white parchment, written in black ink

3) *I am the unreachable boundary / Yet the place you wish to go,*
I run away as you approach. / But I am always there.
What am I?

Answer:
The horizon

4) *At night I come without being fetched*
And by day I am lost without being stolen.
I am like a diamond, / But I am no jewel.
What am I?

Answer:
A star